ALSO BY MARTIN WALKER

FICTION

Bruno, Chief of Police

The Dark Vineyard

The Crowded Grave

The Caves of Périgord

NONFICTION

The Iraq War

Europe in the Twenty-first Century (co-author)

America Reborn

The President We Deserve

The Cold War: A History

Martin Walker's Russia

The Waking Giant: Gorbachev and Perestroika

Powers of the Press

The National Front

Black Diamond

Black Diamond

Martin Walker

HARPER
WEEKEND

Touis '13 March
Ottawa
harsh winter

Black Diamond
Copyright © 2010 by Walker and Watson Ltd.
All rights reserved.

Published by Harper Weekend, an imprint of HarperCollins Publishers Ltd

Originally published in Great Britain in slightly different
form by Quercus, London, in 2010

First published in Canada by HarperCollins Publishers Ltd
in a hardcover edition: 2011
This Harper Weekend trade paperback edition: 2012

HarperCollins books may be purchased for educational, business,
or sales promotional use through our Special Markets Department.

HarperCollins Publishers Ltd.
2 Bloor Street East, 20th Floor
Toronto, Ontario, Canada
M4W 1A8

www.harpercollins.ca

Library and Archives Canada Cataloguing in Publication
information is available upon request.

ISBN 978-1-55468-269-0

Printed and bound in the United States
RRD 9 8 7 6 5 4 3 2 1

To Commandant Raymond Bounichou,
old barbouze, *great cook, good friend*
and one of the few to be given the honor
of lighting the sacred flame at the
Arc de Triomphe

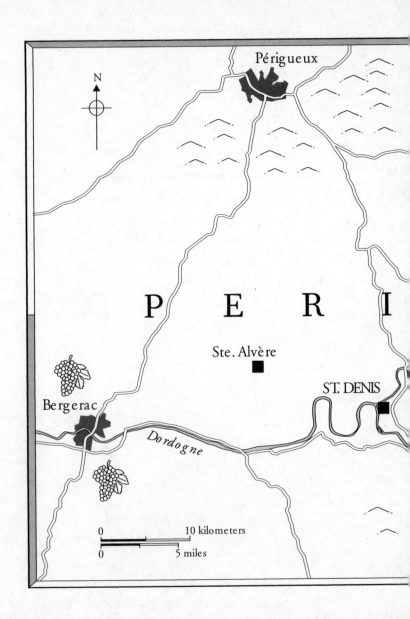

N

Périgueux

P   E   R   I

Ste. Alvère

ST. DENIS

Bergerac

Dordogne

0   10 kilometers

0   5 miles

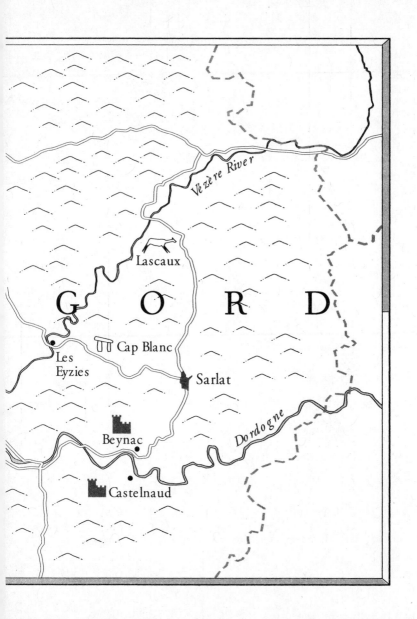

Lascaux

G O R D

Cap Blanc

Les
Eyzies

Sarlat

Beynac

Dordogne

Castelnaud

Vézère River

Black Diamond

1

There were not many times that Bruno Courrèges disliked his job. But today was certainly one of them. The weather was not to blame, a crisp day in late November with thin, high clouds trailing feebly across a sky that was determined to be blue. And even this early in the morning the sun was warm on his face and lending a rich gold to the few remaining leaves on the line of old oaks that fringed the town's rugby field. It gave warmth to the aged stone of the *mairie* across the river and to the red tile roofs of the houses that climbed the hillside. The season was still mild enough, he noticed, for the women to have thrown open their windows and the blue wooden shutters. Splashes of white and blue, stripes and floral patterns, adorned the townscape where they had heaped out bedding to air on the balconies, as their mothers and grandmothers had done before them. It might be the last day of the year that would be possible. A touch of frost had silvered the grass outside his cottage when Bruno walked his dog just after dawn that morning, and he had heard the first of the Christmas Muzak in the supermarket over the weekend.

Bruno turned back to the scene before him, the small

crowd waiting outside the silent sawmill, its chimney no longer sending plumes of smoke into the clear sky. The fork-lift trucks that usually scurried like beetles around the warehouses under their loads of timber were all parked neatly in their garage. The air still carried the wholesome scent of fresh-cut wood. But the memory would soon fade, since this was the day that the sawmill, one of the biggest and oldest employers in St. Denis, was to close its doors.

Bruno himself, acting under orders, had two weeks earlier delivered the formal notice of closure from the prefecture, citing the legal judgment against Scièrie Pons and its owner for breach of the new rules on pollution in urban areas. As the town's only policeman, Bruno had tied a copy of the order, wrapped in plastic against the weather, to the sawmill gates. Now he had to stand watch as the law took its solemn course and the court ruling was carried out. And of course he was obliged to deal with whatever ill feeling followed from this long-running feud between the jubilant Green Party and the man they called "the arch-polluter of St. Denis."

"Pons out, Pons out," chanted the crowd, led into a chorus by a handsome man with a bullhorn, an expensive leather jacket and a white silk scarf. His long blond hair was tucked into a neat ponytail, and he wore a large Green Party button on his lapel. The posters the crowd carried explained the closure. There had been no economic calamity, no financial embarrassment, no sudden shortage of timber that the woods and forests of the Dordogne region had produced for centuries. There was no shortage of demand for the oak and chestnut, pine and hemlock. Indeed it was known that Boniface Pons, the owner of the sawmill that had been in his family for generations, was simply shifting his entire enterprise to another commune with wide forests and fewer than two hundred voters, where he had been assured there would be none of the angry demonstrations and the endless lawsuits that had driven him from St. Denis.

AT LAST, OUR CHILDREN CAN BREATHE, read one of the posters, which made Bruno roll his eyes at the exaggeration. He had played countless hours of rugby on the nearby playing field and endured dozens of training sessions while the chimney still spouted and never felt out of breath.

ENVIRONMENT 1—PONS 0, read another poster, which for Bruno was closer to the truth. Pons's sawmill had, over the decade of Bruno's time as the town's policeman, installed two separate sets of scrubbing equipment for the steam and smoke that belched from the tall chimney. Each installation was supposed to be the latest in clean-air technology, yet within a few years each had been overtaken by new pollution directives from the European Union in Brussels. The most recent directive, which required any business with a polluting chimney to be a minimum distance from the nearest housing, had been the final straw for Boniface Pons. It was not his fault, Pons maintained, that the commune of St. Denis had decided, years before the latest directive had been thought of, to erect a block of cheap flats for public housing just one hundred and fifty feet from the fence around his sawmill. But with the new regulation, that meant his business was twenty-five feet inside the limit required by the EU.

"I've had enough of this green crap," Pons had announced at the last, heated council meeting. "If you don't want the jobs I bring and the two hundred thousand euros I pay in taxes to this town's budget every year, then fine. I'll go where my jobs are wanted."

Bruno had hoped to avoid trouble this morning, wishing that Pons would leave his building, lock his gates and make a dignified departure while the crowd of *écolos,* the town's environmental activists, calmly relished their victory. But from the gossip in the cafés and the grumbling around the market stalls, he had known that the closure might not go so smoothly. He had discussed with the mayor, Gérard Mangin, whether they should call on the gendarmes for reinforcements. But the moment they envisaged Capitaine Duroc blundering his way in, they had dropped the idea. Had Duroc been away on a course, and the gendarmes under the experienced command of Sergeant Jules, their presence might have been a sensible precaution. As it was, the mayor and Bruno knew they could count only on themselves and on the years of trust they had built with their neighbors.

The crowd was bigger than Bruno had expected, swollen by curiosity and perhaps also by a sense that an era was passing and that history was finally overtaking the timber industry that had sustained St. Denis for centuries. Through wars and revolution, through boom times and recessions, the trees had always provided wine barrels and the boats that carried them; beams and floorboards and furniture for half the homes of France; desks in the schoolrooms and fires in the grates. Walnut trees provided oil and food and the young green fruit that produced the local *vin de noix.* Within living memory, in the hard times of Vichy and the German occupation, chestnut trees had even provided flour to make a kind of bread.

So the closure of a sawmill was much more than simply a matter of jobs for the people of St. Denis, Bruno reflected, as he watched knots of pensioners shuffle up the road from the retirement home. The oldest, Rosalie Prarial, the last inhabitant of the town who claimed to remember seeing young men going off to the final battles of the Grande Guerre in 1918, was being helped along by Father Sentout. Like many of the other pensioners, Rosalie had worked at the sawmill all her life, starting under Boniface's grandfather. Montsouris, the town's only Communist councillor, must have taken the day off from his job as a train driver, for he and his even more radical wife were approaching, followed by a delegation from the town's chamber of commerce. Bruno raised his eyebrows; it was a rare event that brought the left and the town's small businessmen together in common cause.

Half the town appeared to be gathering for the event, and Bruno suspected that most of them would be unhappy at this triumph of the Greens. But he knew his townsfolk to be on the whole levelheaded and law abiding, and while any such assembly brought the prospect of trouble, they were not lined up in opposition but gathered in separate knots and groups. A bit like a funeral, thought Bruno, when people hung back on the outskirts in deference to the family.

The mayor stood under the trees that guarded the rugby field, deliberately keeping his distance from the crowd and the sawmill gates. Beside him stood the baron, the main landowner in the district who was also Bruno's tennis partner. Albert, the chief of the town's fire brigade, was out of his customary uniform and smoking a pipe. A pickup truck lumbered around the corner from the public housing block, and Lespinasse, the local garage owner, clambered out with his sister from the florist's shop and his cousin from the *tabac*. They all shook hands with the mayor and his party and waved at Bruno.

Then the unmistakable clatter of an elderly Citroën *deux chevaux* signaled the arrival of Pamela, the woman with whom Bruno was sometimes privileged to spend his nights. Few people now called her the Mad Englishwoman as they had at first, at least in Bruno's hearing. Indeed, now that residents from other European countries had been given the right to vote in France's local elections, the mayor had talked of running her for a council seat at the next election. The mayor hoped to secure the foreigners' votes, but it was a sign that Pamela was accepted as a daughter of St. Denis.

Despite his pleasure at seeing her and the bright smile she beamed at him, Bruno bit back a surge of irritation at Pamela's arrival. It was less that her presence would be a distraction, and more that he felt self-conscious at playing his public role under her gaze. Usually he rather enjoyed Pamela's teasing and the slightly mocking attitude the British seemed to adopt toward their police, but he was beginning to feel nervous about the way the crowd was building.

He sized up the situation. Other than scattered knots of spectators, the crowd was splitting into two camps. Opposite the main gates of the sawmill were the *écolos,* and at the front of the crowd that flanked them were young women with carriages and strollers. Some of them Bruno knew well, the wives and infants of the men who worked at the sawmill, men who now faced unemployment until Pons's new plant was ready. The women, glaring at the chanting *écolos,* had gathered by the small side gate their husbands used. Touching the peak of his cap, Bruno strolled across to greet them and to tousle the hair of the toddlers. He'd danced with the mothers at the feast of St. Jean and taught the younger ones to play tennis; he had attended their weddings and the baptisms of their children, hunted and played rugby with their fathers.

"A sad day," he said to Axelle as her twin daughters peeked out at Bruno from behind her skirts.

"Bloody *écolos,* always putting their noses into other people's business," she snapped. "How come the law doesn't look after people like us for a change?"

"Emile will be back at work soon," Bruno said, hoping to sound reassuring. "And I hear you got a job at the infants' school. I suppose Emile's mother can look after the kids."

"Lucky for some," sniffed another of the mothers. "There's no job for me, and whatever Pierre gets today will be the last money we see for a while. It's going to be a pretty thin Christmas."

"I hope you're satisfied, you bastards!" Axelle shouted at the *écolos.* "Our kids will be going hungry because you keep whining over a whiff of smoke."

"Pons out, Pons out," the Greens chanted back, led by the dashing man with the bullhorn. To Bruno, he was the strangest feature of this drama, a long-lost son of St. Denis, home from his years of travel with a brand-new Porsche convertible, enough money to buy an old farm and convert it into a restaurant and exotic tales of life in Hong Kong, Bangkok and Singapore. And he had returned with an evident interest in local politics, a passionate commitment to the Green cause and an eagerness to fund the lawsuit that had finally succeeded in winning an order for the closure of his father's sawmill. For the young man was Guillaume Pons, who insisted that everyone should call him Bill, and seemed intent on pursuing his family feud against his estranged father by any available means.

Bruno wandered back to the crowd of chanting *écolos* and tapped Guillaume's shoulder.

"Do you think you could stop the chanting for a while? The women over there are worried about their men losing their jobs and they're getting upset. It won't help if you rub their noses in it."

"I know, it's not their fault. But it's not ours either," Guillaume said pleasantly. As he put down the bullhorn to answer

Bruno the chanting died away. "We just want clean air, and we could create clean jobs as well, if we put our minds to it."

Bruno nodded and thanked him for the pause in the chanting. "Let's keep this calm and dignified. It's a sad day for some, and we don't want tempers raised when the men come out."

"Perhaps the *mairie* should have thought of that when this campaign began, instead of using our tax money to subsidize the sawmill," Guillaume countered.

"We can all be wise after the fact," Bruno said. The last time Pons had threatened to close his sawmill, Bruno and the mayor had managed to scrape up some funds from the town's budget to help pay for the scrubbing equipment. It had gained them four years, until the new directive came in. The sawmill's four extra years of taxes had more than repaid the modest subsidy.

"Right now, I'm just concerned that we don't have an angry shouting match," Bruno added. "You're the one with the bullhorn, so I'm holding you responsible."

"Don't worry," Guillaume replied with a smile that in other circumstances Bruno might have found charming. He put a hand on Bruno's arm. "I can also use the bullhorn to calm them down. They'll listen to me."

"Let's hope so, monsieur." Bruno moved on to greet Alphonse, the elderly hippie from the commune in the hills above the town, and the first Green to have been elected to the town council.

"Can I count on you to keep things calm when the men come out, Alphonse?" Bruno asked, shaking the hand of the man who made the best goat cheese in the district.

"We don't want trouble, Bruno," said Alphonse, a hand-rolled cigarette bouncing on his lower lip. "We've won this battle."

"I don't know some of these people you've gathered here," Bruno said, surveying the crowd behind Guillaume and Alphonse.

"It's mostly the usual Green campaigners from Périgueux and Bergerac, plus a couple all the way from Bordeaux. It's been a big campaign for us in this region. Don't worry, Bruno. It's just that we haven't had too many successes lately and this one's important."

There was a sudden alertness in the crowd, and Bruno turned to see the door of the sawmill office open. The employees, or rather the ex-employees, filed slowly out. The first ones paused as they saw the crowd at the gate, and a couple began to wave when they spotted their wives and children. Bruno walked across to the small side gate and gestured to the men to use it, thinking the sooner the men mingled with their families the less chance there would be of a scene. But Marcel the foreman shook his head and advanced to the main entrance, where he unlocked the padlock and began to slide open the big iron gate.

"It's the last day, Bruno. We leave by the main gate," Marcel said. "We didn't start this damn mess and we aren't slinking out by the side door." He moved on to embrace his wife and then turned, his hands on his hips, to stare grimly at the *écolos*.

Bruno moved to block Marcel's view and solemnly shook hands with each of the workers as they left the premises, murmuring briefly to them by name and suggesting it was time to go home with their families. Most of them shrugged and moved on to the waiting women and children. The mayor appeared at Bruno's side, following his example and shaking hands, and taking by the arm two of the younger men who were looking aggressively at the *écolos* to steer them gently away from any confrontation. It seemed to be working, the mood more mournful than angry, some of the married men taking children in their arms and starting to drift away.

Then the main door of the showroom opened and Pons himself appeared, straight-backed and powerful despite his seventy years. His heavy shoulders bulged in his jacket, reminding Bruno that Pons had in his youth captained the town's rugby team. He still served on the club's board. He looked every inch the prosperous businessman in his suit, white shirt and bow tie, his bald head shining in the winter sun. Pons nodded courteously as two women who worked in the office left the building quickly and scurried away through the side gate. He locked the door of the business he had inherited and expanded and then turned to gaze impassively at the crowd.

"Pons out, Pons out," came the first, almost hesitant chant from the *écolos,* not amplified with any bullhorn. Bruno saw that Pons's son was gazing silently back at his father, their poses almost identical. But the bullhorn was by his side, and Guillaume didn't move as the Greens behind him began a chorus of boos and jeers at the solitary businessman.

Bruno walked quickly through the gate toward Pons senior and spoke to him as a friend of many a rugby club dinner rather than as the chief of police of St. Denis. "Your car is parked around the side, *mon vieux.* I'd strongly advise you to get into it and leave now before we have trouble. There are women and kids here."

"Don't tell me what to do, Bruno, not on my own property," Pons said quietly, not bothering to shift his gaze from the crowd at his gate. "I didn't start this *bordel de merde,* but I'm walking out with my head high."

"I'm going to have to walk with you then," Bruno said.

"Suit yourself."

Pons began striding toward the gate. The boos increased in volume, and some of the *écolos* began a surge forward, only to be restrained by Pons's son, who stretched out his arms to hold them back. There was a cold smile on his face as his father approached him.

Too fast for Bruno to intervene, the older man didn't even break stride as he slapped his son across the cheek, so hard that Guillaume staggered and fell to one knee, dropping his bullhorn. Pons stalked on into the crowd of his workers, not looking back and not pausing as some of his employees cheered and slapped him on the shoulders.

White-faced except for the flaming red patch on his cheek, Guillaume shook his head and rose quickly, fury in his eye, surging forward after his father. Bruno wrapped his arms around the man to hold him back as Guillaume shouted, "You bastard, you dirty bastard!"

Bruno felt hands wrenching at his arms, then someone was hauling him back by the neck as Guillaume's *écolos* came to free their leader. Goaded into action, two of the younger workers from the sawmill piled in alongside Bruno, followed by a shrieking Axelle, who waded into the fray, raked her nails down Guillaume's face and pulled on the lapels of his jacket to butt him hard in the face. She pushed him back, spitting in his eye as blood began to spout from his battered nose.

Bruno rammed an elbow into the man wrenching his neck and kicked back hard to free himself. He turned, picked up Axelle by the waist and thrust her back behind him, luckily into the path of Montsouris, who was steaming into the brawl with Marcel and a couple of the younger workers. Then the mayor and the baron were at each side of him, their arms in the air, advancing to make a gap between the two crowds and calling for calm. Bruno held up his hand to restrain Montsouris, and suddenly he heard the cawing of the rooks from the oak trees as a silence fell and all the angry energy seemed to leak away.

Everyone seemed chastened by the eruption of violence and the sight of blood. Axelle was sobbing quietly as Father Sentout led her back to Emile, who was kneeling as he held his dumbstruck children. The priest helped Bruno steer the townspeople back along the fence to the road that led to town.

"I'll see the old ones back," said Father Sentout. "That was a very sad moment, the son and the father."

"Whatever happened to the Pons family, it was all before my time. Do you remember any of it?" Bruno asked.

"There was a very ugly separation when the boy was twelve or so, and he left for Paris with his mother. I think they got divorced in the end. I heard she died in Paris, it must be fifteen or twenty years back."

Bruno nodded as Father Sentout gave his arm to two elderly women. Old Pons himself was helping Rosalie. The mayor would know the background, thought Bruno, or perhaps the baron. Whatever the origins of the family feud, the return of the son meant that it could become Bruno's problem. He turned back toward the sawmill and paused to take in the arresting tableau.

But for the chimney and buildings of the sawmill, the scene reminded him of one of the religious paintings in the church of St. Denis. Guillaume Pons lay on his back, his head on Pamela's lap and blood all down his shirt, while Fabiola, the young doctor from the St. Denis medical center, tended to his battered face. The mayor and the baron stood solemnly at each side of them, and Albert was kneeling at Pons's feet. Around them stood the silent *écolos,* looking down at the son felled by his father.

Bruno remembered precisely the last time he had studied the painting. He had been sitting near it during the Easter choral concert in the church, when Father Sentout had spent weeks rehearsing the choir for a performance of Haydn's "Seven Last Words of Our Savior on the Cross." Bruno had remembered studying the photocopied text of the work and Father Sentout's short commentary. One of the phrases had stayed with him, and emerged again now, unbidden, into his head. *Eli, Eli, lama sabachtani*—Father, Father, why hast thou forsaken me?

2

Bruno loved to drive in the baron's old Citroën DS, a car that had been built before he was born. He enjoyed the way the car hardly leaned when cornering and how it still looked like the most modern car ever made. Bruno had heard the baron sing its virtues a score of times: that it had been the world's first car with disc brakes and hydraulic suspension and some other features he could never quite remember. But one thing the baron had ensured Bruno never forgot was that it had saved the life of the baron's hero, Charles de Gaulle, whom he always called le général, rather than president. During one of the several assassination attempts in the 1960s by the OAS, the military and colonialist rebels who wanted to keep Algeria French, the car's tires had been shot out, yet it could still drive away at full speed. Every time the baron's DS came in for service, Lespinasse at the garage would almost purr with pleasure.

"Did you know I bought this car from Pons?" the baron asked, his eyes on the narrow road ahead, dense trees on either side flickering past in the glow of the headlights. It was still an hour before dawn, but they had wanted to be at the Ste. Alvère market before it officially opened at 8:00 a.m.

"It must be over twenty years ago, maybe more, not long after his wife left him. I got it cheap. These days they can go for over a hundred thousand at classic car auctions."

"You'll never sell this," Bruno said. "It's part of you. But I wanted to ask you about Pons. How come the wife left?"

"I'm told he used to beat her. She came from the south, near Carcassonne. Got a job teaching at the college here. A real beauty, blond hair but with that lovely golden skin you sometimes get in the Midi. I was living in Paris then, and Pons had already grabbed her when I came down one summer. Olivia, her name was."

"Jealous?"

"I certainly was." The baron laughed. "But then things changed. Pons was never known for fidelity. She put up with it for a while. Then she started taking her revenge. I was one of the lucky ones. Not the only one, though. When Pons found out, that was the end of the marriage."

"How was she doing, financially?"

"I helped her get a lawyer. She did okay. Pons was never mean about money, at least not where the boy was concerned. But I know he complained the boy never wanted to see him, that Olivia had poisoned the kid's mind about him."

"Did the boy know about you?"

"I doubt it. I'm pretty sure Pons never knew about me either, we were always discreet. I was married by the time she came to Paris."

"Why the delay before she got a divorce?"

The baron shrugged. "Divorce wasn't so easy in those days, not with the kid, and even trickier after she took the boy to Paris. Pons claimed she'd abandoned the family home, but the lawyer got her a decent settlement."

"What happened then?"

"She taught for a while. Later she got a management job in a good hotel by the Opéra and then opened her own restaurant. I helped her a bit, but it was never a great success. Then she got breast cancer, and everything fell apart. The boy went off backpacking around Asia, didn't even make it back for the funeral. It was just me, some other old boyfriends and the staff from her restaurant. Pons didn't come. At least he sent a wreath."

They had arrived, just a few minutes before seven. Bruno climbed out of the car's warm interior and shivered as he pulled on his old army greatcoat. He looked up to see if he could discern the first hint of lightness in the eastern sky. Not dawn yet, he thought, and pulled his small basket from the backseat. It was a modest haul he had to offer, and he only had the second grade of truffle, the *brumale.* The real black diamond, the *melanosporum,* would not be traded until later in December. The best of them, ones that could go for more than a thousand euros a kilo, seldom came onto the market until January.

Bruno had planted the alley of white oaks that would nourish the growth of truffles on his land soon after his arrival in St. Denis, knowing that it would be a few years more before he would have the chance of a real harvest. But he had six small and knobbly *brumales* of different shapes and sizes, three from his own trees and three from his forays in the woods behind his home. They weighed in total something less than half a pound. The largest was just a little bigger than a golf ball. He might with luck get a hundred euros for them, but the price would depend on the market. He dipped his nose into the basket to smell the deep, earthy scent. He wrapped the truffles inside a page of *Sud Ouest* and stuffed it into his pocket; they smelled better when they were kept warm.

He had left the two best of his *brumales* at home, steeping in virgin olive oil. They would be for his own use. Normally, he would not bother to attend the market until late December, even with his *brumales,* but the baron had said Hercule wanted to see him, and Bruno owed Hercule a great deal.

When Bruno had first seen the tiny darting fly beneath one of his trees that signaled the presence of truffles, he had begun to think about investing for the future. The baron had introduced him to one of his old army friends from the Algerian War, Hercule Vendrot, who lived near Ste. Alvère, the town that was to truffles what Château Pétrus was to wine lovers. Hercule had visited Bruno's property, lunched well, given his advice on what trees to plant and where and returned every year since to enjoy a meal and to stir up the leaves under Bruno's young oaks to see if the flies might be dancing. The two men had exchanged war stories, admired each other's dogs and become friends.

At first, they made a point of hunting and then dining together at least twice a year, once on Bruno's land and again on Hercule's. Their meetings had steadily become more frequent, lubricated by the fine wines on which Hercule spent the money he made from his truffles. Three years ago, Hercule had pointed out the first sign of *terre brûlée* around Bruno's sapling oaks, the ring of dark earth that seemed to have been scorched. Bruno had his truffles and had made two hundred euros in his first year, but fewer than a hundred in the second. He was hoping for much more this year and a steady future income that would never come to the attention of the tax man.

The formal market started when the doors opened to the modern glass-walled building that the city fathers had constructed beside the churchyard. Now they even had an online market, but Hercule had taught Bruno that the real business was transacted before the market opened. And much of the trade was done outside the building as it always had been, men in ancient overcoats with patient dogs at their heels, discreetly slipping from their pockets small handfuls of truffles wrapped in newspaper. Some were standing there already, each of them solitary, glancing almost furtively at his neighbors along the street, wondering what treasures the rivals might bring. They looked, to Bruno's professional eye, deeply suspicious, like a collection of voyeurs trying to summon the courage to spy through bathroom windows. It made the prospect of joining their ranks unappealing. He planned to sell his own truffles in the town market.

The baron led the way up the steps onto a small terrace and into the café opposite the church. The windows were steamed up, and as he opened the door a rush of noise came from inside, where thirty or forty men and their dogs crowded into a space designed for half that number. Desirée, the only woman in the room, was serving croissants and *tartines,* ringing up sales at a furious pace, while her husband manned the espresso machine.

Hercule was taking his coffee at the corner of the bar and signaled to Desirée for two more when he saw them squeezing their way through to him. A big man, his back starting to stoop now that he was well into his seventies, Hercule had sharp blue eyes and a fringe of white hair under the beret he invariably wore. His thick white mustache was brown in the center from the Gauloises he smoked. His elderly mongrel Pom-Pom, a legendary truffle hunter, craned his head forward to sniff at Bruno's trousers, picking up the scent of his dog, Gigi. The three men shook hands and turned to the counter where Desirée had placed three coffees, three croissants and three large cognacs. Like the cognac at dawn when they went hunting, it was a ritual.

"*Salut,* Bruno, show me what you've got."

He nodded when Bruno turned toward the bar. Sheltered by the baron and Hercule, he took out his small parcel and opened it so that only Hercule could see. The beret dipped, and even over the noise in the café Bruno heard him sniff.

"Not bad for *brumales.* Mine aren't ready yet, and prices always go up the nearer we get to Christmas. I know who'll want some of that. But let's finish our breakfast first." He downed his cognac and ordered three more to tip into fresh cups of coffee.

Thirty minutes later, they were in the churchyard and talking to a *renifleur,* one of the scouts who bought on behalf of a group of Bordeaux restaurants. The scout pulled out a small scale, and Bruno was pleased to receive six twenty-euro notes in return. He offered one of them to Hercule as commission, but he waved the money away.

"I asked you here," he said. "We need to talk. But I'll take a look in the market first, just to show our faces."

A small knot of men was gathered at the door. Bruno recognized his counterpart in Ste. Alvère, the town policeman, Nicco. Bruno shook hands with him, a much older man close to retirement, saying he was off-duty and just there for the market. Nicco introduced him and the baron to the town's mayor, a live wire who had pushed for the online truffle market and had gotten European funding to turn Ste. Alvère into a pilot project for alternative energy. Just before 8:00 a.m., a plump man appeared with a key in his hand, almost breaking into a trot when he saw the mayor. It was Didier, the market manager, an ingratiating grin on his face, scurrying to unlock the door into the large room with a series of tables covered in white cloth. A gleaming digital scale held pride of place beside the new computer that ran the online market. Three webcams covered the room. And on a side table in the corner stood a high-grade microscope, to help settle disputes about the grading of the various truffles. Bruno understood enough of the technicalities to know that some unscrupulous dealers tried to pass off a *chatin* as a *brumale*.

"It's a joke," Hercule murmured in Bruno's ear. "All the real deals are still done outside, between people who've known each other for years and don't need fancy machines to know what's what. You'll see the *renifleur* didn't even bother to come inside. There'll be another auction at the end of the day for the stocks left over, but there's something fishy about that."

Hercule prowled around the tables where the sellers were laying out their wares in small baskets. He bent to sniff a couple of times but moved on. A third time he bent and then turned to Bruno.

"Sniff this one. It's good, maybe even a bit better than yours." He turned his back on the vendor to whisper into Bruno's ear. "He's asking fifty euros a hundred grams. You did better, and you didn't have to pay the market fee."

Hercule plucked Bruno's sleeve and jerked his head at the baron to lead them outside. They walked up the hill past the tower of the ruined castle, its stone improbably pale in color after enthusiastic cleaning and its surroundings of fresh turf looking too picturesque to be true. Hercule's dog paused to lift a back leg on the base of the ruin, and the old man led them at a brisk and warming pace up the lane to his home.

Each time he visited Hercule's house, Bruno was curious

that such an evidently learned and cultivated man should affect the style and dress of a country hayseed. The walls were filled with books. From the way they were stuffed sideways onto crammed shelves, with small note cards and bookmarks in the pages, it was clear they were constantly being used. In the spaces between bookshelves were paintings and hangings with foreign calligraphies. Bruno could not have identified, far less read, them had Hercule not explained the difference between the Viet, the Khmer, the Thai, the Lao and the Mandarin.

The furniture was old and heavy and comfortable, of a dark, dense wood and a style that Bruno now knew to be Vietnamese. A vast desk squatted by the window, covered by newspaper clippings, a laptop computer and framed photographs of an Asian woman and child, plus several of French soldiers in uniforms of an earlier era. The baron moved to the desk and picked up one of the photos, turning it to the light.

"Bab el-Oued, when they still loved the French army. I recognize that corner by the St. Eugène Cemetery," the baron said as Bruno looked over his shoulder. "That's General Massu himself on the right, so it must be fifty-seven, when he was running the battle of Algiers. I didn't know you knew Massu that well, Hercule." He put it down and looked at his old friend. "You had something on your mind. Tell us."

"I don't know if you can do anything to help, but I've got to get this off my chest." He knelt to put a match to the nest of newspapers beneath the kindling in the fireplace and then stood, watching the fire catch hold.

"A drink? Coffee?" They shook their heads. "It's the market. There's something nasty going on, and they won't listen to me. When they think of fraud, they think only of the old tricks like people dyeing the white summer truffles and selling them as blacks. But this is different. One of the *renifleurs,* not the one you met, says a couple of his big clients in Paris claim they've been fobbed off with fakes, cheap *sinensis,* Chinese black truffles. It's common enough in oils and prepared foods, but each of them reckoned they got some Chinese rubbish in a shipment of tailings, that's the small and crumbled stuff they use for truffle oil and stews."

"No official complaints yet?" asked Bruno.

"The big hotels hate to do it because it could hurt their reputation. These are places where they'll pay a thousand, fifteen hundred euros for a good Périgord black. But if they feel cheated they just won't buy any more."

"You said nobody will listen to you. Who did you tell?" asked Bruno.

"Didier, the market manager. When he said I was crazy I went to the mayor. But he's invested a lot of money in the market and new equipment designed to make sure this kind of thing doesn't happen. He gave me the brush-off. And Nicco is so close to retirement he didn't want to know. So I thought of you, Bruno. You know truffles, you know what they mean to this part of the world."

"How do these Chinese truffles get here?"

"Straight from the thirteenth arrondissement in Paris, down around place d'Italie. It's the biggest Chinatown in Europe. The truffles come in from China, and we're the next stop. There's a lot of money to be made, but it's going to ruin Ste. Alvère. Look, I'll show you what I mean."

Hercule went to his kitchen and came back with a tray. It held a cheeseboard with a quarter of what looked like Brie de Meaux, some slices from a baguette and three small bottles, each filled with oil covering a layer of small black lumps.

"I want you to try this," Hercule said, putting down the

tray as a rich, almost gamy scent reached Bruno's nostrils. "A couple of days ago, I sliced this Brie in half horizontally and slipped three slices of truffle between the halves. I just took them out, but the perfume will be wonderful."

He smeared thin wedges of Brie onto three slices of bread and handed one each to Bruno and the baron.

"Glorious," said Bruno. The rich and succulent cheese had suddenly developed whole new depths and layers of taste, as if . . . Bruno tried to think of a way to put it. And then he thought that it tasted as if it had grown up and gone to university and won doctorates and become a professor and had a loving wife and handsome children and won a Nobel Prize and spent the money on expensive mistresses and vintage champagne.

"Smells like a *poule de luxe*," said the baron, and Bruno wondered why truffles made men think of sex. It had the same effect on him.

Hercule turned to the bottles on the tray. "This first one is the real thing. Olive oil with one of my decent blacks from last year." He held it out for them. "Now try this. That's a Chinese black in the same oil. Can you tell the difference?"

Bruno could. There was a sour note to the odor, like poor soil baked into dust by the sun. And another flavor lingered behind it, almost like gasoline.

"Now try this. That's what they're getting in Paris. It's mainly Chinese, with a bit of the real thing to add flavor."

This time Bruno smelled the real black Périgord first, but then the flavor seemed to die away. The sample had the same woodsy smell, but the vegetation had a touch of rankness.

"It starts off okay, but after a few moments my *brumale* is better than that," he said.

"Big difference." The baron nodded.

"Any idea who might be behind this?"

Hercule shrugged. "It has to be one of the regulars, some-one we know and trust. It takes a long time to accept strangers in the market."

"If the mayor decided to take you seriously, what could be done to stop this?" Bruno asked.

"Constant spot checks of everything that's shipped out. It's tough to fool the locals and the *renifleurs*. It's no coincidence that this has started to happen with the online market. People buy over the Internet, and it gets shipped in vacuum packs. But checking all the shipments would mean time, extra staff and money."

"And it wouldn't catch the bad guys," the baron said thoughtfully.

"I think this is a lot bigger than it looks," Hercule went on. "It's not just the odd Chinese merchant pulling a fast one. Or if it is, then it's like reconnaissance to see if they can expand this business and start making real money."

"How big is this?" Bruno asked. "Could organized crime be involved?"

"We harvested over fifty tons of truffles in France last year, and they went for between seven hundred and fifteen hun-dred a kilo. That's a fifty-million-euro business, enough to attract some big players. China bought more than five million euros' worth of Périgord truffles. It's our fastest-growing mar-ket. Just three years ago, they bought nothing. It's like cognac; anything that's really rare and expensive has a snob appeal for China's new rich. So if you can add a few scraps of our good stuff and then sell cheap Chinese truffles as if they were from France, there's real money to be made at the Chinese end. But it won't last long before they get caught and the market collapses in scandal. And that means the end of our truffle business, just as it's about to take off."

"You mean with these new plantations I've heard about?" asked the baron.

Hercule nodded. "A hundred years ago, we'd produce seven hundred tons a year here in France, mostly from plantations as people learned to infect young trees with truffle spores. But the trade collapsed with the Great War. Truffles weren't just common in the old days, they were used in huge quantities. Did you ever hear of Escoffier's great recipe for his Salade Jockey-Club, composed of equal parts chicken, asparagus and truffles? Nobody could afford to do that these days. But now the plantations are starting up again after that Spanish guy, Arotzarena, began producing ten and twenty tons a year down in Navaleno."

"I remember old Pons started a plantation near here a few years back," the baron said. "Then he got into that lawsuit over his sawmill, and he needed money fast. He cut down the trees for the timber and lost a fortune."

"He must be doing better because he's started a new plantation," said Hercule. "And he's not the only one. That's why the mayor launched the new market building. These new plantations can produce a hundred kilos of truffles per acre, which makes a lot more money than the four hundred euros you'll get from an acre of wheat. It's a growth industry for this region, unless it all gets ruined by these frauds."

"What would happen if one of these Paris hotels made a formal complaint, or even a polite inquiry?" Bruno asked.

"That would certainly get the mayor's attention. If you're prepared to help me it's worth trying him even though he probably thinks I'm just an old fool."

"I don't think any real Frenchman would dare think that," said the baron, looking at the corner beside the desk where Hercule's Croix de Guerre hung, with his citation for the Légion d'Honneur in pride of place above it.

"I have a plan," said Hercule. "I told our mayor that if he doesn't call in the police now, the least he needs is an outside security review. If this blows up he has to be able to say he tried something. I suggested he ask for you, since you know truffles, you're independent and you're a cop with no jurisdiction in Ste. Alvère. You're qualified, friendly, independent and deniable. That makes you perfect."

"What you need is a complaint, even a letter of inquiry, to the mayor from these big clients, something to force the issue," said Bruno. "Call your *renifleur,* get that letter sent and then suggest your mayor call mine and ask for me to be made available for a discreet inquiry. And I'll see what I can do."

"The guy in trouble will be Didier, the market manager," said Hercule. "I don't trust him an inch."

"He seemed like a fussy type," said Bruno, recalling the scurrying figure, half trotting to open the market building as the mayor stood impatiently waiting. "How did this Chinese stuff get past him?"

"They're trying to do everything too fast with this Internet market," said Hercule. "And Didier's not that good. He used to run that truffle plantation that Pons set up. Didier only got that job because his wife was Pons's cousin. But when Pons had to sell the timber, Didier was out of work. Then they built the new market and he got the job. His sister's husband is related to the mayor's wife."

Bruno nodded. Family connections were the way it worked around here, probably the way it worked everywhere. And his own mayor would be eager to help, since the support of Ste. Alvère would help him get elected to be the next chairman of the Conseil Régional.

"Now to more pleasant matters," said Hercule. "It's my turn to host the hunting. When's your next day off?"

"Thursday."

"I'd like some venison this winter, and the season's open. We've got some roe deer on the land and some of your favorite *bécasses*."

"I'll have to join you late, maybe around ten. The mayor won't fork out for a new police van, so I'll have to take the old one into the garage for the *contrôle technique*."

"Thursday at ten it is. I'll go out early, take a look around. We can meet at the farthest shack, the one on the track that leads off the road to Paunat."

"I know the place," said Bruno. "I'll bring a thermos of coffee."

"And I'll bring the cognac," said the baron.

"One thing I wanted to ask you," Bruno said quickly. "That place you mentioned—Bab el-Oued. What was it?"

"It's a suburb of Algiers, where the *pieds-noirs* used to live before we lost the war and they fled back to France. They were French settlers, the poorer ones, but they wanted Algeria to stay French. When de Gaulle decided to pull out, Bab el-Oued became the heart of the OAS. But that photo was taken before then, when they still loved us, before de Gaulle decided that there was no choice but to grant Algeria its independence."

"Like the rest of the army, I found some very welcoming girlfriends there," said the baron. He was staring into the fire. He looked up. "You were already married, Hercule."

"This was all before I was born," Bruno said, who read enough history to know the broad outlines of the Algerian

War. "Still, every time I ride in the baron's Citroën he tells me how the car saved de Gaulle's life when the OAS tried to assassinate him."

"Organisation de l'Armée Secrète. Not only did they come close to killing de Gaulle, they came damn close to staging a military coup back in sixty-one, with half the army on their side. They took over Algiers, and people were panicking about parachute drops on Paris. De Gaulle ordered the air force to patrol the Mediterranean coast with orders to shoot down any transport planes heading north. The baron was one of the few in his unit who didn't join the OAS."

"Would you still be friends if he had?"

"Absolutely not," said Hercule. "I'd probably have shot him."

3

Pamela turned her *deux chevaux* into the gate and down the newly built road that led to the restaurant. Bruno whistled softly and tried to calculate how much money had been spent on what had been a derelict old farm. It lay at the extreme edge of the commune of St. Denis, nearly five miles from the town, atop the ridge that overlooked the river and the road to Les Eyzies. Newly planted fruit trees formed an avenue on each side of the lane that led to a large old stone archway guarding the entrance to the farmyard. Beside the arch stood a large and floodlit sign, white scrolled letters on a green background, that read L'AUBERGE DES VERTS.

"Ah, I got it wrong," said Pamela. "It's not the Green Inn but the Inn of the Greens. It's still meant to be the first bio-organic restaurant in the department and the first to have a zero-energy footprint." Impulsively she took her hand from the steering wheel and squeezed Bruno's knee. "I'm so glad you agreed to come. I've been wanting to try this place."

The original farmhouse was still there, its honey-colored stone lit by carefully situated lamps, but most of it was obscured by a new conservatory that linked the house to the neighboring stables and barn. Through the big windows that had been built into the stables, Bruno saw a chef's white toque and kitchen workers moving through glittering rows of stainless-steel ovens and shelving. The facing wall of the barn had been removed to leave it open to the elements, but lights picked out the huge beams of ancient chestnut. Paved in gravel, the barn gaped emptily as if waiting for warmer times and summer customers. Most of the conservatory windows were screened by thick curtains, but through two wide gaps Bruno could see customers around tables lit by candlelight and covered in white cloths.

Pamela turned off the ignition, and in the sudden silence he heard a low shirring sound and looked up to see two curious windmills that bore none of the usual propeller blades. Instead, three curved and vertical blades whirled around a central axis, going remarkably fast in what was still a gentle breeze. The parking lot was dimly lit at ankle level by a row of solar-powered garden lights. A larger spotlight illuminated a large vegetable garden, picking out the bright orange of pumpkins and lines of fat cauliflowers. Behind the garden glinted some greenhouses with two more windmills beside them. Beyond the garden stood another small grouping of buildings, presumably where the staff lived.

"They spent a lot of money on this place," said Bruno, thinking about the likely size of the dinner bill.

"Fabiola doesn't want to be treated by the baron, so she's asked us all to pay our own way," Pamela said, as if reading his mind. "And don't worry about me. Thanks to Fabiola I've got a tenant through the winter for once, so I'm feeling unusually prosperous."

She was suddenly backlit by the flare of headlights, and Bruno recognized the baron's DS as it turned and parked. His friend emerged and moved swiftly to the passenger door to hold it open for Fabiola, who was renting one of Pamela's vacation cottages.

"Fabiola came straight from work," Pamela said. "Otherwise I'd have brought her. But I'll take her back with me." She looked at Bruno, her eyes twinkling affectionately. "And you too, if you're good."

"You'll get a reputation," he replied, watching her as she swept her hair back from her forehead, tucking it behind her ear in a way he knew well. Usually she wore no makeup but for this evening she had applied a dark red lipstick and mascara and done something artful that made her eyes look larger. She was wearing a long black raincoat that flared from her hips, a white silk scarf and high heels that gave her the same height as Bruno.

"You ruined my reputation months ago," she said, taking his arm as the others joined them.

The restaurant was more than half full, rare in Périgord for a weekday evening in winter, with an unusual mix of customers. Some were well dressed in suits and ties and cocktail dresses while others were in dowdy casual clothes that probably counted as Green chic. Among them Bruno recognized a couple of people who sold organic foods at the St. Denis market and his friend Alphonse the councillor, who patted his stomach and gave Bruno a thumbs-up of approval for the food.

At the table beside Alphonse, Bruno noticed Didier, the manager of the truffle market in Ste. Alvère, dining in silence with a plump woman who wore a discontented air. There was a long table at the rear for a dozen that was filled this evening by a festive family group. A large balloon that read JOYEUSE ANNIVERSAIRE floated above a woman with white hair who was beaming at the well-dressed children beside her as they attacked two large pizzas.

"Welcome to L'Auberge des Verts," said Guillaume Pons, signaling a young waiter to take their coats. Pons was wearing crisply pressed slacks and a starched white dress shirt, open at the neck. Its sleeves were rolled to his elbows, revealing what Bruno thought might be a Rolex. Pons's good looks were marred by two black eyes and two thin strips of white tape across the bridge of his nose. His voice was thick and nasal, as if Axelle's butting had given him a heavy cold.

"All my rescuers here at once," Pons said, smiling gingerly, and pointed across the room to where Albert, the chief *pompier,* was dining with his wife. Albert raised a hand in salute.

"I'm afraid I ruined your clothes with my bloody nose," he said to Pamela. "I had to throw my favorite shirt away, and I suspect you had to do the same with your shirt. I insist on buying you a new outfit. Good Samaritans shouldn't have to pay for their kindness."

"Not at all," said Pamela. "It was an old skirt, anyway. I soaked it in cold water. It's fine."

"Are you sure?"

"Absolutely."

Pons turned to Fabiola. "There must be a bill for your medical treatment."

"Forget it. The damage doesn't look too bad," said Fabiola, in her brisk, professional way. She was wearing one of the dark trouser suits she always wore at work. It set off her trim figure. "Your bruises will go down in a few days, and the nose should heal by itself. Come and see me again in a week, and I'll check your sinuses. You can pay me for that."

Suddenly the door to the kitchen opened and the face of a small and very serious Asian girl peeked out. Pons turned and said something loud and firmly in what Bruno assumed was Chinese, and a tall Chinese man in a chef's hat appeared behind the girl and pulled her back.

"Excuse me. One of the nieces of Minxin, my chef," Pons explained. "You know how curious kids are."

"In the meantime, Monsieur Pons, I'm getting hungry," said the baron.

"Of course. But I do want to apologize for the way things got so out of hand at the sawmill," Pons said. "Now let me show you to your table. And please call me Bill. When I hear 'Monsieur Pons' I look around for my father. Not a happy relationship, as you know."

He smiled to take any reproof from his words and led them to a table by one of the large windows, screened by thick red drapes. He held a chair for Pamela, who somehow made the little black dress she was wearing look festive rather than formal, a wide red suede belt emphasizing her waist and the curve of her hips. Bill pointed to the ice bucket where a bottle of Bollinger awaited their arrival between two tall beeswax candles.

"With my compliments." He ripped off the foil to open the bottle. "A small thank-you." Bruno watched approvingly as Pons twisted the cork, not the bottle, and gave a gentle tap to the bottle's base to reduce the foam. He carefully filled their glasses, and a young waitress appeared with four leather-bound menus and a wine list.

"I hope you know that this is an organic restaurant, and as much of the food as possible is grown locally," Bill went on. "We want to offer a full wine list so we are not so strict there, but the bio wines are all marked. If you have any questions, just ask for me, and bon appétit."

"The champagne is a pleasant gesture," said Pamela, smiling, once their host had gone. She raised her glass and called for a toast to Bill's generosity. Bruno nodded and sipped with the rest of them, despite the sense of discomfort he felt at accepting a gift for doing no more than his job. He had seen too many policemen taking free meals and other favors, and he knew that at some point they usually came with a price attached. That may have been the way Bill learned to do business in Asia, but that was not something Bruno wanted to see in St. Denis. Still, he smiled across the table to the baron, and he looked with pleasure at the two handsome women who flanked them, Fabiola's dark hair piled almost formally high and Pamela's hair glinting now bronze, now chestnut, in the candlelight.

"This place is grander than I'd expected," said Fabiola.

"I'm not sure about this *foie gras poêlé en étoile d'anis.* It sounds like it would ruin a perfectly good foie gras," grumbled the baron from deep within the menu. "Nor this fresh trout with lemongrass; you won't be able to taste the fish. Still, the prices aren't too bad."

"But you like the way Bruno does his *foie* with honey and balsamic vinegar," said Pamela. "This kind of change is just what we need around here. But do you think people in St. Denis will ever forgive Bill for closing his father's sawmill? You were born here, Baron. What do you think?"

"The people who worked there will never forgive him. But that's a small minority. Old-fashioned types like me regret its passing. But I do wonder about a son who breaks with his father like that, in such a public way."

"It was the father who slapped him," said Fabiola.

"After the son had tried to destroy the father's business. And we all know how much we need jobs around here. So I'm reserving judgment on our inventive restaurant owner, at least until we've eaten his food." He turned to Bruno. "Did you see Alphonse was dining with Jean Marillon?"

Bruno nodded. Marillon was one of the town's pharmacists, and expected to be the Socialist Party's candidate for mayor in the elections in May. He was a competent man but a lackluster candidate who had been beaten twice before by Bruno's boss, the current mayor. If Marillon stood down and his Socialists forged an electoral pact with Alphonse's Green Party, Bruno's mayor could be facing a tight race.

"You think young Pons is going to be the joint candidate?" Bruno asked.

"Not only that. I think he's going to win," said the baron, handing a sheet of paper across the table. Bruno found himself reading a printed appeal from Boniface Pons, owner of the old sawmill, to sign a petition to support his independent campaign to be the next mayor as candidate for the St. Denis Alliance for Jobs. "He only needs sixty signatures on that petition to get on the ballot, and he'll get that from the sawmill employees and their families."

" 'Ban all immigration so long as French workers remain unemployed,' " Bruno read aloud.

"So he gets the Front National vote, and a lot of the conservatives who usually vote for the mayor," the baron said. "If the Reds and Greens put up a decent candidate, they could win. And I think they might just have one in the guy who bought us this bottle of champagne."

"You think our mayor could lose?" Bruno asked. With young Pons heading that Red-Green list and his father running on the right, a lot of media attention could be guaranteed, Bruno thought. That would mean more work for him, trying to keep St. Denis calm during a heated campaign with TV cameras and reporters hunting for Oedipal drama as father faced son on the hustings. If the mayor lost, it might well be his final task as the chief of police of St. Denis.

"Voters get tired of the same old face. And there's a recession. And young Pons is a fresh new political face with some new ideas. Yes, I think our old friend could lose."

Bruno handed back the paper and looked across to the table where Alphonse and Marillon were raising a glass to each other. They could have been sealing a pact. The baron followed his gaze.

"Would anybody mind if we treat this like a Chinese restaurant and share one another's dishes?" asked Pamela. Startled, Bruno turned his attention back to the table.

"Sure, good idea," said Fabiola as Bill approached the table to take their orders.

"Tell me about this Pekin-Périgord duck on the menu," the baron said.

"It's like the usual Pekin duck, wrapped in a crepe with strips of cucumber and spring onions," Bill explained. "But instead of hoisin sauce we use a reduction of *vin de noix,* and the ducks are from here, but we wind-dry them in the Chinese way. My chef, Minxin, says he can't wait to try it back in Hong Kong." He poured the remainder of the champagne.

"I'm pleased you're having the risotto. It's an attempt to do with our truffles here what they do in Piedmont with white truffles," Bill went on, when Fabiola told him her choice. "And there's an organic sauvignon blanc from a small vineyard near Thénac that goes wonderfully well with it, and with the duck."

The baron chose the duck and the white wine and as usual asked for a carafe of tap water. The price that restaurants charged for mineral water was one of his standard grumbles. His dinner companions were used to his ways. The four of them had eaten and played tennis together often enough to be comfortable in one another's company. Only when they were alone did the baron tease Bruno about his relationship with Pamela, saying how much more suited he was to her than Isabelle, the dashing police inspector from Paris with whom he'd enjoyed a brief but passionate affair that summer. When you get to my age, the baron had said, you'll know that it's better to be suited to a woman than to be besotted with her.

Looking across the table at Pamela's perfect complexion and lively eyes, and feeling the soft pressure of her foot resting on his beneath the table, Bruno knew that he was more than a little besotted with her, possibly because their affair had begun just a few weeks ago. And Bruno was still trying to adapt to the rhythms that Pamela imposed. He was accustomed to a blaze of passion, spending each night with a new lover and plunging into the relationship as if he were diving headlong into a river. As loving as she might be when they were together, that was not Pamela's way. She made it clear when he was welcome in her bed and when he was not. When she wanted a weekend to herself she told him so with firm affection, and she never spoke of their future. It was a very controlled affair, and she insisted on their living separate lives. She said it was because she did not want to become a subject of St. Denis gossip, which just showed how little she understood the way a small town comes to know things by a kind of osmosis. She'd talked of her failed marriage back in England and told him she was wary of living with a man. She remained elusive and something of a mystery to him, and Bruno was sufficiently honest with himself to admit that was part of her attraction.

They all shared the baron's duck, and then Pamela took command of the table, passing around spoonfuls of her *gado-*

gado salad, described on the menu as an Indonesian dish of bean sprouts with a peanut sauce. She quartered her trout to serve it around the table, and even the baron nodded approvingly at the lemongrass sauce. The wine was pronounced perfect, and all the dishes were empty by the time the young waitress returned with the Pruneaux d'Agen soaked in brandy.

"I think I'll become a regular here, even though they didn't get the risotto quite right," said Fabiola. Murmurs of satisfied approval around the table made it clear she spoke for them all. The baron was nodding happily as he signaled for the bill. But before it came, Pons ambled over, bringing a tray with four small pottery cups and a stone bottle so cold that beads of moisture sparkled and ran down the sides.

"This is something special I'd like you to try," he said. "We offer it to all our guests on their first visit. It's called *mijiu*. It's a Chinese rice wine that's usually drunk warm. But I find it makes a fine digestif served very cold."

"How long were you in China?" Pamela asked. "And why don't you come and join us? Most of your other guests have gone." She waved a hand at the almost empty restaurant.

"I'd like that," Bill said, pulling up a chair between Pamela and the baron. "I lived in Hong Kong and Macao for nearly ten years, but with lots of trips to the mainland. I was in Shanghai for nearly a year, Beijing for a few months. And I spent time in Singapore and Bangkok. I loved Asia. Still do, but suddenly I started to feel a little homesick. Believe it or not, I hoped for a reconciliation with my father."

"But you weren't prepared to compromise on the sawmill," said the baron, "despite the family tie."

"No. But I offered to help pay for a new chimney scrubber."

"The latest problem was less the pollution than the location," said Bruno. "It was too close to that housing block."

"It would have meant demolishing one building," said Pons, with a bitter laugh. "Just a small storage shed, and donating about a hundred square meters to the commune. Then the sawmill would've been outside the excluded area. I offered to pay for the land and for a replacement storage building, but my father saw it as a matter of principle. Or perhaps he saw it as good business—he's getting a generous grant to build the new sawmill over in St. Félix and a tax write-off for the old place. Anyway, he made it pretty clear that he wanted neither my help nor my company. But that's enough about my dysfunctional family. Thanks again, especially to you, Monsieur le Chef de Police. I'd heard all about you from our mutual friend Alphonse, and I think it was mainly thanks to you that it didn't turn out worse than it was."

"If violence breaks out, even one brief incident, it means I've failed," said Bruno, feeling uncomfortable. "I can't count that as one of my better days."

"Let's try this Chinese wine," Pamela said into the sudden silence.

Bill poured. "Tell me what you think."

Bruno sipped and made polite noises, but it wasn't to his taste at all. The baron put his cup down after a sip and muttered about having to drive and beware of the gendarmes. Fabiola, who made a point of putting honesty first, said it was not her idea of a digestif.

"It's interesting, different from what I expected," said Pamela. "What did you do in Asia? Did you get a job or teach French or start a business or what?"

"All of those," he said, with a charming smile that even his bruises could not dilute. "At different times, of course. I was a cognac salesman in Shanghai, ran a wineshop in Vientiane, taught French in Bangkok and even worked as a croupier in a Macao casino. But my primary business was to have a small share in what became a very successful restaurant in Macao and then Hong Kong. That's where I met my chef, Minxin Hu. He's become a good friend. Let me introduce him." He rose. "Anyone want coffee?"

"I have to work tomorrow, so I don't want to be too late," said Fabiola. "Let's say hello to your Chinese partner as we get our coats."

Bill headed for the kitchen and quickly reappeared with the tall and solemn-looking Chinese man. The clothes were impeccable, gleaming white and freshly pressed, as if he had just put them on. Bruno, who had seen Chinese cooks drenched in sweat after working close to their steaming woks, was surprised. "Thank you for a memorable meal," said Bruno, rising to shake Minxin's hand. The man gave a tight-lipped smile and a short bow.

"*Merci, merci*—my French very bad," the chef said, and shook hands all around as Bruno asked Pons once more for the bill.

"You are my guests tonight," he said airily.

"No, it's kind of you, but we can't accept that," Bruno said firmly. "Policemen can't accept free meals. We'd like to pay."

Bill studied Bruno for a moment, his bruised face impassive. Then he nodded and turned aside to the small reception table and scribbled out a bill. It said simply "4 fusion menus at 20 euros, 1 bottle wine 20 euros. Total 100 euros."

"By the way, Minxin's nieces need to be registered for school," said Bruno, handing over two fifty-euro notes. He turned to help Pamela on with her coat. The baron helped

Fabiola, and the two men voiced a cheerful good night as they steered the two women into the darkness, ignoring their protests about paying their share of the bill.

"We'd have been there all night if we'd stopped to hand over four credit cards," Bruno explained. "You can all pay me back later."

"It's just as well, Bruno. I really do have to be at work early tomorrow," said Fabiola, clambering into the back of Pamela's car. "Good night, Baron. It was a wonderful meal."

Pamela drove off in silence, Bruno beside her. He realized that it was one of those deafening silences that only women knew how to manufacture, a silence that any mere male broke at his peril. He looked glumly at the road ahead, knowing that he needed to think about his own future if the mayor lost the election. Despite his political neutrality, Bruno was the mayor's appointee and was widely known as one of the mayor's right-hand men. A new mayor would be wary, even suspicious, and might well want to appoint his own nominee to the post. Not that Bruno could be fired; French employ-ment law didn't work that way. But he could be forced to transfer elsewhere in the *département* or the region, or even to a much larger municipal police force in a big town. He'd hate that. And with his rank, Bruno would probably be catapulted into a senior post ahead of some bright young man who was expecting promotion. He'd have an enemy from the start. Worst of all, he'd probably have to move, sell his house and find somewhere else to live that would take his dog. He'd have to give away his chickens and his ducks and geese, leave his vegetable garden and his truffles to a new buyer. He would have to make new friends, build new relationships, carve out a new life. And where would that leave him and Pamela?

Fabiola interrupted his thoughts. "That violence at the

sawmill wasn't your fault, Bruno. And you stopped it pretty fast. Don't brood about it. And don't worry about Bill. That pretty face of his looks a lot worse than it is."

"I wouldn't call him pretty," said Pamela. "Handsome certainly, but there's too much character there to call him pretty. He's had an interesting life. I wonder if one of those windmill things would work for me."

"You can get grants for that these days," said Bruno. "And for adding insulation to your roof. We've got some pamphlets about it at the *mairie*."

"It's not just about money," Pamela said crisply, and Bruno lapsed into silence again.

When they reached Pamela's place, Fabiola pecked them both on the cheek, said a quick good night and darted into her own house.

"Perhaps I'd better walk back to town," Bruno said.

"Don't be silly. It's far too cold," Pamela said, going through her kitchen door and shedding her coat. "Help yourself if you want coffee or anything. You know where it all is." She served herself a glass of water from the tap, leaned against the sink and turned to face him. He hung up his coat and sat at the kitchen table. "You seemed rather down this evening. Don't you approve of Bill?"

Bruno shrugged. "I don't know enough about him to approve or disapprove. But it's a good restaurant, and I certainly approve of the energy saving. What surprises me is his sudden decision to go in for politics. He's only been here a few months, and now there's talk of him running for mayor already." Bruno wondered how to put into words his discomfort at the threatening pace of change, at the disruption of the calm and ordered way of life in St. Denis that he cherished.

"You mean you spent ten years sinking your roots into

St. Denis and this attractive young prodigal son blazes back into town and starts to take over. It sounds as though you're jealous."

Bruno looked her in the eye. "I've got nothing to be jealous about. If you find him attractive, you're a free woman. I have no claims on you." But the moment he said it, Bruno knew that it didn't reflect quite what he felt. He smiled at her, trying to make a joke of it.

"I take you as you are," he said. "Whatever the terms."

"The terms are still under negotiation," she said, unfolding herself from the sink and coming across to take his face in her hands and kiss him softly on the lips. "Come on, dearest Bruno, and take me to bed."

4

Didier, the manager of the truffle market, was a short man with a clammy handshake, a potbelly and a bad haircut. Bruno tried to damp down the instinctive dislike he felt even as he turned himself a little sideways to avoid the man's sour breath. Didier was explaining the various steps required to match a basket of truffles sold in the market hall with an Internet order. Bruno tried to concentrate on the process as he observed Didier for any signs of nervousness. Bruno had assumed even without Hercule's hints that a successful fraud would require somebody on the inside who was familiar with the way the market worked. Didier was his guide to this process but also an obvious suspect. Bruno had expected defensiveness, but that was not the way Didier seemed to be reacting.

"The difficulty is that we don't have the authority to control the whole market," Didier said, sounding more aggrieved than nervous. "If all the sales had to go through us, there'd be no problem. But the mayor doesn't want to upset the *renifleurs*. He might lose their votes, and some of the big customers insist on using them anyway."

Bruno nodded encouragingly. "Politics always seems to get involved, that's true."

"It's politics all the way in this town. Especially now that the elections are coming up. I suppose that's why the mayor called you in. The last thing he wants is a scandal, which would explain why you're not in uniform."

"I don't have any jurisdiction in Ste. Alvère," Bruno said. "But I don't think it's just the elections. The new plantations are going to increase the truffle supply and make the trade even more important for the town."

Didier nodded and helped himself to more coffee from the jug that a young woman had brought in when Bruno arrived. It was weak and slightly stewed, and Bruno had left his cup unfinished. From his chair in front of Didier's desk in the office of the market hall, Bruno had a clear view of the tower of the ruined castle that dominated the town center.

"The growth is for the future. But right now, because the mayor doesn't want to upset the *renifleurs,* we have to have a double system," Didier said. "There's the market we control, where we buy in the truffles and then sell them. And then there's a consignment system, where we sell the truffles on behalf of the grower or the hunter. We only pay him once we get paid. We charge a small fee when we give a guarantee of quality."

Bruno had already looked over the account books that lay open before him. Last year, the market had issued certificates for almost eight million euros' worth of truffles, so the fees for the certificates amounted to a quarter of a million. The figures had surprised him. There was more money involved here than he'd thought. The market was required by the *mairie* to take a five percent profit on the truffles it bought and sold directly, and last year that had been worth another quarter million.

"It looks like half a million a year in income for the *mairie*," said Bruno.

"I'm proud to say that I run the most profitable single department of the *mairie*," said Didier, sitting back in his chair with a smug expression on his face. "Of course, buying and selling on our own account means there's another problem because of the cash flow. We pay cash to buy the truffles, but we don't get paid until we resell them. That's a problem when there's a surge in supply like we get in January. We have to pay interest on the bank overdraft, and that cuts our profit."

"The profit looks pretty healthy to me."

"It is, and that's how the mayor wants it. And I think our controls are good, so I was surprised when we got word of a complaint."

"More than one," said Bruno. "The first came from a hotel group in Paris and the second from a brasserie in Montparnasse. They both said the same. The individual truffles were fine, but they weren't satisfied with the quality of the tailings. I suppose those are the scraps that they use to make truffle oils."

"And in stews and risottos," said Didier. "The quality's always lower. The chefs want to get some truffle flavor without paying for real truffle quality."

"But their complaint states that they had your tailings analyzed and they included some *sinensis,* cheap Chinese truffles."

"They say that, but who knows when the *sinensis* were added? It could've been during the delivery or even in Paris. We've never found any trace of *sinensis* in the stocks here. I think they're saying that just to try to get us to give them a discount."

"It doesn't sound like good business to accuse your customers of pulling a fast one," said Bruno. "And they've never complained before. I'd take this more seriously if I were you. Is there any point in your operation where low-grade truffles could be sneaked into a shipment without your knowledge?"

"Theoretically, I suppose you could have some sleight of hand, but I think I'd spot some *sinensis* in a batch. Once a basket leaves the market hall it goes either to the test lab or to the shipping point and that's all controlled."

"How do you mean 'controlled'?" Bruno asked. This was what he needed to understand.

"Once we accept a basket it leaves the market hall through that hatch in the wall and goes onto a table in the hall behind us. Anything to be tested is put on the left and goes to Madame Pantowsky in the lab. Items for shipment are left on the right for Jean-Luc and Alain, who pack them for shipping. Nobody but us is allowed through that door."

"So in theory, you could have the cheap truffles added at any stage by any of the staff."

"In theory, yes, but I trust them all. I presume you'll want to question them?"

"Of course, but that'll be later. Is it possible that this sleight of hand could be done on a crowded market day?"

"Yes, but even when it's crowded the public can't get close to the hatch. And every basket is weighed. Anybody trying to take out good scraps and put in bad ones would have to make an exact match of the weight. I don't think it's possible. Once we accept a basket, we weigh it. The weight and basket number are the two identifiers we put on the label for each basket. Everything is checked at packing, so if the weight changed, Jean-Luc would spot the difference and call me."

During this exchange, Bruno had been drafting a diagram

of each step in the process, from the arrival of a hunter with a basket of truffles through to final shipment. He showed the diagram to Didier.

"Is there anything I've left out? I want to make sure I have every single step tracked."

"No, it's all there, except for a final bid. Once we've ful-filled all the orders on hand, we then let the *renifleurs* bid for any stock that's left over. It's like an auction. I don't like to keep stocks here, so we try to ensure that everything gets sold."

"Where does that happen?"

"Here in the market hall at the end of the day. We list each sale by weight, quality, price and name of buyer, and of course the date."

"I'd like to see those records, please."

Didier seemed to hesitate. "All the logbooks and records were put into storage at the *mairie*."

"So I'll be able to find them there?"

Didier nodded. "They're not very well organized. I don't have any secretarial help."

"Why not? The truffle market makes enough money, and I've never heard of a mayor who wouldn't like to find some-one a job."

Again Didier seemed to hesitate, and then spoke slowly, as if choosing his words with care. "He seems happy enough for me to do it as part of my duties. Of course, my figures are then checked by the town auditor for the taxes and social security charges."

Bruno resigned himself to a day in a dusty basement file room. "The complaints refer to truffles bought in two differ-ent ways," he said. "The hotel group bought from you direct, but the brasserie bought its truffles from a *renifleur* who

attached one of your quality assurance certificates to his shipment. Would he have got that in such a bidding process?"

"Yes. But he could then have substituted some cheap tailings for what we'd approved. He'd have to open the vacuum-
sealed bag we use, put in the cheap stuff and then get another
vacuum pack. He'd have to steam off our quality label from
the original pack."

"Why not use a steamproof glue for your labels so he
couldn't do that?"

"Good idea. I'll look into it, see what special glue we
might need."

Bruno paused. The procedure seemed sound enough as a
safeguard against adulteration. That left the human element.

"Tell me," Bruno said, "just as a hypothetical, if you ever
wanted to cheat the system, how would you go about it and
not get caught?"

"I really don't know," Didier replied with a shrug that
turned into a confident half smile. "I've asked myself that and
I don't see how because at the end of the day the final step in
quality control rests with the customers. If they aren't happy,
we're out of business, and I'm out of a job."

Didier switched his half smile to full beam and spread his
arms wide. Bruno forced himself to smile back.

"Who designed this system you have?"

"I did, and had it approved by the mayor. We've had three
years with no trouble."

"Until now."

Didier's smile was still in place, but his eyes glinted. An
innocent man angered at unjust suspicion, or a guilty one
worried that his deception wasn't working? Bruno had no
idea. Most of the usual little clues and the local knowledge
that helped him in St. Denis simply did not work here. He

knew little of Didier, his family and his reputation. Ste. Alvère was virtually unfamiliar territory, and he was groping in the dark, trying to decide whether his hackles were up because he was suspicious of the man or whether he just disliked him and his bad breath.

"Do you ever see any Chinese in the market?" Bruno asked.

"We get the occasional tourist. We have some regular customers. There's a Chinese supermarket chain and an import-export firm in Paris that sells our truffles into the Chinese market. But they get all the profit, so we're looking at arranging our own distribution in Hong Kong."

"I'll be in touch," Bruno said, rising now that his list of prepared questions had run out. "And now I'd like to see your chemist. Should I stay in this room?"

"I'll send her in," said Didier. "By the way, I know you're a friend of Hercule Vendrot. Could you ask him to let us borrow his truffle journal? It's got all the prices and supplies in the market for years past plus weather reports and all sorts of other historical data. He's turned down me and the mayor. You might have better luck."

"Why should I do that?"

"It would help make the market more efficient if we tracked sales and output over time, and since you're on the payroll now . . ."

"How do you mean, 'on the payroll'?"

"Well, I presume you're not doing this security review for nothing." He winked, rubbing his thumb and index finger together.

Since the thought of payment had never entered his head until this moment, Bruno said nothing but simply stared at Didier. Why did people think of everything in terms of money? He was doing this for a friend, Hercule, and because his boss, the mayor, had also asked him to perform this small service. If it helped the truffle trade, it helped Bruno and all the other truffle hunters of St. Denis. And where would the Périgord be without the truffles that symbolized its culinary distinction? Evidently embarrassed by Bruno's silence, Didier scooped up his papers and bustled out.

The fair-haired young woman who had earlier brought the coffee came in and stood quietly by the door. Bruno was about to decline more coffee when he suddenly realized he was about to make a fool of himself. Despite her demure pose, there was a sharp and watchful intelligence in her eye.

"You're the chemist, madame . . . ?"

"My name is Florence Pantowsky. Yes, I'm a chemist, employed here part-time." Her voice was quiet and low, and she kept her eyes downcast, although her posture was upright. She had a fine complexion, and strong cheekbones gave elegance to what would otherwise have been a rather plain face. Bruno noted that while her hair was neatly brushed it was dry and lifeless. She was wearing a very unflattering floral dress that was about thirty years too old for her and canvas tennis shoes. With a little effort, she would have been handsome.

"Thank you for bringing the coffee earlier. Won't you please have a seat?"

"Thank you." She tucked her slim legs beneath the chair and smoothed her dowdy dress down so that it fell below her knees.

"What kind of chemist becomes an expert on truffles?" he asked.

"The unemployed kind with a divorce and two children to raise," she replied calmly, without hint of humor or resentment. She might have been discussing the weather.

"How old are they?" He glanced down through her personnel file. She was thirty, born in Amiens. Pantowsky was her maiden name, so she was probably from one of the Polish families that came to work in the coal mines, when there still were coal mines in France.

"Three. They're twins, a boy and a girl. But I don't think they've anything to do with this meeting."

"Very well, madame. But I need your help. I'm trying to understand how it is that a fraud might be committed here. We've had complaints that some of the truffles coming from this market are Chinese."

"It's simple. Somebody must have made a substitution."

"Where and how?"

"I've no idea." Her eyes looked up at him. They were pale blue, almost gray. He thought of the Baltic Sea and remembered her Polish name.

"Take a guess."

"It's pointless to speculate." Her face was impassive.

"Why?"

"It could take place anywhere along the supply chain, either here at the market or during delivery or at the end user. Proper controls could be installed at each stage, but it would be very expensive."

"What proportion of the truffles do you analyze?"

"I am supposed to make random checks of an average of three percent. In rush periods, like the one that will last into February, the volume is simply too big for that scale of testing. In January, I might not even be checking one percent. The mayor and the market manager know this. They allow me to average out the three percent over the year. That means we are most at risk during the key period, when the really valuable items are being traded."

"Does that worry you?"

"Yes, a great deal. I've proposed hiring a couple of part-time assistants during January. Any high school graduate could be trained to do the work, under proper supervision. The cost would be minimal, perhaps a thousand euros. But the manager refuses."

"Did he give a reason?"

"Cost," she said coolly.

"Did you find this convincing?"

"Of course not."

"What do you think was Didier's real reason?"

"I've no idea. That is, I don't know if there is a real reason. He's a man who often finds it necessary to show that he is in charge."

"Is that why you make the coffee?"

"No, I make the coffee because I need this job." Her voice was flat. A robot might have shown more emotion, more involvement in the conversation. Accustomed to the instinctive warmth of the people of the region, Bruno felt disconcerted.

"You really think you could lose the job if you refused to make the coffee?"

"I'm a part-timer on a contract, so I have no job security. It's not a risk I want to take."

"What a pity you show it by making such bad coffee," said Bruno, determined to provoke some kind of response from her. "A woman of your education and intelligence could make excellent coffee if she tried."

For the first time, she smiled. It was not a very convincing smile, but Bruno felt encouraged. He let the silence build.

"I'm not used to dealing with the police," she said.

"Who told you I was a policeman? I'm doing a security review."

"You're Bruno of St. Denis. I saw you at the closing of the sawmill."

"You were one of the Green protesters?"

"I'm a Green Party member, yes. A lot of scientists are."

"I see you got your degree and your diploma in Paris. What brought you down here?"

"Marriage, and then I grew to like the place more than I liked my husband. It's a good place to raise my children. So I'll do a lot to keep my job."

"Would that include turning a blind eye to some irregularities?"

"No, I know there are irregularities. But I can't prove it. I don't know who's doing what. I do know that by investigating these Chinese truffles you are looking at the molehill rather than the mountain."

"I don't understand," he said.

She was studying his face as if trying to assess his character and whether she could trust him. He looked back at her, doubtful that he could control his features nearly as well as this woman controlled hers.

"You might check the average price being paid at the final biddings for those items not sold by the end of the day," she said eventually.

"Why would you recommend that?" he asked. "Please understand that I'm new to this. I want to understand what exactly I should be looking for, and why."

This time she responded quickly, as if her decision on whether to trust him had already been made.

"The prices recorded at the end-of-day auctions seem unreasonably low to me, week after week. I don't think that happens by accident."

"You suspect the bidding process is being rigged?"

"Yes. But I'm aware my judgment might be flawed by personal prejudice." She looked at him knowingly.

Bruno paused, then the realization dawned. Having met Didier, and seen something of the way he chose to treat Florence, Bruno felt pretty sure he knew what lay behind her prejudice. There was no subtle way to confirm his guess. She might even appreciate the frankness of an open question.

"Please look at me, madame," he said. When her eyes raised reluctantly to his own, he waited for a long heartbeat before he spoke. "Are you being sexually harassed at work?"

"No more than usual, and not anymore," she replied, so brisk it was almost businesslike, but her eyes were suddenly blazing. "I can deal with it. He's a pig, but he's also a coward."

5

The Tuesday morning market of St. Denis, which in summer stretched the length of the rue de Paris from the place de la Mairie to the parade ground in front of the gendarmerie, shrank in the autumn after the tourists departed. In the quiet months of November, January and February the stalls barely filled the town square. But it always expanded again for the month before Christmas, which meant eager competition for the favored spots among the pillars in the covered market beneath the *mairie*. The rule was always that the first arrivals chose their sites, but the definition of what constituted an arrival was sometimes in dispute.

Usually, it required the placing of a couple of trestles to establish a presence, and Bernard the basket maker had his trestles firmly in place and stood grimly between them, his arms folded. Margot, the housekeeper at the home for retired priests in St. Belvédère, stood equally grimly, her arms also folded, her wide hips defending her small table with its beeswax candles and jars of honey that stood in front of Bernard's trestles. Fat Jeanne, whose shape became more spherical with each passing year, was supposed to umpire such confrontations as she collected the five euros per meter of frontage that the *mairie* charged each stallholder. But Margot, who refused to pay any more than two euros on the grounds that her table measured only eighteen inches a side, tested even Fat Jeanne's inexhaustible cheeriness.

"I won't move," Margot declared. "I was here first."

"My trestle was already here when you arrived," countered Bernard.

"Only one of them, and one trestle doesn't count," she snapped, brushing aside Fat Jeanne's offer of an alternative spot beside Fauquet's café.

"Margot," said Bruno, attempting his most winning smile. "Just the woman I wanted to see. The mayor needs some help, and I told him we could count on you. It's for the children."

Bruno needed both hands to hold up the big placard that he had collected from the Info-Boutique. THE MAYOR'S FUND, it read, with a picture of Father Christmas and some smiling infants. TO MAKE A REAL CHRISTMAS FOR THE CHILDREN OF THE UNEMPLOYED.

Bruno leaned the placard casually against Bernard's trestle, kissed Margot on each of her cold cheeks and handed her the collection plate. "Can you take care of the collection here under the pillars?" he asked. "And you know everyone in the market, Margot. Who do you think I should ask to take care of the collection outside?"

"Now there's a question," said Margot, preening. "Your friend Stéphane's a reliable type, at least when he's not drinking. Or perhaps Aurélie, she'll have time on her hands, since nobody wants to buy her scrawny ducks." She cast her eyes over the rest of the market, wondering who might be worthy to share with her the honor of the mayor's special task.

"Give me a hand with that other trestle, Bernard," Bruno

said to the basket maker. Catching on, Bernard quickly assembled his stall, and Bruno placed Margot's small table alongside it and then put the placard atop both of the stalls.

"So you stand here, Margot, right beside your table with the honey so everyone can see the placard and can see that you're in charge of the collecting," Bruno said. "I think you're right about Aurélie for the other collection box. Why don't you go and ask her?"

"I don't know how you do it," Bernard murmured as Margot strode off.

"Do you think anybody would dare *not* to make a donation with Margot looming over them?" Bruno replied. "She's just what this project needs."

"Since when was it the mayor's fund?" asked Fat Jeanne. "The last I heard it was your idea."

"Ever since the mayor thought it was his idea," said Bruno, grinning. "He'll be along in an hour or so, rattling a collection box. And I've got to get dressed up as Father Christmas."

But first he had to make his usual tour of the market, shaking the hands of the men and embracing the women and hearing snippets of gossip along the way. Léopold the Senegalese, who sold leather belts and wallets and sunglasses in summer, wanted to sign up his son for Bruno's rugby lessons. Raoul, who kept a summer stall selling wine to tourists and did odd jobs in the winter, had gotten a job at the new winery that he'd feared would put him out of business. Vinh, who sold hot fried Vietnamese *nems* and assorted Asian foods throughout the year, showed off his new Paris St. Germain shirt for the soccer club, whose fortunes he followed with devotion. His tiny wife offered Bruno a beignet, so hot he had to toss it from hand to hand while trying to reach for some coins.

At Alphonse's stall, the usual display of the tiny round *crottins* of goat cheese, divided into neat columns of dry, semidry and fresh, were almost obscured by a large placard that announced GIVE THE CHILDREN A GREEN CHRISTMAS. THE GREEN PARTY ANNOUNCES A FREE CHRISTMAS PARTY FOR ALL CHILDREN OF THE UNEMPLOYED AND THOSE ON MINI-MUM WAGE. L'AUBERGE DES VERTS, DECEMBER 21. ALL DONATIONS WELCOME. A small basket containing a couple of five-euro notes and some coins stood before it.

"How long have you been planning this?" Bruno asked Alphonse, shaking hands.

"Since last night when I saw Bill at the restaurant. We were talking before you arrived about the kids of guys who worked at the sawmill. At first I thought of hosting it myself up at the commune, but Bill had the facilities and he offered to do it."

"The mayor's organizing one too," Bruno said, brandishing his collection box.

"The more the merrier," Alphonse said. "Not a bad thing if the kids get two parties, or maybe we could combine them."

"Makes sense to me. I'll talk to the mayor, if you see what the others say. But I suspect everything will be political from now until the elections. By the way, it's amazing how fast young Pons seems to have taken over the leadership of you Greens," Bruno said. "You've been fighting the good fight for twenty years and more, so why aren't you leading the list?"

"They all know me as that old hippie, the *soixante-huitard,* and I wasn't born here, so that means lots of people won't vote for me on principle," Alphonse replied. "Bill was born and raised here, however long he's been away. He's a better speaker, more dynamic. I've never wanted to be mayor anyway."

He turned away to serve a customer, and Bruno headed for

the bustle of Fauquet's café, the tables of old men taking their first *petit blanc* of the day at the zinc bar as they scanned the sports pages of *Sud Ouest*. Tante Sandrine, as everybody called Fauquet's wife, came from behind the counter to embrace him and accept a collection box for the bar. Bruno greeted the rest of the company, and as soon as the hissing of the espresso machine died away Fauquet began to tease him about the competing parties.

"I've put the Green collection box over there on the pâtisserie counter and yours goes on the bar," he said. "An interesting experiment, to see whether the cake lovers are more generous than the drinkers."

"Depends how much you give them to drink," Bruno replied.

He paid for his coffee and went across the alley and up the stairs to the storage room of the *mairie* to look for the Father Christmas costume. He found it in one of the boxes that contained the decorations for the town's Christmas tree, which reminded him that he'd have to check when the tree would be delivered and get Michel from the public works office to test the town's Christmas lights. The suit smelled musty and needed dry cleaning, and the beard was straggly, but it would do for today. He took off his thick blue uniform jacket but kept his trousers on, donned the tunic, beard and hat, picked up his handbell and headed out toward the men's room to check his appearance in the mirror.

"Now I know it's Christmas," called Claire, the secretary, as he crossed the open-plan office. "Are you going to come down my chimney this year, Bruno?"

"Your reindeer's got a parking ticket," chimed in Roberte, who looked after the Sécu, the social security paperwork.

"Where's my present?" called Josette as Bruno stomped

down the stairs, deciding that he'd skip looking in the mirror rather than go back through the gauntlet of the tired old jokes he heard every year.

Bruno felt odd to be wearing such festive garments in sunshine, however thin and wintry the rays and however good the cause. He'd be teased about it in endless markets to come. But he strode into the rue de Paris, ringing his handbell and thrusting his collection box at stallholders and shoppers alike.

"For the children of the sawmill," he called out. "For the children of those who lost their jobs."

It seemed to work. One- and two-euro coins rattled into his tin and a few five-euro notes, one of them from a young, single man who had lost a sawmill job. Bruno thanked them all and turned down Vinh's offer of one of his hot *nems* as he strolled on to rattle his box at Léopold. As he paused at the stall, Bruno was jostled by two young men in a hurry who seemed to come from nowhere, and he half fell over Léopold's stall of cheap leather belts. Turning, he saw that the two men were Asians, presumably acquaintances of Vinh.

But then the first one pushed Vinh's wife aside and delivered a vicious chop to Vinh's neck with the side of his hand. The second man, burdened down with something heavy, staggered up to Vinh's stall and with his companion launched the contents of a large bucket into the display trays containing *nems* and *lumpia,* the samosas and prepared curries and winddried ducks. They tipped the last of some thick black liquid into the bubbling deep fryer, hurled the bucket into what was left of the trays and began kicking at Vinh and his wife where they lay huddled on the ground.

Overcoming his surprise and outrage, Bruno realized he was carrying his handbell and launched himself at the pair of them. In an instant, he knew that his costume was the perfect disguise. How could Father Christmas possibly be a danger? Bruno slammed one of the attackers on the side of the head with the bell, and without bothering to watch him fall he slammed the collection box, heavy with coins, into the back of the neck of the other. Just before he connected the man twisted, and Bruno hit his shoulder instead, and he turned to launch a swift sideways kick at Bruno's groin.

The thick skirt of the Father Christmas costume saved him, and he raised the handbell to hit again. But the young Asian had managed to win enough time to step back and pull out a khaki-colored stick, about the size of a runner's baton. Bruno recognized it from his army days, a stun grenade, all noise and stunning flare of light but not lethal. Yet it would probably serve to ignite whatever black oil now drenched the remains of Vinh's stall.

Bruno used the only weapon he had, hurling the handbell at the Asian's face. Then scooping two long belts from Léopold's stall he used them as whips, aiming the flicking leather at the Asian's eyes before darting forward to get between him and the oil that was now flooding over the prostrate figures of Vinh and his wife. But a hand was gripping his ankle and holding him back—the other Asian. Bruno stomped down hard while constantly flicking his leather belts and shouting for support. He felt rather than saw Léopold alongside him and the hold on his ankle gave way so he could move again. But the Asian now had a grip on the leather belts with one hand. At least he could not ignite the grenade.

Bruno dropped the belts and picked up a thick bolt of brightly colored African cloth from Léopold's stall. Thrusting it before him like a battering ram, he charged at the Asian, forcing him back into the tiny alley that led to the rue Gambetta. Behind the retreating figure, Bruno saw a car, its doors open and with another Asian at the wheel, leaning out and calling for the others to join him. Bruno's opponent ran back toward the car, clambering in and shouting in a language Bruno didn't understand.

But Bruno knew the geography of his town. With the market stalls and the parked ranks of the vendors' vans blocking the side streets, there was only one exit from rue Gambetta. He ran back down the rue de Paris, seeing Léopold sitting solidly on the chest of the fallen Asian and holding the man's hair. Vinh, soaked in black oil, was helping his wife to her feet. Bruno's van was parked in the place de la Gendarmerie, near the exit from the rue Gambetta. He knew he wouldn't have time to start the engine. He opened the door, released the hand brake and heaved the van forward a few feet to block the exit from rue Gambetta just as the Asians' escape car navigated the slow twists and turns between the parked vans and accelerated toward him.

Bruno dived out of the way as their car slammed into the side of his van, crumpling the front of their own car against one of the front wheels.

The two Asians came out as Bruno clambered to his feet, the driver whirling a stick on the end of a short chain as he advanced, shrieking angrily. Trying to keep one eye on the second man, Bruno backed away slowly and saw his attacker put one hand across his eyes as his partner tossed something in Bruno's direction. Suddenly there was a huge noise and a great flare of light and he was stunned and blind and deaf. The stun grenade had gone off.

Bruno felt a sudden assault of cold water and a familiar scouring of his face before the sponge moved to the back of his neck. Sergeant Jules from the gendarmerie had learned his rudimentary medical skills on the rugby field, where an icy sponge was deemed sufficient for anything short of a broken limb. The sergeant's lips were moving, and Bruno tried to concentrate, but his head was throbbing. At first he heard nothing. Then Jules's voice seemed to come from very far away.

"They stole your van," said Jules. In his hand was Bruno's Father Christmas hat. "I've sent a car after them, and Capitaine Duroc is putting out an alert. We should catch them before they reach Périgueux. We'd better get you to the medical center."

"There's another one, a prisoner at Léopold's stall," Bruno said, shaking his head to clear the stars from his eyes. Gingerly, he rose to his feet, still swaying; Jules put out a protective arm. Then there was another flash as Philippe Delaron, who ran the camera shop and took pictures for *Sud Ouest*, snapped a bedraggled and battered Father Christmas in the supportive arms of a gendarme.

"You run that photo and you'll never get another story out of me," said Jules, his voice hard. "And you'll be breath-tested every time you step into your car."

Leaving Delaron to take photos of the wrecked getaway car and the scraped and broken wing mirrors that marked its passage through the vendors' vans, Jules helped Bruno limp back up the rue de Paris toward what was left of Vinh's stall. There was no sign of Vinh or his wife, but Léopold was squatting beside his prisoner, a pocketknife pressed against the Asian's throat. He wasn't going anywhere. Fat Jeanne was sitting on his chest.

"This little animal will know better than to attack our

market again," said Léopold, slapping the youth almost play-fully across both cheeks and grinning widely at Bruno. "And I saved your collection box," he added, gesturing toward his stall as Bruno nodded his thanks.

"Vinh said he was going to take his wife to the medical clinic," Jeanne said as Jules bent to handcuff the young Asian, whose eyes were squeezed tightly shut. His face was smeared in blood. Bruno searched the man's pockets for a wallet or some identification but found nothing except three hundred euros in new twenty-euro notes, a cheap mobile phone and a slip of paper with a single telephone number typed on it. Starting with the digits 0553, it was clearly local.

"We can sort this out at the gendarmerie," said Bruno. Jules attempted to haul the young man to his feet, but he crumpled back down again, whimpering as he tried to crawl behind Jules and away from Léopold. "We'll need to bring in the forensics experts to look at his mobile phone. They'll have to try and identify the source of that stun grenade, if there's anything left of it. That means bringing in the Police Nationale from Périgueux."

"It looks like this boy might need an ambulance," Jeanne said, to be howled down by other stallholders who were clus-tering around. Melanie from the cheese stall was close enough to give the young Asian a kick in the ribs with her heavy win-ter boots. Bruno began pushing the crowd back, but they were in no mood to listen. Two more gendarmes arrived.

"To hell with the ambulance," said Jules. "I'm putting this little bastard in jail. We can always call a doctor to the gendarmerie."

"You know that Vinh had trouble in Sarlat last Satur-day?" said Léopold. "Same thing, some young Chinese telling him they wanted his spot. There were some hard words exchanged, a bit of pushing. But all the stallholders backed Vinh, and the others left."

"Thanks for your help," Bruno said to the big Senegalese, shaking his hand. "I'd have been in much worse trouble without you. And let us know how much that bolt of cloth cost." It was lying in a pool of oil, clearly ruined. "The *mairie* will reimburse you."

Léopold pulled from beneath his stall the small dolly he used to load and unload his van, and they pushed the half-conscious youth onto it, and with Sergeant Jules beside him, Léopold pushed the prisoner down the rue de Paris.

Bruno bent down to dip a finger into the dark oil and raised it to his nose to sniff and shrugged. Probably fuel oil, but he'd better check. He turned to Jeanne. "Please, can you call Michel at public works, get him to clean up this mess. Not that there's much to be saved of Vinh's stall. But tell him to keep some of this oil for the police lab. And ask him to hang on to the bucket they used. Thanks, Jeanne."

He pulled out his own phone and rang the Police Nationale switchboard in Périgueux, reporting the assault, the use of explosives and the theft of his van and asking for assistance and a forensics team. The word "explosives" would get swift and top-level attention.

6

By the time Bruno reached the gendarmerie, his police van had been found, rammed into a concrete lamppost at Lespinasse's garage on the outskirts of town. Two Asian men had abandoned it, leaped into an almost-new silver Renault that had just been filled with petrol, and driven off leaving the driver with the gas cap in his hand. The registration number had been circulated to all police, but there were many silver Renaults on the road. The young Asian had nothing to say. He sat silently in the interview room, his head bowed and his hands on his knees, refusing even to acknowledge questions or the offer of a glass of water. The telephone number he carried turned out to be that of a lawyer's office in Périgueux, who did not seem much surprised at the call from the gendarmerie. A lawyer would be there within the hour, accompanied by a Chinese translator.

"So at least we know the nationality," said Capitaine Duroc. "I tried calling the most recently dialed numbers on the guy's phone, but all I got was a burst of Chinese or something. We've got France Télécom looking up the subscribers."

"Has a doctor seen him?" Bruno asked, suppressing his

irritation at the way Duroc worked. It would have made more sense to check the subscriber names first, and then probe the numbers that they called most frequently. It was called a tree analysis, from the way that a trunk led to branches, which led in turn to twigs. Once the computer had churned through the numbers it could chart entire networks of connections. But now that Duroc had started calling, cell phones would be ditched and numbers changed.

"He looks okay to me," Duroc said.

"He could have a possible concussion from a blow to the head," said Bruno. "Regulations say a doctor has to check him out. And his lawyer will make a fuss if we don't." He took out his own phone and called Kati, the receptionist at the medical center, and asked for a doctor as soon as would be convenient. "It'll give us a chance to strip his clothes off and check for identifying marks or tattoos," he added.

Duroc went down to the communications room to monitor the search for the stolen car. Françoise, the only woman among the small team of gendarmes, came in waving an evidence bag, looking pleased with herself. A curl of charred plastic was visible inside the bag along with some scraps of paper.

"It's what was left of the stun grenade," she explained. "There are some numbers and other markings that might help identify it." She reached over the desk, pulled a magnifying glass from the drawer and turned on the desk lamp to shine it onto the evidence bag. "See there. Are those letters or what?"

Bruno's phone rang, and the screen showed it was a familiar and expected caller. "What's this about explosives?" demanded Jean-Jacques Jalipeau, the chief of detectives for the Police Nationale in Périgueux. Bruno counted him as a friend, with a touch of caution. Usually their interests coincided, but Bruno's boss was his mayor, while J-J reported to the prefect of the Département of the Dordogne and to the Ministry of the Interior.

"The explosive was a stun grenade, used by some young Asians after attacking a market stall. They got away in a stolen car. We're looking at the stun grenade now, or what's left of it. It looks like one of the grenades we had in the army, but it's not French issue. We've got one of the attackers in custody plus his cell phone. He had the phone number of a Périgueux lawyer in his pocket."

"Which one?"

"Poincevin. His office is supposed to be sending someone here. Do you know him?"

"More than I'd like. He runs a big criminal defense practice, and he's not particular about who he takes on, lots of lowlife clients and some shady councillors. This is the first time I've heard of him representing Asians. I'll make some calls and send you down a forensics guy to look at your grenade and check out the cell phone. Hold the Asian under *garde à vue* until I can sort out an interpreter. When should I expect your incident report?"

"By the end of today, but it'll be very basic."

"Before you go, read me out the recent numbers he called on the mobile. There's a special unit in Paris that deals with Asian crime. Our old friend the brigadier is involved. I'll see if any of the numbers spark any interest."

"They're mostly mobiles, but there's a couple for Paris," Bruno said, reading them out. "Anything going on with Asians I should know about?"

"We had a tip from Paris. The biggest Chinese restaurant in Périgueux, owned by a guy with his own supermarket attached, just got taken over. He borrowed money from some big boys in Paris, loan shark stuff, and they screwed him on interest rates. It seems they did the same thing to a Chinese supermarket in Bordeaux a couple of months ago. The Paris cops think it's organized crime, Chinese triads getting established in France. I'll keep you posted."

As they hung up, Fabiola walked in with her medical bag and asked, "Where's this prisoner?"

"It's Bruno you should look at," said Jules. "He had a stun grenade go off beside him, and he was out like a light for about a minute. The Asian kid's just groggy."

"I'm fine," Bruno protested. But Fabiola was already turning him toward the window and pulling back his eyelids to look into his pupils. She took a small flashlight from her bag and shone it into his eyes.

"No bleeding from your nose?" she asked, as she poked the flashlight into his ears.

"No, Doctor. Jules here dosed me with a cold sponge, just like he does on the rugby field. I'm fine, just a bit of a headache, and I've got work to do."

"I want to see you at the medical center just before noon, and I'll look again. And I want you to take the afternoon off. Otherwise I'll put you in an ambulance to the hospital right now and insist they keep you overnight for observation."

Bruno knew better than to argue with Fabiola in professional mode so he grumpily agreed. She told him to take two aspirin for the headache and went downstairs to the interview room with Sergeant Jules to see the Asian. Bruno called the gas station to ask about his van. It had been new when he started the job as the municipal policeman of St. Denis, but that had been ten years, one reconditioned engine and more than two hundred thousand miles ago.

"Looks like they didn't know about the brakes," said the garage owner when he came to the phone after a long wait. Jean-Louis Lespinasse, whose passion in life was to restore old Citroëns, took great pride in keeping Bruno's van on the road. But the brakes needed special care. Bruno found that a combination of a low gear, pumping the brake pedal and prayer usually worked.

"They only stopped when they ran into the lamppost," Lespinasse went on. "If you ask me, the frame's gone and it's a write-off. I'll get the boy to take some photos and e-mail them to you for the insurance. Meantime, what should I tell this guy whose car they took?"

"Tell him the gendarmes have an alert out for it, and I'll be along as soon as I can and give him the number of the incident report, but he might want to inform his insurance company."

Fabiola and Jules came up the stairs as the main door to the gendarmerie opened. A middle-aged man with a self-important air approached the main desk. His clothes looked expensive.

"I'm Poincevin," he announced. "I'm here to see a client who's been detained."

"And I'm the arresting officer," said Bruno. "One moment please." He turned to Fabiola. "Okay?"

"He's in better shape than you are," she replied. "But one thing. I thought that Vietnamese friend of yours was supposed to be bringing his wife to the medical center. Neither of them turned up."

"I'd better check on that," said Bruno. "Thank you, Mademoiselle le Médecin." He smiled, her formal title a private joke between them. He turned back to Poincevin, who clearly did not like to be kept waiting.

"Perhaps you did not hear me," the lawyer said coldly. "I'm here to see my client."

"We intend to charge the prisoner with one count of criminal damage, three counts of assault, one of them on a policeman, and attempting to evade lawful arrest," Bruno said. "So far, we have no name, no statement and no proof of identity. If this detainee is your client, I'm hoping you can help us with that."

"I will see my client at once," said Poincevin, waving aside the list of charges. "And I wish to see the gendarme *officier* in charge of this station. I'm not in the habit of dealing with village policemen." He made the phrase sound like "village idiot."

"Now just you wait a moment . . . ," began Sergeant Jules, but Bruno held up a restraining hand.

"Which client, Monsieur Poincevin?"

Jules settled back, leaning against the doorframe, a smile on his face. He always enjoyed it when Bruno started calling someone "monsieur" and using that tone of icy politeness.

"What do you mean, 'which client'?" Poincevin snapped. "The one in your cell, of course."

"And the name of your client, monsieur, would be what?"

"The Chinese boy."

"Ah, monsieur speaks Chinese."

"I do not, but I have an interpreter waiting in the car outside, a member of my staff."

"And does your interpreter know the name of your client?"

"He will once I as his lawyer am allowed to see him."

"Monsieur, am I to understand that you think you have a client here, but you do not know his name?"

"My office was telephoned from this gendarmerie some two hours ago and informed that a young Chinese boy had been arrested and had offered them the number of my office. He is therefore my client."

"Monsieur, you are mistaken," Bruno said. "When that call was made, we had no idea whether he was Chinese or an Eskimo. We informed your office that a young man of Asian appearance had been arrested and was in possession of your phone number. But now you tell us he is Chinese. That represents progress. Now, if he is indeed your client, you will have his name and some means of identification. If he is not of French nationality, presumably you have his passport or some proof of his legal presence in this country. Otherwise we shall have to invoke the procedures for illegal immigration."

Fabiola was smiling broadly as she stood by the door, watching this exchange. Jules gave her a wink, but quickly returned his face to its usual stolid expression when Poincevin began casting his eyes around the room as if daring anyone to witness his frustration.

"This is ridiculous," he said, his long nose looking white and pinched while two red spots flared on his cheekbones.

"Chef de Police Courrèges is quite correct, monsieur," said Sergeant Jules. "I'm currently the officer on duty and as a lawyer you will understand that the regulations do not permit anyone to visit a detainee unless he or she has the proper authorization. I've never heard of a lawyer being unable to identify someone he claims to be a client. May I see your own identification papers, please?"

His thin lips tightening, Poincevin pulled out his wallet and handed over his identity card. Jules took it, went to a desk and formally copied down the particulars.

"*Merci,* monsieur," said Jules. "And who is it you are here to see?"

"One moment," said Poincevin after a long pause. He

pulled out a mobile phone and a notebook, juggled with them both but finally put the notebook on the counter and began to punch in some numbers. Once he had a connection, Poincevin squeezed past Fabiola and walked out the main door to speak in private. As the door closed behind him, Fabiola let a gust of laughter escape from the lips she had held tightly closed.

"Did you get them, Jules?" Bruno asked urgently. He had seen Jules discreetly scribbling the numbers down on his palm. Jules nodded and showed his hand so Bruno could see. It was a French mobile number, and Bruno punched the digits into the memory of his own phone and then called J-J, to pass them on to his contacts in Paris. Fabiola rolled her eyes and left them to it.

Poincevin returned, slipping his phone into an elegant pouch at his waist. He was followed by a young Chinese in a black suit, white shirt and dark tie. The lawyer, back in control of himself after his mysterious phone call, kept his voice flat and his face immobile as he announced that he wished to see his client, Yiren Guo. The client was twenty-two, a Chinese citizen and student, visiting France as a tourist. He read out a passport number from a notebook. Jules wrote it all down and then solemnly led the way downstairs to the interview room.

7

They took the baron's hunting car for the rendezvous with Hercule. It was one of the few vehicles that had ever aroused Bruno to pure, burning lust. An old French army jeep, still bearing the markings of the baron's former regiment of Chasseurs, it had all its old military fittings, including the can of fuel on the back and the circular canvas bag to carry the towing chain. Bruno had spent a considerable part of his military career in jeeps such as this, and his sense of nostalgia was almost as powerful as the four-wheel drive that could haul the vehicle over any terrain that wasn't vertical, and even that could usually be tackled with the winch. And it was simple, quite different from the computerized mysteries of modern cars. Bruno knew that, armed with a basic tool kit, a little ingenuity and a lot of patience, he could fix just about anything that went wrong with a jeep. The speed might be modest and the cornering dangerous and there was zero protection from the weather. But for the woodland trails and the muddy, boulder-strewn streambeds and the steeper slopes of the Périgord hills it was perfect.

Not that the current journey needed the jeep's special

attributes. The tract of forest that was reserved for Hercule's hunting club—covering a long ridge with wooded valleys on either side—was easily reached via the road from Ste. Alvère to the medieval abbey church of Paunat. A gravel road rose gradually into the woods for a kilometer and then became a dirt track for the final sweep to the shaded clearing where Hercule's elderly Land Rover was parked.

A narrow footpath through the trees led to the small shack that was formally known as the hide. In reality, like most such structures used by the region's hunters, it was more of a clubhouse, with a long table and battered benches, a cast-iron stove and barbecue stand. In a locked cupboard they kept tin plates and enamel mugs and an old shovel that did service as a frying pan on the hot embers of a fire. A stream tumbled down the hillside nearby and offered running water. Over the years they had built a little dam that provided a pool large enough for two or three tired hunters to stand and sluice off under the tiny waterfall. Below that was a washing place for utensils and for the knives used for bleeding and gutting the deer and wild boar. The dogs they brought ensured that there was little left to bury.

The rule among Bruno, the baron and Hercule was that the guests provided the *casse-croûte,* the hunters' morning snack. As always, they erred on the side of generosity. In the baron's rucksack were two cans of his own duck pâté, three beefsteaks and some of his crop of apples. His hip flask was filled with cognac. Bruno carried two bottles of the Lalande de Pomerol that he and the baron bought each year in a barrel, to spend a happy afternoon bottling it themselves. He also supplied half a dozen of his own eggs, hard-boiled, two baguettes of fresh bread and half a Tomme d'Audrix, a local cheese made by his friend Stéphane.

Leaping from the back of the jeep as soon as it was parked, their dogs were already sniffing up the trail after Hercule as Bruno and the baron pulled out their rucksacks and guns and followed. The baron used his father's old gun, a venerable English-made Purdey that was worth more than Bruno's annual salary. Bruno had a secondhand St. Etienne model from Manufrance, a serviceable gun with a walnut stock that had still cost him a month's pay. For hunting *bécasse,* the elusive game bird that could dart almost from beneath one's feet, they carried shells of standard small-gauge bird shot. Each man had a couple of slug rounds in case they met wild boar. They'd done the tests and safety courses required by the Fédération de la Chasse to receive a hunting permit, and they carried their guns safely broken open at the breech as they followed their dogs up the trail to the hide.

"Quiet," said the baron, stopping. "Listen to the dogs."

A well-trained hunting dog is silent until his master authorizes the animal to give voice. Bruno's Gigi and the baron's Général were very well trained, and yet they were whining from the trail up ahead.

Something was wrong. The baron moved on cautiously while Bruno automatically stepped out to his side. They saw their dogs backing hesitantly away, with haunches low and tails down. Bruno circled slowly, trusting the baron to take care of whatever lay ahead while Bruno peered through the trees behind them and up the slopes on both sides. He kept his gun open but gently eased two shells into the barrels. The dogs had stopped their whining, and the woods were almost silent but for the distant sound of running water. Nothing stirred except the faintest of breezes, and then Bruno caught the first scent of something on the wind. His back to the baron, he sniffed again; fresh blood.

Too well trained to turn and look, Bruno moved his eyes first and let his head follow slowly. Their rear and both flanks were clear. But still Bruno did not turn. The baron, an Algerian War veteran who had seen combat and knew its rules as well as he knew the skills of the hunt, would warn him when he was ready.

Bruno heard rather than saw the baron's dog, alerted by a hand signal from his master, start ranging out to flank the clearing and come in from the other side, exactly as he would if the baron wanted a *bécasse* cleared from a thicket. His own Gigi had come quietly to his side, awaiting orders. Bruno went down on one knee to hold his gun steady against his thigh and signaled Gigi to skirt around the other flank. He waited until he heard the baron start to move forward again.

Then he heard his friend, speaking so softly he was almost breathing the words, *"Putain. Putain de merde."* And then more loudly as the baron closed the breech of his gun, *"Ah non, ah mon Dieu. Non."*

Still Bruno did not move, although every nerve was quivering, for he could hear the fear and dismay in the baron's voice.

"Bruno," he called, and finally Bruno turned and went through the last fringe of trees and into the clearing where the baron stood before the sight of Hercule. He seemed to be hanging in midair, his head and neck craning forward like some medieval gargoyle thrusting outward from a cathedral roof. And he had evidently been made to suffer before his death. Hercule's dog lay dead at his feet.

"Don't touch anything," Bruno said, and pulled out his phone. No signal, this deep in the woods. He could not touch Hercule without stepping in the pool of blood, too fresh to have dried. Bruno looked into the hide, where Hercule's broken gun lay on the table. A hand ax and a small pile of kindling was beside it. Hercule's jacket hung on the back of a chair. He had probably been chopping wood for a fire when he was surprised. Bruno walked across to the jacket and tapped the pockets. Hercule's wallet was still there and so were the keys to his Land Rover. That would have to be searched. Bruno wrapped his hand in a handkerchief, pulled out the keys and slipped them into his pocket.

There was something else in the pocket. He hooked a finger over the pocket's edge, peered in and saw an object wrapped in newspaper, but the smell had already informed him. He pulled out two perfect examples of *melanosporum,* the famous black diamonds, weighing perhaps a pound between them. They could not have been fresher, so they must have been picked that morning, Hercule's last act before starting to prepare a fire for a *casse-croûte* with his friends. Hercule wouldn't want them to go to the ambulance men. He pulled out the truffles, showed them to the baron and put them in his pocket.

"Stay here, keep the dogs away from the blood and I'll go to phone," Bruno told the baron. "Keep your eyes open and I'll be back as soon as I can. I'll whistle when I come up the trail so you'll know it's me."

The baron tossed him the keys to the jeep, backed into the hide and settled down on one knee, his back against the stove.

"This is not just a murder," he said.

"How do you mean?"

"This is a killing that triggers phone calls to government ministers. Hercule was a *barbouze,* one of the top ones. He'll have files and secrets that could shake la République."

"You didn't tell me."

"I didn't need to, until now." The baron gestured with

his head toward the hanging corpse. "Somebody's out for revenge."

"From his Algerian days?" Bruno asked. "Or is it something else?"

The baron shrugged.

Had Hercule been Deuxième Bureau, military intelligence or the SDECE foreign intelligence and counterespionage service or what? Bruno's head spun a little at the thought of all the vague and shadowy organizations that had been charged over the past few decades with guarding France's security by fighting her secret wars. "I know somebody in Renseignements Généraux, but that's about it."

"He'll do. Call him and just say Hercule was an old *barbouze*. Indochina and Algeria and the OAS. He'll know what to do."

Bruno left, avoiding the footpath, in case forensics could find something useful on the trail, and kept a keen watch for any other signs of life. Before he reached the clearing where the jeep and Land Rover were parked, he slowed down, skirting around to approach the cars from another direction. Hercule's vehicle was locked and showed no signs of tampering. Bruno's phone still gave no signal. Before starting the jeep he looked carefully for any signs of different tire tracks in the clearing and on the track leading back to the road. He saw two possible tracks. He marked each one with a large stone and crossed branches, and then drove down the track toward Paunat, eyes darting to his phone for the first sign of a signal.

As soon as the first bar appeared, he began to call J-J, but then paused. This was one report he had better make by the book. He began by calling 15 for the SAMU emergency ambulance service and told them he'd wait by the junction with the Paunat road. Then he called a number in

Paris that he had been given previously, in the course of a different inquiry, gave his name and asked for the brigadier. Apparently his name was still on the approved list at Renseignements Généraux because the brigadier was on the line within seconds.

"How's life in the Périgord, Bruno?"

"Dangerous for some," Bruno replied. "I've just found a body left hanging in the woods, murdered, probably tortured. He's been killed within the last hour or two, and he's one of yours. An old *barbouze* from Indochina, Algeria and the OAS, is how I was advised to put it by one of his military friends."

"What was his name?"

"Hercule Vendrot. He had a Croix de Guerre and was a member of the Légion d'Honneur."

"*Putain,* Bruno. Hercule's a legend in this business. You said he'd been tortured?"

"I think so. It reminded me of some of the things I saw in Bosnia."

"*Putain.* Someone thinks he was an informer. What had he been up to? How did you know him?"

"He's been retired for as long as I've known him. He spent his time hunting for truffles. He was worried about some dirty goings-on at the truffle market in Ste. Alvère, where he lived. He and I go hunting together, and we were supposed to meet today in the woods."

"Have you told anyone else?"

"Yes, I followed procedure and called the SAMU, told them it was a suspicious death. They'll automatically inform the gendarmes and the Police Nationale when they send the ambulance. Next I'll call our mutual friend J-J. Meantime, I'm waiting at a road junction to direct the SAMU guys into the woods. They'll never find it otherwise."

"I need a favor, Bruno. As soon as you've directed them to the body, would you go to Hercule's house and make sure nobody else gets in until one of my people shows up? They'll have identification."

"I can't keep the gendarmes out."

"I'll take care of them. You've got your hunting gun. Just get to Hercule's house as soon as you can and keep it secure. Whatever happens, I'll back you. Even if you have to use the gun. Does anybody else know of this?"

"Yes, my chum the baron. We were all going hunting together. He was the one who told me to call you and say Hercule was a *barbouze*. I left him at the scene."

"Fine. You call J-J while I sort things out with the gendarmes and get somebody to the house in Ste. Alvère. I've got people in Bordeaux; with a chopper from the military airfield, expect them anytime after a couple of hours. But nobody else gets into that house."

"I need to do this by the book," Bruno said. "Once I get the SAMU guys to the body and they pronounce him dead, the rule is that any available law officer has to secure the scene until relieved by a senior officer or by the scene-of-crime unit. So we'd better get a gendarme out here fast. I'll call one of the motorcycle teams from Sarlat to stand by until the SOCO guys turn up."

"I'll fax your mayor with a request for you to be seconded to us as a matter of national security. You'll be covered."

Bruno made his calls and waited, wondering what kind of *barbouze* Hercule had been. The word meant simply someone with a false beard, but had come to mean somebody operating undercover or in the murkier areas of security and intelligence. In the Algerian War the *barbouzes* had been outright killers, some of them taken straight from prison and offered a pardon if they joined the underground war to kill members of the OAS, the secret army fighting de Gaulle in a quixotic bid to maintain the French empire. Deals had been done with the Union Corse, the mafia of Corsica, to turn a blind eye to some of their organized crime work in return for help against the OAS. They had kidnapped, tortured and assassinated each other and had become almost indistinguishable, except that one group had the backing of the French state and the other did not.

Somehow, despite the gruesome manner of his killing, Hercule did not strike Bruno as that kind of *barbouze*. You learn a lot about a man from the way that he hunts, Bruno thought, and Hercule was subtle. He did not go charging into the woods, gun blazing. He considered his quarry, tried to think the way it did and to anticipate its moves. He seldom fired more than a single shot in a whole day of hunting, but it was always a shot that found its mark. Bruno pondered Hercule's knowledge of foreign languages, the books in his home. However basic his education may have been, Hercule was thoughtful, learned and well read, something of an inspiration to Bruno, who was learning that he need not be limited by the inadequacies of his own schooling but that he could read for himself, learn by himself, think for himself.

Hercule had been no thug, no gangster lying in wait to kill renegade French officers in Madrid nightclubs or to kidnap *pied-noir* nationalists in Rome brothels. The brigadier had called him "a legend in this business," which meant a strategist, a planner. Who would want him dead? Bruno thought as he heard the siren and saw the red SAMU van coming over the far hilltop. The method of the murder itself had to be the message. It was a killing designed to demonstrate the ruthlessness of the killers and to intimidate by its very brutality.

But anyone who sought to intimidate, thought Bruno, needs to be known. There is no point in anonymous terror. One has to be frightened of someone or something. And once that someone emerged, Bruno would have his target, both for justice and for vengeance.

8

Bruno parked the baron's jeep on the slope behind the ruined castle and looked up the lane to Hercule's house. It seemed normal, as if waiting for its owner's return. He rang the medical center in St. Denis to ask if Vinh or his wife had turned up for treatment, but there had been no sign of them. Bruno rang Vinh's home number and his mobile, cursing himself for not doing it earlier, but got no reply from either. This was ominous; he'd have to visit Vinh's home as soon as he was relieved here at Hercule's place. But there was no telling how long that would be. He called the gendarmerie, and Sergeant Jules answered the phone.

Bruno explained his anxiety about Vinh and asked Jules to send someone to check on the house. Then he told Jules what had happened to Hercule.

"Hercule from Ste. Alvère? Who'd want to murder the old boy?"

"It's complicated and I'll explain later, but can you check on Vinh?"

Jules said he'd put Françoise onto it. Then he told Bruno that Poincevin had returned to confirm that the Chinese student was an illegal immigrant who would plead guilty to all charges, pay the costs of all damages and accept deportation back to China. The Chinese prisoner had not uttered a single word while detained and had now been transferred to the custody of the magistrate in Périgueux for trial.

"But he's the only link we've got to all this. We've got to get him properly questioned," Bruno said.

"I know. And Capitaine Duroc"—Jules weighted the rank with a heavy irony—"says this fits the pattern of events on his checklist for organized crime. It must be reported to the Police Nationale. So we had your old pal J-J on the line."

"J-J's now tied up in the murder investigation. I'll call him later. Look, I've got to go and check out Hercule's house, but don't forget Vinh."

Bruno next called Nicco, his counterpart in Ste. Alvère, as a courtesy to explain his presence on Nicco's turf, but if he wanted to share the guard duty at Hercule's place he was welcome. Nicco was a member of Hercule's hunting club and knew him well.

"Murdered? Our Hercule? Christ, I'd better tell the mayor."

"You'd better tell the rest of the hunting club to stay away for a while. The murder took place at the hide. They're both dead, Hercule and his dog."

"The best truffle hound in the valley? *Putain,* what sick kind of devil would want to do something like that?"

They hung up. Bruno tucked his opened shotgun under his arm and walked up the lane past Hercule's house. A man with a gun was commonplace in rural France in the hunting season. He continued through an old archway and an alley that led to the back of the house. The place looked undisturbed. Just in case, he took an empty paint can left by the garden shed and placed it against the rear door. If anybody left the house in a hurry he'd hear it. He went around to the front and used Hercule's keys to let himself in.

The house smelled clean, with a touch of mustiness from old books and Gauloises mixed with wood smoke from the previous evening's fire. The kitchen was tidy, a washed cup and plate and an ashtray on the drying rack. The desk and papers in the big living room looked undisturbed. Bruno went upstairs and found again the signs of a neat and well-organized man. One small bedroom was filled with boxes of files and papers, and Bruno left them for the brigadier's people to examine. The iron-framed single bed in Hercule's room had been made and covered with a brightly colored cotton spread. Old tribal rugs were spread on the floor, and Bruno assumed they were antiques. Hercule's clothes were hung in a large wardrobe, and there was no indication of anyone else ever staying, no women's clothing and only the most simple masculine toiletries in the bathroom. The walls were papered in a design from another era, pale red prints of eighteenth-century scenes against a gray background.

The books by Hercule's bed were works of history. Bruno put down his shotgun and picked up the first. It was on the French war in Vietnam, Jean Ferrandi's *Les Officiers français face au Vietminh*. But most covered the Algerian War. Bruno recognized Axel Nicol's *La Bataille de l'O.A.S.* and Claude Paillat's *Dossier secret de l'Algérie*. There were several bookmarks inside General Massu's memoirs, *La Vraie bataille d'Alger*, and even more inside General Paul Aussaresses's *Services spéciaux*. Bruno remembered the scandal it had provoked when published a few years earlier. Aussaresses had confessed to the routine use of torture and claimed that François Mitterrand as minister of justice had approved the practice, twenty years before he had become president of France. Bruno looked at the marked pages, all of them referring to torture.

He put the book down and returned downstairs. There was no sign of a safe, and the cellar contained only wine. Bruno could not help himself. He squatted down to examine some of the bottles and handled them reverently: Château Angélus from St. Emilion, Château l'Evangile and Château le Pin from Pomerol, Château Haut-Brion from Graves. He smiled to himself and envied Hercule's heirs.

Back in the living room, which looked as if Hercule might return any moment, there were press clippings on the desk in what he assumed to be Chinese and Vietnamese. Another book had been left open with an old-fashioned lead-weighted leather bookmark holding the pages in place. It was in English, called *SOE in France,* and written by M. R. D. Foot. The publisher was Her Majesty's Stationery Office, which made Bruno assume it was an official volume on the work of British intelligence in France in World War II. The English was almost too much for him, but Bruno made a note of the number of the page that had been held open. The text on the page seemed to be about a British officer named Starr who had become the mayor of the small commune of Castelnau-sous-l'Auvignon in Gascony, and whose role allowed him to provide quantities of official but false documents. Why would Hercule be interested in that?

Also on the desk was a thick file of notes and what looked like the draft of a book of Hercule's memoirs, almost all of it about Vietnam and Algeria. On top of the file were two transparent plastic file folders. The first contained an account of a farm at a place called Ameziane, a detention center in Algeria run by a Centre de Renseignement et d'Action, one of the counterinsurgency intelligence units based in the nearby city of Constantine. Hercule's notes said that torture had been practiced there on an "industrial scale" and added that more than eleven thousand Algerians had been detained at the farm, all of them tortured with a hellish blend of electric shocks, beatings, starvation, mock drowning, cigarette burns and rape. There was a page, headed with the word "Ameziane," with a list of French names and military units beneath. Some of the names were just initials. A final sheet was the photocopy of a news clipping from *Vérité Libre* with a passage marked that said some inmates had been able to bribe their way out. Against this Hercule had written another list of names, military ranks and initials.

The second plastic folder was titled "Crevettes Bigeard," which sounded to Bruno like food. But as he read on, he saw that General Bigeard's shrimps were corpses or survivors of torture who were loaded into helicopters, taken over the Mediterranean and dropped into the sea. After some of their bodies floated ashore, the torturers began taking the precaution of putting the feet into a large plastic bucket filled with cement before dumping them. These, with a kind of black humor that Bruno found repellent, were known as Bigeard's shrimps. Again, Hercule had appended a list of names and units.

Bruno put the folders back in their place. No wonder the brigadier was alarmed. Hercule's memoirs would open a lot of old wounds. He looked at the photographs, all expensively framed in silver, which took up part of the wide surface of the desk. The one the baron had recognized was still in the front row, but pride of place was held by a studio portrait of a beautiful Asian woman with a small child in her arms. Another photo of the woman showed her arm in arm with a much younger Hercule. Yet another showed her sitting in the middle of a row of young Asian girls, all wearing the tabard, the traditional French school uniform.

There were more photos of young Hercule in army camouflage, one of him in a jeep wearing the shoulder bars of a captain and looking up at a cluster of parachutes dropping from the sky. A MAS-38 machine gun was balanced across his knee. Bruno thought he recognized the event from other photos of the same scene. It was the relief of Dien Bien Phu, when the Foreign Legion paratroops were dropped in to reinforce the doomed French outpost whose defeat heralded the end of France's empire in Indochina. In an adjacent photo, this time in Algeria from the look of the buildings, he was surrounded by young Asian troops, presumably some of their Vietnamese allies the French took with them when they withdrew after Ho Chi Minh's victory.

By now Hercule was a major. More photos showed him with a very old de Gaulle pinning the rosette of the Légion d'Honneur to his chest. At the back was a much smaller photo of Hercule with an impressive-looking uniformed black man with a beard and a white man in commando camouflage with a face that was vaguely familiar. Half the history of modern France was spread out in the photos before him, some of it doubtless secret, and Bruno marveled at the way a man such as this had been content to sit back and help him learn about truffles.

He thought of the manpower it would take to go through Hercule's mounds of files and papers, looking for whatever embarrassments or secrets the state wished to guard. But there was one book he expected to find and so far he had drawn a blank. It was Hercule's truffle journal, the one Didier had been so eager to see. Bruno assumed that Hercule kept the journal with him, and it would thus be found by the police forensics team. He made a mental note to check with J-J.

The drawers of the desk all seemed to be unlocked. Using his handkerchief on the handles, he opened them and found bills and bank statements neatly filed. But in the central drawer, he saw an envelope marked "Testament" and handwritten below was a note saying that the original will was filed with a *notaire* in Ste. Alvère. He closed the drawer again and went back through the kitchen to the outside toilet, pushing aside the paint can he had left there. He put it back where he'd found it by the shed and went in to pee, smiling at the torn-up squares of *Sud Ouest* hanging on a nail. Hercule was old-fashioned in such matters. It reminded Bruno of the orphanage of his youth.

He was washing his hands in the kitchen sink when he heard a small noise behind and the words "Hands up—police." It was a female voice, and instantly familiar. Isabelle.

"May I finish washing them first?" he asked, trying to control the catch in his voice and the thrill in his heart. The last words she had said to him nearly three months earlier had been "I miss you," and he could remember each timbre and tone and the sound of her breath on the phone when she spoke them. "It would be good to see you again, Isabelle, if I'm allowed to turn around."

"You're supposed to be armed with a shotgun and on watch," she said.

"And you're supposed to show me an item of identification from the brigadier," he said, shaking the water from his hands and turning. How marvelous it was to see her!

She held the shooter's pose, knees bent, arms straight out before her and hands clasped together on a Pamas G1 pistol, the new standard issue for French police. Since Bruno never carried his old gun, he'd seen no point in burdening the budget of St. Denis for the cost of a new one. Isabelle's eyes were cool, but there was a twinkle somewhere behind them. As always, her hair was cut short, and she was dressed in black, a floor-length raincoat over slacks and a turtleneck. She was wearing black lace-up shoes with low heels and even in the semi-uniform she managed to look the height of elegance.

"Nothing sexier than a woman with a gun, particularly when I know how good a shot you are," he said.

"Where's your shotgun?"

"It must still be on Hercule's bed. I got interested in his books and put the gun down."

"You're going soft, Bruno."

"Perhaps I need you to keep me on the straight and narrow."

"Perhaps." She lowered the gun, straightened to her full height as she turned on the safety catch and came across to exchange kisses on both cheeks. She smelled the same, some sporty soap or shampoo rather than perfume. She held him a moment longer than required by the courtesies of old lovers, and he felt again her supple strength and the muscle tone of a trained athlete.

"How did you get here so fast?"

"The brigadier arranged a helicopter. I was in Bordeaux already. What books were you looking at?"

"Algerian War, mostly. The house is stuffed with them— and photos. Come, I'll show you."

He led her into the main room and showed her the ranks of framed photographs, the trail of lost empires from Dien Bien Phu to Bab el-Oued and of lost leaders from de Gaulle to Giscard and one photo of Hercule lighting the flame at the Arc de Triomphe.

"Who's the woman?" she asked. "And the child?"

"No idea. And who's the African?" He pointed to the small photo. She leaned in closely to see, putting her hand on his shoulder as if simply keeping her balance.

"The guy in camouflage is Rolf Steiner, German, ex–Foreign Legion. He became a mercenary," she said. "So I guess the African must be Ojukwu, the man who ran Biafra when it tried to break away in the sixties. Steiner fought for them as a mercenary."

"What was Hercule doing there?"

"Looking after French interests, as always," she said, stepping back, leaving a space between them. "I recall hearing something about Total Oil hoping for a deal with Biafra, breaking Shell's monopoly in Nigeria. This other photo here is Jacques Foccart, who ran our African policy for the past thirty years. It didn't matter who got elected president, Foccart always stayed in power."

"And that's the kind of work you're in these days?" he asked, thinking, The kind of work that you were pressing me to do so I could come and live with you in Paris.

"I'm still on the personal staff of the minister of the interior, in a section run by the brigadier." She was all business now.

"Does that make you a *barbouze* like Hercule?"

"Do people really use that old slang these days?" She laughed. "No, I'm still part of the Police Nationale. Mostly, I do liaison, which means keeping an eye on what other police and security forces are doing so that our minister avoids the embarrassment of being surprised. You'd be amazed how much politicians hate to be surprised."

"So what's happening in Bordeaux?"

"Can't tell you," she said, and then grinned. His heart

warmed to see it, the first genuine expression her face had worn since their meeting. They'd been dancing around each other, too aware of the history between them to lower their guard. That grin was the first sign that it was the same Isabelle he'd fallen in love with. "It's all straightforward stuff. Liaison with customs and the military and Europol, and our neighbors across the Channel," she went on.

"The British?"

She nodded. "I just did six weeks in London, seconded to their counterterrorism unit, and they sent one of theirs to Paris. We work closely together on radical Muslims, but this latest operation is about illegal immigration, which is why the navies are involved, ours and theirs. It's all run by organized crime."

"The brigadier thought Hercule's death was more important than that?"

"Well, perhaps more urgent. And it's not his death that matters, it's his files. He ran a big section of the old SDECE so it's routine to check over his papers. And then his being murdered makes it a real problem. No surprises, remember?"

"What's your role in all of that?"

"I just babysit the house until the archives team gets down from Paris, which should be later today. They were taking a high-speed train to Bordeaux. But if you found anything interesting while poking around . . ."

"I know he was reading about the Algerian War and about British intelligence in World War II. He was writing something that looked like memoirs. It's that folder on the desk, but it's a long way from being done. And I found a copy of his will in that central drawer, but I didn't open it."

"Show me," she said, pulling a pair of surgical gloves from her shoulder bag. She opened the drawer and took out the envelope. It was unsealed, so she removed a thick wad of papers, unfolded them and sat down on an easy chair to read.

"I presume I can go, now that you're here to look after the premises."

"What?" She looked up. "Just hold on a second, Bruno. There's something interesting here about you. He says you and the baron are the only real friends he's made since his retirement. He's left the baron his wine cellar. Some journal that he kept on truffles goes to you, along with his old Land Rover."

"What did you say? His journal? And his Land Rover?" He sat down. He felt overwhelmed with a mixture of surprise and affection for Hercule. He had never been bequeathed anything before. The pleasure faded as he thought of Hercule, so animated when last they met.

"He's also left you some books. A lot of books, it sounds like. He must have been really attached to you." She looked up and smiled widely at him. "You're thinking of the Land Rover, I can tell." She laughed. "Oh Bruno, I do like you."

He felt himself blushing, but also profoundly moved. He'd respected the old man deeply, but he'd never suspected that Hercule thought of him as anything more than a casual hunting companion and as an amateur truffle cultivator. To bequeath his journal, a master's guide to the truffles of the region and of the secret sites where they might be found, was a mark of real affection. But had there been no family?

"Who is his main heir?" he asked. "Is that Asian woman mentioned?"

"I'm still reading. I can't see anything about the woman in the photo, but there is a reference to his late wife. There's nothing specific about the young girl in the photo. The main beneficiary is a scholarship trust fund he seems to have established more than twenty years ago, for the education of Vietnamese who fought for France. There's more that goes to the Daughters of St. Paul, an order of teaching nuns. And there's a codicil. The house and contents, less the books, go to a woman called Gioan Linh Nguyen-Vendrot, if she can be found. I assume that may be the daughter, but it doesn't say so. If she is not traced by his executors in a reasonable time, the house goes to the commune of Ste. Alvère. The latest available information on her whereabouts is with his *notaire* in the town here. He is named as an executor of the will, along with you and the baron."

She put down the will. "And that, my dear Bruno, means that I had better arrest you. And your friend the baron when he turns up. You two found the body. You are the heirs. Obviously you had the motive and the opportunity, and presumably you had the means. How was he killed?"

"That's not funny, Isabelle. He was tortured, left hanging by his wrists."

"Mon Dieu!" She shuddered. "Do we have a time of death yet?"

"No, but the baron and I were there a bit before nine, and the blood was still wet. He can't have been dead long, and we saw nobody on the trail up to the hide where we found him. There are other ways out from there, but you'd have to know those woods pretty well."

"Not in these days of GPS. But they'd still need to rinse the blood off themselves, most likely. Was there water nearby?"

"Yes, a stream. I'll make sure the forensics guys check that. But Hercule was a hunter and a trained soldier. And he was armed. It wouldn't have been easy to sneak up on him or take him by surprise. He knew those woods like the back of his hand."

"One of the things they'll be looking for in the archives is anything that could point to a motive for his murder. It's a bit complicated because of the way he left the service," she said. "I don't know the details, but he was one of the victims of Mitterrand's big cleanup in eighty-two, when he closed down SDECE and started the new foreign intelligence department. It was all political. Mitterrand thought the old guard was a bunch of right-wing anti-Communists, and his coalition government depended on Communist support. So he closed the old bureau down and put the new organization under the Ministry of Defense."

"And Hercule was one of the sacrificial lambs."

"Exactly. And when they fired him Hercule was running the Action Division, that's the clandestine service. So you can imagine, one of the top priorities of the new organization was to keep an eye on the disgruntled veterans of the old one, just in case they used their files to make trouble."

"But he never did."

"Not Hercule, no. But some others caused Mitterrand a lot of problems, leaks of files to *Le Canard Enchaîné* and *Figaro*. And remember back in eighty-two Mitterrand was running a very left-wing government, nationalizing the banks and big companies, and there was a run on the franc. Closing down la Piscine was seen as part of that, a big move to the left. The Americans were very worried."

"La Piscine," he said, almost to himself. "I haven't heard that for a while." It was the old slang term among insiders for French intelligence, named because its headquarters on boulevard Mortier in Paris adjoined the big Tourelles swimming pool. "So how closely would Hercule have been watched?"

"Very closely, but that's long over," Isabelle replied. "I checked before I came, and there's no surveillance here, no microphones and not even a phone tap. Hercule was listed as 'inactive' until the brigadier got your phone call this morning."

And now it all starts up again, thought Bruno. Hercule's old outfit was taken over by the defense ministry, and Isabelle works for the minister of the interior. There would be turf wars over this.

"So when do we expect the defense ministry guys to turn up?" he asked.

"We don't," she said firmly. "At least not officially. This is an internal French matter, so it's our affair, not theirs. I'll call you on your mobile as soon as the archives team turns up," she continued, a touch of hesitation in her voice. She looked at him almost shyly. "Perhaps we can have a drink before I get a train back to Bordeaux?"

"I'd like that, but what happened to the helicopter?" He was smiling at her, despite himself, despite having been through all this before. He knew that theirs had been an affair without a future, but the grip of the past was very strong.

"The chopper just dropped me off. Getting here was urgent, not getting back."

9

So big and boisterous that he always seemed to fill every room he entered, J-J threw open his arms to embrace Bruno and then lumbered around the office of the mayor of Ste. Alvère to deliver bone-crushing handshakes to the others present. His dominance thus established, Commissaire Jean-Jacques Jalipeau, chief detective of the Police Nationale for the Département of the Dordogne, looked around for a comfortable place from which to give his briefing. He perched his ample buttocks on a windowsill and waved the mayor imperiously back to his own chair at the head of the council table.

"What we know so far is mainly from forensics. There were at least three people involved in yesterday morning's attack on Hercule Vendrot," J-J began, not bothering to look at the manila file that seemed to Bruno as small as a bus ticket in his large paw. "A fourth person may have stayed in the stolen Mercedes four-by-four whose tire marks we found about six hundred feet down the dirt track. They seem to have been waiting since daybreak, as if knowing that their victim would arrive. Then they killed him in a most brutal way that would have left at least one of them covered in blood."

"Do we know how they took him by surprise?" Bruno asked. "Hercule was armed, and he had his dog."

"The dog was dying," J-J replied. "Poisoned meat had been left at the entrance to the hide. The poor creature would have been in no shape to give much warning. Maybe they had guns pointed at the victim, we don't know. Forensics says that Vendrot was handcuffed inside the hide and then taken outside to be murdered. They think that time of death was between seven and nine, which is not very helpful. The knife used on the victim was about eight inches long, an unusual length, and single edged with a sharp point. We haven't found it.

"The stolen Mercedes was found early this morning in the parking lot at Toulouse Airport." J-J paused. "That might tell you how much effort we're putting into this. It had been cleaned and vacuumed and was empty. Garbage cans at the airport and at rest spots on the obvious autoroutes are being searched."

J-J looked up from his file, and then he scanned the room, making eye contact in turn with Bruno and each of the other men present.

"Hercule Vendrot was a prominent man, and an honored son of France," he said. "The minister of the interior has personally instructed me to give this case top priority, and all other agencies of the state have been ordered to provide full cooperation. This includes the DGSE, whose predecessor agency our victim used to serve. We have a representative here today." J-J nodded at an anonymous-looking middle-aged man in a dark suit and tired gray shirt sitting at the foot of the table. He nodded in acknowledgment.

"Do you have any hypothesis so far?" asked the mayor.

"That's about all we do have," J-J replied. "It might have been revenge for something from his past, or something more recent, possibly connected with the truffle market here in Ste. Alvère. That's why you gentlemen are here, because we need your local knowledge of Hercule and his concerns, his enemies . . . anything that might be useful."

Bruno had one new fact to contribute, but he would inform J-J in private rather than share it with this bunch of local gossips. Still, he knew it was a good tactic for J-J to bring in the members of the town council and brief them. Feeding their self-importance would ensure their support, and their local knowledge might be useful. But the copies of Hercule's will and the note he had left with his *notaire* seemed more important. Bruno had been to see him already that morning. The *notaire* was a member of Hercule's hunting club and knew Bruno well. He'd confirmed that a formal notice of death had been filed, so Bruno had no difficulty in obtaining Hercule's papers. He'd also provided a copy of the letter being sent that day to the legal attaché of the Vietnamese embassy in Paris, asking for assistance in tracing one Gioan Linh Nguyen-Vendrot, a possible heir. Such letters, the *notaire* had said, were quite routine.

The terse sentence in Hercule's will on the possible heir was written in the dry tones of an official report, and yet Bruno could almost feel the personal sadness that had gone into its drafting. When reading it in the *notaire*'s office, Bruno had wondered aloud at the self-control that had kept Hercule from ever mentioning his loss. The *notaire* had been able to fill in some of the gaps.

When Hercule had left Vietnam with the French forces in 1954, he'd brought with him a new Vietnamese wife. Still attached to military intelligence, he was based briefly at the NATO headquarters in Fontainebleau and was then posted to Algeria soon after learning that his wife was pregnant. She stayed in Paris with Vietnamese relatives and died in childbirth. Hercule had remained in Algeria, and the daughter had remained in Paris. He had seen her only on his occasional leaves, and she barely knew her father. For security reasons, even these brief contacts ceased when the generals launched their coup attempt in 1961 and the war with the OAS had begun. Hercule had been one of their targets. To visit his daughter would have put her at risk.

Now, looking around the council table in the *mairie* of Ste. Alvère, listening to the predictable questions from the mayor and the council members, Bruno found it daunting to comprehend a France that had been so close to civil war. Bruno recalled Hercule when last they met saying he would have shot the baron if he had joined the OAS. Bruno had assumed he was joking, or at least exaggerating for effect. Now he knew better. Had some fearsome echo of those OAS years cost Hercule his life?

Suddenly aware that J-J and the rest of the gathering were looking at him and evidently awaiting an answer, Bruno hauled his attention back to the meeting. J-J had been talking about full cooperation, and Bruno had spent years learning the army rule that one could seldom go far wrong repeating an officer's words back to him and adding "sir."

"Full cooperation, Monsieur le Commissaire," he said, which seemed to suffice. J-J's penetrating gaze lingered on him a moment, but moved on.

The mayor began to explain ponderously that Hercule's death could have had nothing to do with Ste. Alvère, since the truffle market was thoroughly monitored. Bruno tuned out again and looked gloomily at the DGSE man in the gray shirt who had arrived so late from Paris yesterday that after meeting with him there had been no time for a drink or even much of a conversation with Isabelle as he had raced her back to the station at Le Buisson to catch the evening train to Bordeaux. A little less speed, a bit more braking on the corners and just slightly more caution before passing other cars and she'd have missed her last train and been stuck for the evening. The thought had crossed his mind with a brief flutter of temptation. It was not that he wanted to restart their affair but that he still felt baffled and frustrated at the way it had ended. It felt unfinished and untidy; there were still matters between them to be resolved.

But there was other unfinished business that nagged at him. Once he had dropped Isabelle at the station, he had driven to Vinh's house on the outskirts of St. Denis. It was one of the small modern homes, built from prefabricated kits for a hundred thousand euros and the cost of a small tract of land. They had been spreading around the region since the foreigners and the Parisians had pushed the price of the traditional Périgord houses out of reach. Bruno understood the need for them, but disliked them all the same with their shallow roofs of rounded red tiles, as if they were in Provence or Italy rather than the Périgord. But he remembered Vinh's pride at his single-story home with two small bedrooms all on a flat platform of cement, and the feast he and his wife had given to celebrate his new status as a man of property.

The house had been closed and silent when Bruno arrived, the window shutters closed and no sign of Vinh's small truck that he used to get to the local markets. As he tried to peer through the shutter gaps and poked around the tiny rear garden for any sign of life, Bruno remembered his mild surprise at finding Hercule among the guests that evening of Vinh's feast. Hercule, the only Frenchman there who was not in some way attached to the St. Denis market, had made a brief speech, reminiscing fondly of his own days in Vietnam and his admiration for the *nems* and *pho* that Vinh's wife made. Probably Vinh had taken his wife away for a few days to get over the shock of the attack. But he was not answering his mobile phone, and Bruno had no other Vietnamese contacts in the area, which meant he was stuck, although he very much wanted to know why Vinh had been attacked by a Chinese illegal immigrant with an expensive lawyer.

Beside him, the councillors were starting to pack away their papers and Bruno saw J-J moving to shake the mayor's hand in farewell when there was the sound of a commotion outside the room and a flustered young woman came in.

"Monsieur le Maire, Nicco," she began, stammering nervously as she looked round the room. "I'm sorry, but there's a fight, some trouble in the market. . . ."

Nicco, old and slow, looked at Bruno for support, and the two of them went out to the street. There were shouts from the stalls to the right and the angry whine of a high-revving motorbike disappearing down the side street opposite the castle ruins. Bruno found himself looking at a scene he had seen before, a wrecked stall smeared with black stuff and angry stallholders and customers splashed with it. An Asian woman stood beside it screaming, smeared from head to foot in what Bruno could now smell was fresh black paint. Beside her, an Asian youth was hauling a big five-gallon paint can away from the wreckage of a glass-fronted cold display case and a deep fryer. Bruno peered under the deep fryer and turned off the butane gas bottle. They were lucky the paint had doused the burner or they could have had a fire along with everything else.

"Silence," he shouted. Some of the stallholders were known to him. "Marie, please call the medical center to have someone come and check out this lady for any injuries or just to help clean her up." He turned to the Asian youth. "You stand there and try to remember everything that happened. I'll come to you in a moment. Now, Léopold, let's start with you. What happened?"

Apparently a motorbike with two people wearing helmets had driven through the market, weaving in and out of the shoppers. The one on the rear of the seat was carrying the paint can and threw it directly into Madame Duong's stall. Then they rode off before anyone could stop them. That was it. Not a word had been said. The bike had barely slowed.

"Anybody get a look at the people on the bike?"

"Not in those helmets," said Léopold. "It was all over so fast."

"Who are you?" he asked the young Asian, black paint still dripping from the sleeve of his shirt. He looked frightened and very young. No more than sixteen, Bruno thought.

"I'm her son," he replied, speaking in a local accent. "Pierre Duong. I just came today to help her. Usually it's my dad, but he was busy."

"Any idea who attacked you? Or why?"

The young man shook his head. "I have to call my dad." His hand dropped to the mobile phone at his waist, but it was sodden with paint.

"Where's your father?"

"Back at the office."

"Look after your mother until the medics get here. One

more thing, Pierre. Do you know Vinh, runs the stall in St. Denis?" The youth nodded and Bruno handed him his own mobile phone. "I'd be grateful if you could call your dad, tell him he'd better get here fast and probably with some clean clothes."

Bruno turned to the crowd, gathered in a circle and waiting to see what he'd do next.

"Anybody who saw the registration number or knows the make or color of the motorbike, anything that might help us identify them?"

"I'll take some statements," said Nicco, pulling out a dog-eared notebook and pen.

"Maybe you could organize a cleanup crew," Bruno told him, thinking of the protocol. This was Nicco's town. He was always doing this, Bruno chided himself, jumping in to take charge when something obviously needed to be done and nobody else was doing it. "You'd better take over here, Nicco. It's your turf."

"The cleanup crew is on the way," the mayor said, putting away his mobile phone. "And we'll pay for the turpentine and towels," he added as Marie scurried up toward them, laden with a large pack of paper towels. Suddenly Bruno heard an ambulance siren, getting louder.

"Bruno," J-J called from across the street, standing in a shop doorway and beckoning for Bruno to join him.

"Is this like the incident at your market the other day?"

"Yes and no," Bruno replied. "Paint instead of fuel oil and the attackers came by motorbike rather than car. I think it's a safe bet they're linked, but they learned something from what went wrong in St. Denis. I need to talk to Vinh, the man whose stall was trashed earlier. I've no idea what's behind this.

And Vinh's disappeared along with his wife. At least now I've got another Asian victim."

"So have I," said J-J heavily. "Just got a call from the office. You know that big Chinese restaurant in Périgueux, the Golden Dragon, beside the Asian supermarket?"

Bruno nodded. "The one you told me the big boys in Paris were interested in."

"That's the one. It got burned down last night, or rather early this morning. Gasoline bombs through the windows, front and back."

"Vinh was hit by a Chinese in St. Denis, and now the Chinese get hit in Périgueux." Bruno paused. "I'm out of my depth here, J-J. If this is turning into some kind of Asian gang war, I wouldn't know where to start looking."

"Let's not jump to conclusions. The restaurant could have been firebombed by the aggrieved former owner."

"Maybe, but he'd be a brave man, taking on the big boys like that."

"A fool, more likely. It could be an insurance scam. The Chinese do a lot of that."

Suddenly young Pierre was looming at Bruno's shoulder, holding out Bruno's mobile phone. "My father's on his way, stopping off first for some clothes." He paused. "I was careful not to get any of this paint on your phone."

"Thanks, Pierre," said Bruno, quickly saving the last number dialed so he'd be able to keep contact with Duong. He didn't want to lose him like he'd lost Vinh. He turned to Léopold and led the big Senegalese away so they could talk quietly.

"Remember you told me that Vinh had a bit of trouble last Saturday in Sarlat market? Is that the only other incident?"

It was, Léopold said, the only one he'd seen. But he'd heard of scuffles in Bergerac and in Rouffignac where Chinese vendors were trying to muscle in on the best locations at the markets. There were only enough customers for one Asian food stall, particularly in winter. In the summer, the big tourist trade might have meant enough business for many stalls. But in winter the Vietnamese knew their livelihood was at stake, and they couldn't afford the Chinese competition. They would fight back, all of them.

"And they're friends, the Vinhs and Duongs, not rivals?" asked Bruno.

"Some kind of cousins, I think. You'd better ask them," Léopold said. "And I'd better get back to my stall. All these interruptions are bad for my business too."

When he had gone, Bruno spoke quietly to J-J. "Hercule Vendrot was a friend of the Vinh family. He's murdered. They've disappeared after being attacked. Now their cousins are attacked. Smells like a connection to me."

"That's how I see it," J-J replied. "But we need to get the Duongs to talk, and to find your man Vinh."

"That son of theirs, Pierre, was born and brought up here and speaks like a local. If the Duongs have been here that long, they'll be naturalized by now. Do you think your office could check out their citizenship applications? We might find something useful, other family members and addresses, sponsors, that kind of thing."

J-J eyed him doubtfully. "How's that going to help us with Hercule's murder?"

"I don't know. But Hercule served in Vietnam, had a Vietnamese wife who died young. He may have a Vietnamese daughter somewhere, but if we can't find her, his will leaves his money to a Viet scholarship fund. If that's the connection, we'd better follow it. Unless you have a better plan."

J-J shook his head, pulled out a pack of Gauloise filters and flicked his old-fashioned gasoline lighter.

"The only plan I have is to wait for the DGSE to tell me what clues they find in Vendrot's papers," he said, blowing out a plume of smoke. "But I suspect they're more worried about what little embarrassments he's left behind than with solving a murder. What about this truffle business he was stirring up? Where does that fit in?"

Bruno shrugged. "Do you see truffles as a motive for murder?"

"Depends how much money is involved. But it's a line I have to pursue."

"One thing you should look out for is Hercule's truffle book, a journal where he recorded all his finds and sales and prices. Everybody in the market knows about it. Apparently he left it to me in his will. I didn't see it in his house, and it's not in his car. That DGSE man promised you full cooperation, and he'll be at Hercule's house now, going through the files. You could go and ask him for it, make it official."

"I'm planning on picking up the records of Hercule's phone calls. We've got a fixed line and a mobile. What about you?" J-J asked.

"Going back to St. Denis, where I'm supposed to work. On the way I'll stop by the medical center to check on Madame Duong."

10

Madame Duong was wearing a suit of white overalls borrowed from a nurse, and she smelled strongly of turpentine. Her son Pierre sat beside her, his face and hair clean, but he was still clad in the paint-drenched shirt and trousers he had arrived in. Sheets of newspaper protected the chair he sat on in the medical center's waiting room.

"I don't know," she said for the fifth time. Whatever Bruno asked about the attackers, or about Vinh's whereabouts, or about trouble in other markets, she gave the same flat reply. He couldn't tell if she was suspicious of the police in general or just wary of anyone who wasn't Vietnamese. Perhaps she was still in shock. Her fingers kept plucking nervously at the white cloth of the nurse's jacket, and her fingernails were bitten down to the quick. From the age of her son, she could hardly be older than fifty, but she looked closer to seventy, with tired eyes and white roots in her hair. She kept her eyes down, refusing to look at him, and her thin mouth was set in a determined line.

"My mother is tired," Pierre said, more resigned than aggressive. "Can't you leave us alone?"

"I don't know anything," she said again, but then the medical center's doors opened, and she rose to her feet as her husband rushed in and embraced her and his son. Probably around forty or forty-five, he was thin and wiry, distinctly shorter than Pierre and dressed in a tracksuit. Through the window Bruno could see the car that had brought Duong waiting outside, one man at the wheel, another standing beside the car and looking tough and vigilant; he reminded Bruno of a professional bodyguard.

Duong handed a bag of clothes to his wife and another to his son and was walking with them into an adjoining room when Bruno cleared his throat and said, "Monsieur Duong, I'll have to ask you some questions about the attack on your wife."

"Who are you?" he said, although Bruno was in full uniform. Unlike his wife, he spoke French without an accent, and unlike his son he spoke it more like a Parisian than anyone brought up in the Périgord.

"I'm a friend of your cousin Vinh, who was attacked like your family was," Bruno said. "I want to find your attackers."

"I know nothing. I wasn't there," he replied.

"Where's Vinh?"

"I don't know."

"Why are Vietnamese stalls being attacked?"

"I don't know." His eyes kept darting around the room.

"You should know I was a friend of Hercule Vendrot," Bruno said. And this time Duong focused on Bruno and gave a slight, sad smile.

"A very good man."

"You know that he's been murdered?"

He nodded and sighed. "These are very difficult times."

"Your wife and Vinh have been assaulted and Vendrot

murdered, very brutally. I need your help if I'm to do something about it."

Again that sad smile, but no words.

"Why are you so frightened? Why do you come here with a bodyguard?"

"He's a friend, not a bodyguard. Excuse me, but I must take my family home now," he said as the door to the adjoining room opened and his wife appeared in black slacks and a sweater.

"These people are trying to destroy your livelihood. Why won't you help me find out who they are?"

"I know nothing that could help you in your work."

Bruno shrugged and pulled out one of his cards. Madame Duong came to stand beside her husband. He put his arm around her shoulders. "If you see Vinh, ask him to call me," Bruno said, and gave him the card. "His friends are worried about him."

Duong looked at Bruno for a long moment and then asked, "Are you the man who fought for them in St. Denis dressed like Father Christmas?"

Bruno nodded. "Vinh is a friend."

"Yes, I remember, that feast he gave when he bought the new house. You were there, I think."

"Along with Hercule Vendrot."

"I'll try to find a way to pass a message to Vinh, but if you couldn't protect Hercule Vendrot . . ." He shrugged.

"You think the people who attacked you also murdered Hercule?"

Duong shrugged again. "How would I know?"

"What will you do, now that they've destroyed your stall, and Vinh's?"

"We'll find something. We have friends with restaurants, we can work there."

"You know a restaurant was attacked with firebombs in Périgueux last night?"

Duong's eyes went blank. He shook his head.

"A Chinese restaurant," Bruno added. "Destroyed."

"Difficult times," Duong repeated as his son came out. He gathered his family and went out toward the waiting car. At the door, he turned. "Vinh will get your message. Thank you for your help."

They climbed into the back of the car. With a last raking look around the parking lot, the bodyguard followed them, and the car took the Bergerac road. That was interesting. Bruno had checked the address on Madame Duong's *carte vitale,* the French health insurance card. Their home was in Vergt, which lay in the opposite direction.

Perhaps I should have been tougher, Bruno told himself. He could have insisted on taking them to the gendarmerie to make formal statements. Another kind of policeman, like Capitaine Duroc, would have threatened them with arrest for obstruction. But the very fact that a Duroc might have tried such a trick was reason enough for Bruno to avoid it. He needed these people's cooperation and their trust, not their hostility.

He walked into the empty waiting room and knocked on the door that led to Dr. Gelletreau's consulting room. He could hear a string quartet on the radio and then the sound of a chair being pushed back and heavy footsteps coming to the door.

"Ah, Bruno," said the plump doctor with white hair and a heavy mustache. "What's wrong with you? You look healthy enough to me."

"I'm fine. I just wanted to ask about Madame Duong, the woman you just treated."

"She's fine, just some bruises and very sore skin after we cleaned the paint off her. Never seen anything quite like it."

"Did she say anything about the attack?"

"Not a word, except to mutter about their livelihood being destroyed and how were they going to live. She was in quite a state so I gave her some tea and that calmed her down a bit."

"Did you tell her to come back and see you again?"

Gelletreau shook his head. "She said she had her own doctor in Périgueux, and she'd go to see him. She gave me his name, another Vietnamese, a heart specialist at the hospital. I was going to give him a call later this evening, make sure he follows up. Her boy seemed like a responsible young man and said he'd make sure she went to see him."

"Did the boy say anything else?"

"Nothing that comes to mind. He did say something about the Chinese, as though he knew they were the ones who attacked them. Do you think it's tied in with the supermarket fire?"

"Could be. How did you hear about that?"

"The prefect's office called. They're making an inventory of burn units and doctors who know how to treat burn victims. I handled a lot of burns in the military so they had me down as a specialist. I got the impression they expected more fire bombings."

"Interesting," said Bruno. "By the way, how's that boy of yours?"

"Doing well at the lycée in Paris. They expect him to get into Sciences Po next year, with a lot of thanks to you."

Bruno nodded. Young Richard Gelletreau had been arrested on suspicion of conspiracy to murder until Bruno had solved the case. "Give him my best wishes and tell him we expect him at the tennis tournament this summer. If he wants a doubles partner, I'd be happy to join him."

The waiting room was no longer empty when he left the doctor's office. Rollo, headmaster of the St. Denis *collège* for pupils under sixteen, was sitting in the corner, leafing through an old magazine. One of Bruno's regular tennis partners, he was still a handsome man in his early fifties, but appeared weighed down by the endless juggling of budgets and the difficulty of finding good teachers prepared to live in the countryside.

"*Salut,* Rollo," he said, shaking hands. "What's up with you."

"More sleeping pills," he replied. "I keep waking up at three and can't get back to sleep, even when I haven't had a drink."

"You're not playing enough tennis. Exercise will cure your ills."

"I wish. No, I heard this week that old Joliot is determined to retire at sixty-two, so I'm going to need a new science teacher beginning in January. I've got the budget for it thanks to the new curriculum, but the only applicants so far aren't really qualified."

"New curriculum? They only changed it last year." Bruno remembered him complaining about it.

"This was part of it, a new course on environmental sciences. Joliot was just about able to handle it, but the kids deserve someone with a proper diploma."

A thought struck Bruno. "Would any science diploma be sufficient? Someone with a chemistry degree from Paris, for example?"

"If you can find someone with a Paris degree in chemistry

to teach at our *collège* I'll make you headmaster. Even with the new budget, we can only pay two thousand a month. I may have to settle for someone with a science *bac* and a teaching certificate."

"Is the teaching certificate essential?"

"Not entirely. Somebody with good science qualifications can get the certificate while teaching under supervision. I'm senior enough to arrange that. Why, did you have someone in mind?"

"A young woman in Ste. Alvère, recently divorced and raising two kids. She's working part-time at the truffle market for about half of what you're offering. She strikes me as a very sharp woman, and she's got a chemistry degree and a research diploma."

"A research diploma? That means she'd qualify for an extra five hundred a month. Do you think she'd do it?"

"I'll ask her," said Bruno, after a quick mental calculation that told him Florence, if she took the job, could be earning more than he did. He thumbed through his mobile phone for the numbers he'd taken down at the truffle market and punched in the call.

After Bruno relayed his conversation with Rollo, there was a silence on the other end of the line.

"Bruno, is this a joke?" she asked.

"No, not at all. Let me pass you to the headmaster. School hours and vacations, that's good for your children. He says you can qualify for the teaching certificate while working. Here he is."

He handed his phone to Rollo and leaned back against the wall while they spoke and arranged to meet. When Rollo handed back the phone, Bruno said, "She's got a miserable job in Ste. Alvère, working for a real bastard."

"You mean Didier at the truffle market? I was at school with him. I didn't know him well, but he wasn't much liked. He used to enjoy making girls cry."

"He still does," said Bruno. "Let me know how you get on with Florence."

"With those qualifications, if she can stand up and see the blackboard, I'll hire her," said Rollo, and he walked toward Gelletreau's office with a spring in his step. At the door he turned. "Will I see you at the meeting tonight? You know the Greens and Socialists are announcing their pact for the elections?"

"Wouldn't miss it."

Rollo paused. "You know this means the mayor could lose?"

Bruno nodded.

"Where would that leave you?"

Bruno shrugged. "I wouldn't lose my job. But a new mayor could have me transferred elsewhere."

"*Merde,* Bruno. Tell people that, and the mayor wins by a landslide." Rollo winked and went into the consulting room.

As he left the medical center, Bruno's phone rang. J-J's number was on the screen.

"They've got four guys here at the house, and they've been through everything. No sign of the truffle journal," J-J said. "But there is a safe-deposit key for a bank in Bergerac, and I'm arranging for an authorization letter to examine the contents tomorrow. And there was no journal listed in his belongings on the forensic report. And talking of forensics, they have some interesting stuff from the stolen Mercedes. Human hair, a cigarette butt and a used tissue, which means DNA evidence if we ever manage to find a suspect. By the way, you'll be in trouble with the investigating magistrate for taking the Land Rover."

"No, I won't. Forensics had already examined it and gave me the receipt to prove it. And I'm an executor of Vendrot's estate. What's more, he left me the vehicle in his will, along with that journal."

"You go on like this and you'll be a suspect," said J-J. Bruno could almost see his grin through the phone connection.

"That's what Isabelle said."

"She'll get her hands on you yet. Listen, I'm going back to Périgueux to take a look at the Chinese restaurant. You get anything out of the Duongs?"

"Not much. They said Vinh and his wife are safe and they'll try to put me in touch."

"No cooperation?"

"Not much. They're frightened and clammed up. Duong came in a car with a driver and what looked like a bodyguard. Did you put in a request for the citizenship papers?"

"First thing I did. And I also spoke to this special unit in Paris that's dealing with Chinese organized crime, and they're sending somebody down to work on the fire. They added their own priority onto the request and say we should get something on the citizenship papers tomorrow."

"We'll talk then," said Bruno, and checked the time before he closed his phone. He'd just have time to take his dog for a run, shower and change and pick up Pamela before the meeting. And he'd better take that side of venison out of the baron's freezer on the way. That was the unwritten rule. When a hunting friend died, you ate some of the last meat you'd hunted together and then drank to his passing.

11

The dining room of the retirement home was the largest indoor space in St. Denis, and by far the most popular for political meetings, since even the most boring event would get at least a modest audience from the old folk. But this time it was more than crowded, with the tables stacked away, every chair occupied and another hundred people standing against the walls and in the doorways. Bruno was impressed. At least one in ten of the inhabitants of the commune of St. Denis was present, and he couldn't remember any previous political meeting getting even half that number. At the far end of the room three more chairs were squeezed precariously onto a very small dais, and Alphonse was trying to stop the microphone from howling every time he brought it toward him.

"Turn your phone off," shouted someone from the front row. Alphonse obeyed, and the electronic howling stopped.

"Friends, comrades, fellow citizens of Planet Earth," he began. "This is a public meeting, but only those with Green and Socialist Party membership cards will be allowed to vote. And we have our party lists here, so we'll know who you are before we hand out the ballots. It will all be democratic and transparent.

"As you know, we've hammered out a joint program for the Greens and Socialists for next year's municipal elections. There are copies of the program here in the hall for anybody who hasn't read it already. If it's approved tonight, we'll present a common list of candidates next year, whose names will be on tonight's ballot paper. So there'll be one box to vote for the program, another box for the common list of candidates and a last one for our joint nominee for mayor. We all know and like Gérard Mangin, but he's been mayor for too long, and it's time for a change. So now let me present our joint candidate, born and bred in St. Denis, as good a Green as he is a Socialist, Guillaume Pons."

The contrast between the mumbling Alphonse and the dynamic and dashing figure of Pons in his open-necked white shirt was more than striking. It was like a shift in time between Alphonse's era of dull but worthy causes and a new politics of image and excitement. Bruno could almost feel a thrill of expectation run through the hall as Alphonse handed over the microphone. Pons climbed up onto a chair and beamed at the crowd.

"Can you all see me?" he asked. A roar came back. "Can you all hear me?" Another roar. "Welcome to everybody, Greens, Socialists, Communists and monarchists, you're all welcome here tonight—just so long as you don't try to build a sawmill where we're trying to raise our children."

Another roar, but this time it was mainly laughter. Bruno found himself warming to the man, Pons's charm somehow coming across in public in a way that Bruno hadn't seen before in St. Denis. People instinctively took to him. Within thirty seconds, Pons had established himself as a born speaker and politician. Even the hard-line old lefties who thought it heresy to have a common program with the Greens were smiling.

"Now I'm sorry to say that here comes the boring part, but it's important for our kids and our town, so we're going to have to put up with it as we go through the common program we've agreed upon." He paused. "And if it's going to be a dull ten minutes for you all, then think about those of us who spent ten hours drafting this."

More laughter, and then a respectful and interested silence as Pons went through the ten points. Bruno wouldn't have disagreed with a word of it, nor would Mayor Mangin, or any other politician in France. It was a list of generalities on jobs, the environment, low taxes and the importance of children and the elderly. It was so bland that Bruno felt his customary skepticism start to creep back.

"He's a good speaker," Pamela murmured, her eyes fixed on Pons. Beside her, Fabiola looked at Bruno and rolled her eyes. He winked back at her, relieved that he wasn't the only one to find this party manifesto less than persuasive.

"Now you may say that this program is not very detailed, and you'd be right," Pons went on, running his fingers through his already tousled hair. "But we have spent a lot of time working together on this and learning that we can indeed work together. What we have produced here is a set of binding principles. I repeat, binding principles. They are our bedrock, our moral and political foundation, and these principles will inform and shape every decision we take as members of your town council.

"I can't tell you tonight what's going to come up. Let's be honest about this. I don't know what new regulations on water supply and sewage we'll get from Paris or what new rules on recycling we'll get from Brussels. Nobody yet knows what the regional council may ask us to do about public housing or about building codes. But what we can promise you is that we'll never violate the principles I have spelled out tonight. Your jobs are too important, and the air your children breathe is too important."

"So why did you close down the sawmill and put me out of work?" came a shout from the crowd. Bruno turned and saw it was Marcel, the foreman at the sawmill.

"We didn't," Pons replied. "The law did that. We put up compromise after compromise to keep the sawmill open and to save your jobs. We offered to buy a piece of land that would have made the sawmill legal. And we all know who turned us down. We've done a lot here in St. Denis, all of us, all of you and every taxpayer, to help hang on to those jobs. Your own taxes helped pay for the last piece of antipollution equipment that was installed. And that was the right thing to do, because jobs and the environment have to go together. We can't be made prisoners of a false choice between the two—that is principle number seven in our joint program."

More cheers. It was a clever answer, Bruno concluded, conciliatory and glib at the same time. And already Pons was changing the subject to talk about the plan to turn the empty sawmill into an industrial eco-park with tax-free premises for green jobs. He didn't know where Pons had learned public speaking, but Bruno acknowledged that he was very good at it. Pamela was right about that. He cast his mind back to the evening in Pons's restaurant when he had spoken of his various careers in Asia. Hadn't he been a salesman, a champagne salesman, or was it cognac? And he'd been a teacher, so had grown accustomed to speaking in public. And he'd been a croupier in a casino, whatever skills that had taught him.

He began to make mental note of the sequence of tricks that Pons was using: the joke, the arms opened wide, the self-deprecating grin, the sudden turn to solemnity as he banged one fist into his palm to make his points, one, two, three. This was political speaking by numbers, Bruno thought. Pons was playing his audience like an angler plays a fish, and from the rapt faces around him, they were enjoying the manipulation.

Bruno glanced down at Pamela. Her eyes were shining, and the warm smile on her face gave way to a look of purpose as Pons struck another serious note. Her hand came up to touch her own cheek, her little finger just brushing the corner of her lips as if unconsciously caressing herself. It was an almost intimate gesture, and he was startled to see it here.

Looking around the hall, Bruno noticed similar gestures among other women, touching their hair or putting a hand to their necks or their temples. The men were reacting differently, their heads nodding or their jaws set firm before relaxing into a smile again. Suddenly he was aware of Fabiola watching him as he studied the crowd. She seemed immune to Pons's skills, shaking her head as she looked at Bruno. She was as unmoved as he.

Fabiola sidled around Pamela and put a hand on Bruno's shoulder. "I don't like this. It feels creepy," she said, too quietly for Pamela to hear.

"I know what you mean," he said.

"Can you do something?" Fabiola whispered. "He seems to have cast a spell over people."

Bruno shrugged. He was known to be close to the mayor. Even if he could think of some way to intervene, it would be seen as a political move, even a hostile one. That might do more harm than good. But almost without being aware of it, he raised his hand and took advantage of one of Pons's dramatic pauses to call out, "Will you take questions?"

"Who's that? I can't see with these lights. Of course I'll take a question."

People were standing back from Bruno, giving him space.

"Oh, it's you, Bruno, our respected chief of police. I didn't recognize you out of uniform," Pons said. "Welcome to the meeting. What do you want to know?"

"It's about the town budget," Bruno began, using his parade-ground voice so that his words would carry. "We all know that the sawmill was one of the biggest taxpayers in St. Denis and we're going to lose that money. How big a hole will it make in the budget and how does your program plan to fill it? Will you have to raise our taxes? Perhaps Alphonse could answer this as well, since you're partners."

Pons studied Bruno for a moment, then glanced around the crowd, as if he were measuring the degree to which their mood had changed.

"That's a very good question, and it's one all of us in this hall are going to have to think about and work together as we try to answer it. But let's hear from my friend Alphonse first. Just one thing, Bruno," Pons said with one of his trademark smiles. "If I've got anything to do with it, your own salary will be safe from any cuts. You're too valuable a member of this community."

That raised a laugh, and Bruno felt himself color slightly, almost angry. Alphonse took the microphone and began stammering about priorities and hard choices while all the energy leaked from the meeting like air from a deflating bal-

loon. People in the crowd began to shuffle their feet and mutter to their neighbors as he tried to come up with a number
that would answer Bruno's question. When he sat down,
nobody was at all clear what Alphonse had said. Pons took the
microphone again.

"I can't give you this year's figures because we don't have
them yet, but on the basis of last year's budget, the sawmill
paid less than five percent of the tax revenue. That's a chal-
lenge, but it's not a desperate one, and it gives us an opportunity to use the old sawmill premises for new businesses and
new jobs."

People began to drift toward the doors at the back. Pons
noticed and changed his tone.

"We don't want to be here all night, so let's move to the
main business of the evening, the vote. We have two voting
tables—Green Party members to my left, Socialist Party
members to my right. Show your membership card and get
your ballot paper, cast your vote and put it in the boxes provided. Thanks to our student volunteers from the college,
we'll have the result counted within five minutes. And let's
give a big hand to our young people for volunteering to come
and help us with our town meeting tonight."

This brought scattered applause, the sounds of chairs
being pushed back and then a chaotic muddle of people moving left and right to get to the voting tables as they paused to
greet one another and shake hands and forget which table
they were heading for.

"Well done, Bruno," murmured Xavier in his ear. "For a
moment there I thought we were going to elect him mayor by
popular acclamation." The deputy mayor squeezed Bruno's
arm and moved on. Then came a thump on Bruno's back, and

Montsouris, the only Communist on the council, put his burly arm around Bruno's shoulders.

"Good question, Bruno. And even better timing," he said, and moved to rejoin his much more left-wing wife.

"I have to go and vote," said Pamela at Bruno's side. "I didn't know you were so serious about the town budget."

"I didn't know you'd joined a party. You have to be a member to vote tonight," Bruno said. "That's why I can't vote. I'm nonpolitical."

"Oh yes, I joined the Greens yesterday," she said. "It seemed like a good idea to get involved. Bill signed me up himself. I'll be right back. Are you still coming for supper afterward?"

"Wouldn't miss it for anything. No time for lunch today."

"You handled that well," said Fabiola, once Pamela was out of earshot. "I didn't know what to do, but I felt we had to do something. I hate that crowd thing, when people all get caught up in an emotion like that. You'd think we'd have learned by now."

"You haven't joined a party?" Bruno asked her.

"I got all that out of my system when I was a student," she said, smiling. "Very militant, I was. I began with straight Marxism and then drifted off to the Trotskyists. I almost became a Maoist, but then the feminist movement got me, then the mountain climbing. The mountains cured me of politics. And there was also a very cute mountain climber who rescued me from the feminists just in time to settle down to study for my medical finals."

"Well, you know the old saying: If you're not on the left when you're twenty, you have no heart."

"And if you're still there when you're thirty, you have no

head. My dad used to say it to me, and he'd been a Communist." She paused. "I get the impression this is Pamela's first flirtation with politics," Fabiola said. "It can be a dangerous experience, when you come to it late."

She looked meaningfully across the hall to the stage, where Pons was bending down attentively to talk to Pamela. Bruno noticed that Pons's Chinese chef was standing watchfully at the side of the stage, getting his first taste of French democracy. He reminded himself that he really needed to check on getting the man's nieces into school, but was distracted when a very pretty young blond girl whirled into his arms and gave him a strong hug. A large paternal presence loomed behind her, his plump face in a wide grin and his hand out to be shaken.

"Stéphane, Dominique," Bruno said, returning the girl's hug with his left arm while shaking his friend's hand with his right. "You're supposed to be at university in Grenoble. Don't tell me your dad approves of your playing truant." Stéphane laughed, proud of his daughter and beaming in delight at her unexpected arrival.

"I came back specially for this," Dominique said. "Cheap travel for students. But I couldn't miss it, the chance of finally getting a Green mayor for St. Denis. And my politics professor was all in favor."

"I'm not sure Pons will be a Green mayor so much as the head of a coalition," Bruno said. "That means compromises."

"We'll see," Dominique said. "I'm glad you asked your question. I hadn't thought about the money."

"Money and how to spend it are what politics is all about," said Bruno.

A howl came from the loudspeakers, and Alphonse had the microphone again.

"We have the results of your votes," he announced. "And I'm pleased to say that majorities of all parties have voted for the common program. The Greens voted for it by forty-six to twelve. And the Socialists voted seventy-six to forty-six in favor. So we have it. And we have even bigger majorities for Guillaume Pons, whom we all know as Bill, to be our joint candidate for mayor. I now hand the microphone to him."

Pons began by thanking them all for coming this evening and promising to organize other evening meetings like this one, so that the town's twelve elected councillors would be accountable to the voters and party members. Then he explained that the list of candidates had some deliberate gaps, to save some places for useful and worthy citizens who are not party members to sit on the council.

"For example, I'd like to be sure we elect one of the residents of the retirement home here, so we never forget our senior citizens and their interests," Pons said. "And I think we need a good local businessman as well, and perhaps a student. Even if they're too young to stand for election to the town council, we can have a representative at the table because it's their future we are talking about."

Pons waved at the young students from the local college who had counted the votes, and they gave him a cheer. Then he made a show of shading his eyes and looking around the hall, peering from one side to another. Then he muttered an exaggerated "Aah," gave another wave and spoke again.

"And seeing our friend Pamela here in the audience tonight, I think it would be an interesting idea to have one European citizen who is not French on our council to represent all those British and Dutch and other nationalities who have homes here and who bring money to our tourist trade. Maybe we could also find a place for our chief of police, who reminded us all tonight of the importance of keeping track of our town budget. What I'm saying, my friends, is that politics is too important these days to be left to the politicians. We need to include everybody if we are to fulfill the promise of this evening of a new day of democracy for St. Denis. Good night, and our thanks to you all, and *Vive la France.*"

"Councillor Bruno." Fabiola sniffed. "I think I prefer you as chief of police. Just to keep you in your place."

12

Bruno woke in his own bed and alone. Back at Pamela's home after the meeting, he and Pamela and Fabiola were invited to share the chicken Pamela had left slowly roasting on a bed of potatoes and garlic. Bruno had opened a bottle of his Pomerol. Fabiola set the table in the kitchen, and Pamela opened a large can of *petits pois*.

"I hope you don't mind, but I'm feeling drained after that event and I'd rather eat at once than wait for some vegetables to be cooked. I think I was pretty tired anyway." She yawned.

Bruno decided to play it by ear, but he'd probably leave after the meal. He stayed the night here often enough to know where everything was, so he pulled down the decanter from the top shelf and went to the sink to pour the wine. It should have been opened a couple of hours earlier, but the decanting would have to serve. Fabiola sliced a baguette and arranged a cheese tray. Nobody was speaking and the silence was starting to become oppressive when they all spoke at once.

"Did you hear . . . ," began Bruno. "Sorry . . . ," said Pamela. "I meant to say . . . ," said Fabiola. "Go ahead, Pamela," said Bruno.

"I'll just get the chicken," Pamela said. "I was just going to ask what you two thought about this idea of Bill's about my going on the council. He mentioned it to me just before he spoke publicly. I think you'd do a better job, Bruno."

"I can't do it, and I think he probably knows that," Bruno replied as the steaming pot came from the oven. He sniffed deeply, savoring the scents of garlic and chicken and lemon. "I'm employed by the mayor and the council. So I couldn't be in charge of myself, it's against the rules. I think you'd be good on the council."

"They still talk of me as the Mad Englishwoman, don't they?" She put the pot in the center of the table.

"That was before they got to know you," Bruno said. "Country people always invent a nickname for strangers. It's a way of placing them when you don't know their parents and grandparents and how they looked when they were babies. Now everybody knows you as Pamela."

"Would it be a lot of work?" she asked.

"It's usually one evening every other week for the council meeting, more in the week when the budget gets approved," Bruno replied. "But you'd have to be available to your voters. In your case, that would mean the other foreigners here, and some of them don't speak much French. You might find yourself acting as an unpaid translator and a guide through the thickets of our French bureaucracy. And then it would depend on which committee they put you on. Avoid the *ponts et chaussées* committee or every farmer will be badgering you to make his cart track into a commune road so that the town has to pay for the upkeep."

"It's flattering just to be considered," said Fabiola as Bruno poured the wine.

Pamela had seemed distracted, picking at her food rather

than dispatching it with her usual appetite. But she drank as much wine as the other two together. After the chicken, Bruno took a small sliver of the Tomme d'Audrix, the local cheese that his friend Stéphane had invented, and a final swallow of wine. Then he rose, pleading an early start in the morning and a busy day and pretending not to notice the brief frown that passed across Pamela's face.

"Don't be upset," Fabiola had said as she walked him to the Land Rover. "She's a bit confused and distracted. A friend of hers in Le Buisson saw you with some old girlfriend at the station yesterday evening. You know how word gets around."

Bruno replayed the scene in his head as he lay in the dark of his bedroom. There had been no time at the station for anything more than a brief peck on Isabelle's cheek as she dashed for the waiting train. He'd always nurture a sweet *tendresse* for Isabelle, but she had made it clear the last time they'd parted that any romance was over. Bruno smiled to himself, remembering the look of her beside him in this bed, the scent she left on the pillows, the way she liked to wear his shirts as a dressing gown.

He opened his eyes and looked at the darkness of the woods through the window. The worst thing about winter was that dawn came so late he always rose in the dark. At least the house was warm, the thick stone walls holding the heat pumped out by the woodstove. He climbed out of bed, opened the door to let Gigi in to smother him with doggy affection, turned on Radio Périgord and began the usual routine of exercises he'd learned in the army. The second item on the news was a fire at an Asian supermarket in Bergerac. This was getting worse.

He made coffee and began toasting yesterday's baguette for breakfast. He'd better start on the venison casserole for Hercule's wake. Gigi looked hopeful at his feet as Bruno took down the large ham that hung from the beam that supported the kitchen roof. He sliced off some of the dense fat with the meat, chopped it into lardons, tossed them into his big casserole dish and lit the gas. He pulled down six shallots from the string that hung from the beam and began to peel them. The toast was ready, and he and Gigi ate slice and slice alike before he began cutting the venison into rough cubes. He stirred the lardons and judged whether there was sufficient fat. Not quite, so he added more from the ham and put the shallots into a separate pan to fry them with duck fat. He put more duck fat into the casserole and threw in the venison to brown.

Radio Périgord had started to play music so he tuned to France-Inter for the news and the newspaper review as he sipped his coffee and began turning the chunks of meat so they browned on all sides. From his larder he removed a large glass jar of the mushrooms he had dried in September. Then he began to peel heads of garlic. When the venison was well browned, he sprinkled flour onto the meat to soak up all the juices and then tipped in the shallots and added half a dozen cloves of garlic, salt and pepper. He took a bottle of the Bergerac red he bought for everyday drinking and poured a splash into the pan where the onions had been and grated what was left of the baguette into the glaze. He then took a fat blood sausage, made from last year's pig, squeezed out the rich, black contents from its skin and added them to the pan, crumbling the sausage meat that would help thicken the sauce, and then scraped the result into the casserole. He added the rest of the bottle of wine, added the dried mushrooms and closed the lid.

Now for the dessert, he said to himself. He had decided on crème brûlée with truffles and began by taking a jar of truffle scraps and trimmings and tying them firmly into a small bag of doubled cheesecloth. Then he poured three quarts of heavy cream into a saucepan, turned on the heat and dropped the bag of truffle trimmings into the thick liquid. As it heated, he began—with thanks to his chickens for their fecundity even this late in the year—to crack two dozen eggs, tipping the egg halves quickly back and forth over a bowl so that the whites slithered out and the yolks were left in their half shell. In a separate bowl, he mixed the egg yolks with a dozen table-spoons of sugar until they were thickened and had turned pale yellow.

The cream was about to boil, and the heady scent of truf-fles began to fill the kitchen. He turned down the heat, poured in the egg yolks and whisked until the mixture began to steam. Careful not to let it boil, he tested it with a wooden spoon to see if it would coat the wood, and once it did he poured the mixture through a sieve into his largest soufflé dish. He chopped one of the black truffles he had been saving into the mix and set it aside to cool. He'd leave it in the refrig-erator throughout the day to set, and then all it would need would be a layer of sugar on the top and a minute with a blowtorch to melt it. The result would be a dessert fit for roy-alty. No, better than that, fit for a hunters' feast. Fit for Her-cule, he thought sadly.

He turned to the sink, washed his bowls and cleaned the kitchen, put on his boots, winter jacket and woolen cap and took Gigi out for their predawn walk. The night was cold and the stars brilliant, throwing enough light to gleam on the white frost at his feet. From his barn came the soft hooting of an owl, and somewhere far off in the woods a fox barked. Bruno took a flashlight from his pocket and checked his chicken coop, and at the sound of his footsteps his cockerel gave the usual hesitant crow of a winter's morning while the hens stayed sound asleep, heads tucked under their wings so they looked like balls of feathers. The coop was secure, and the wire netting around the chicken run was intact. That fox had better look elsewhere. His ducks were stirring, waiting for him to toss them their feed from the large bin where he kept the dried corn. From his vegetable garden he took some sprigs of thyme and plucked two leaves from the bay tree and put them by his door before taking Gigi into the familiar woods behind his home.

It was his best time for reflection, knowing the terrain so well he barely needed to think where he stepped as Gigi darted out to the left and now to the right sniffing furiously. He had the scent of the fox, and Bruno called him back. Once a basset hound had a scent he could track his prey all day. Gigi waited until Bruno approached, and even in the darkness of the trees Bruno knew that his dog would be eyeing him reproachfully, not understanding why he'd been called from his hunter's duty. Bruno bent and fondled his head and stroked the long ears and murmured encouragements as his dog rubbed the side of his muzzle against Bruno's leg. If only he could begin to understand women as he understood his dog.

But that would mean understanding himself and knowing what *he* wanted. What did he expect or hope for from Pamela? She had made it clear that she wanted no permanent relationship and that she insisted on keeping her independence. Bruno had never suggested otherwise, but he knew that she was a woman with whom he could be content. She was considerate and kind, and the cool self-confidence of her public face became wonderfully sensuous in private. There was also the spice of her being foreign. Her French was almost perfect, but her sensibility was altogether different. They did not share the same references to old pop songs and advertising jingles, to the names of old movie stars and the reputations of old politicians.

Pamela would ask him about the different street names that he took for granted. Why was this street called the Eighteenth of June and that one the Seventh of May? And what was the Dix-huit Brumaire and the Twenty-first of April? He supposed he had absorbed all the dates at school along with the memories that were seared forever into the soul of France: the Massacre of St. Bartholomew and the Voie Sacrée of Verdun, the horn of Roland at Roncesvalles and the siege of La Rochelle, the sun of Austerlitz and Léon Blum's Front Populaire. He could define them for her, but not the echoes and the sentiments they carried, that core of Frenchness that loved the sound of an accordion and the taste of *andouillettes*.

But not sharing all that was part of Pamela's charm, he admitted. It made her just faintly exotic, with a touch of the adventure that Bruno relished in his life. Still, had it been adventure he wanted, then life with Isabelle in Paris and working for the brigadier would have been a great deal more attractive. Isabelle was wonderful and tantalizing and exciting in a way that made him want to match her daring and her pace. But not all the time. He sniffed the cold night air, saw the very first light of dawn, and he knew that he loved these woods and his home and St. Denis and never wanted to leave them.

He turned back toward his home, taking the long route along the ridge, strangely comforted that his conversation with himself had ended as it had before, with a realization that both women answered to something essential in his own nature. But neither one of them could offer him all that he needed. He loved Isabelle, but not the life and career she insisted on leading. And he loved Pamela and the country life she represented, and the way she adored this dear corner of France enough to leave her own country for it. She would be a fine woman to settle down with, but she did not want to settle down. And nor, if he were honest with himself, did he— not yet.

He looked at his cottage and at the roof where he'd already drawn the plans for the *chien assis,* the dormer window that would turn his empty loft into an extra bedroom. Why do that, if not because he had a family in mind someday, children who would sleep in that room and smuggle Gigi or his successor up the stairs to curl up with warmly at night? Children to whom he could leave this house that he had rebuilt, this stretch of land that he had turned into a garden.

However generous the gesture, there must have been a touch of sadness in Hercule when he drafted the will that, in the absence of a family heir, left his goods to his friends and to charity. Bruno would miss walking through these woods with Hercule, looking for the darting dance of the fly that indicated the presence of truffles beneath the ground. He'd miss Hercule's special way with dogs, the quick understanding that he brought forth from Gigi when training him to find the truffles and stand and mark the spot without digging. He'd miss the cognacs at dawn in the open air, and the easy camaraderie that he and the baron and Hercule had enjoyed, three old soldiers. They might have known different wars, but it had been the same army.

He walked to the back of the house and took his hay box from the barn and then picked up the herbs and bay leaves and went into his kitchen. The casserole was bubbling gently. He stirred the stew, added in the thyme and bay leaves and a handful of black peppercorns and went off to shower and change into his uniform. When he returned, he turned off the gas, opened the hay box and nestled the casserole inside its thick bed of hay. He settled the small sack of hay on top to keep the heat in and closed the tin lid. Now it would cook itself in the insulating hay for the rest of the day. He checked that he had a fresh towel in his sports bag and headed out to the Land Rover to supervise the setting up of the Saturday morning market. Gigi sat solemnly at the head of the lane, as he did every morning, watching him go. Bruno wondered what he did then. Probably padded back to the chicken coop to pick up the scent of the long-gone fox and patrol his master's land.

13

Bruno walked twelve or thirteen miles on a good day of hunting, ran two or three times a week, played tennis and taught the children of the town to play rugby. But he'd be forty on his next birthday, and he knew that a full ninety minutes of rugby would be rough. It was less the stamina to keep running than the constant bursts of acceleration that the game required. And once again the team had insisted he play at wing forward, where he had to be as fast as the backs and as relentless as the forwards.

He rubbed liniment into his thighs and strapped his sometimes suspect ankle. And then he watched in disbelief as his teammate Stéphane slid on some black tights under his shorts. One of the biggest and toughest men who'd ever played for St. Denis, he was known to be impervious to pain, but suddenly he was dressing up to keep his legs warm. Stéphane saw Bruno looking and said defensively, "It's cold out there."

"Not after the first couple of minutes," Bruno said. "Mind you, that's about all I'll be good for."

"Look at the rest of us," grunted Stéphane. He was right.

As Bruno glanced around the changing room, he saw a bunch of middle-aged men carrying too much weight and capable of too little stamina, each of them probably wondering, like him, whether he'd be able to walk tomorrow.

It was the day of St. Denis's annual youth-versus-age rugby game, the over-thirty-fives against the under-eighteens, maturity and cunning against the energy of youth. There were only two ways for the old men to win. The first was to pile up a huge lead in the first fifteen minutes when they could still play with some of their old fire and then dig in for a solid defense. The other was to crush the striplings with their bulk and ruthless aggression. Bruno had been on teams that played it both ways, and it never quite worked. The speed and resilience of the youngsters always told in the second half. And the one time the oldsters had played rough, the wife of one player had run onto the field to hit her husband with her handbag after he'd flattened their son with a brutal tackle. It was in the hope of another such scene that the town's stadium and the railings around the pitch were always filled for this match, which was one of the club's best fund-raisers of the year.

Raoul handed around a bottle of cognac, but Bruno shook his head. Maybe at halftime, if he lasted that long. He looked around at the team. He knew each of his teammates and had played with all of them before except for the one newcomer, Guillaume Pons. So he was over thirty-five, even if he didn't look it, bouncing up and down on his toes. Bruno wondered how much rugby he had played in China. Still, he looked in good shape and in the little preparation they had done, a few jogs around the playing field, he'd shown himself to be pretty fast. He was playing on the wing.

"Okay, gather around," said Louis, the rugby club chairman who had appointed himself their coach, which was one way to avoid having to play. "Go like hell for as long as you can. We've got to pile up at least thirty points before they know what's hit them. And then just keep possession and kick the ball away if you have to. We're bigger and taller than they are so we can win most of the scrums. And watch out for women with handbags. Good luck!"

Putain! It was even colder than it had been during his dawn walk, thought Bruno as the players trotted out of the changing room and through the crowd to the pitch. The youngsters were already warming up and showing off their speed. Standing by the gap in the railings that led to the field was Father Sentout, a thick black cloak over his soutane, giving his customary blessing to the players. Laughing and cheering at their fathers and uncles and husbands, the crowd gave them a great welcome with the women blowing kisses and shouting out jokes about stretchers and ambulances. Bruno saw Pamela and Fabiola waving as he jogged past, and he gave them a mock salute. Perhaps he should have asked for a handkerchief or a garter, like some knight of old wearing his lady's favor on his breast.

The weather had turned. The sky was dull and gray and the ground had been sodden all week. There was a sheen of ice on the puddles beyond the rugby posts. The field would be mud within twenty minutes, which would slow down the older men, but it meant the kind of grinding struggle between the forwards that should suit their style of play. A firm pitch and easy running would have helped the youngsters. Stéphane was captain and lost the coin toss, so the oldsters lined up to receive the opening kick.

Short and squat and a fine forward, Lespinasse from the garage caught the ball and turned his back on the charge of his son Edouard. Taller than his father but maybe half the weight, Edouard simply bounced off his father's bulk as Lespinasse passed the ball to Raoul, who gained another ten yards before he slipped the ball to Stéphane, who bulled his way forward with three youngsters hanging on to his legs before he flipped the ball across to Marcel.

The big, middle-aged men lurched their way forward through the tackles, Bruno keeping himself out slightly to the flank. Finally the youngsters brought the drive to a halt. But Marcel rose from the melee and tossed the ball back to Jacquot. Just thirty-five, the youngest man on the team, Jacquot ducked and darted his way around to score as the first drops of rain began to come down.

And so it went. Each time the old men got the ball they used their bulk to drive through and score. When the youngsters got possession, Bruno had to make tackle after tackle, and not the easy ones around a running opponent's legs, but a high tackle to grab the arms and keep his man up until his teammates could plunge into the melee and haul the ball away.

The old forwards scored twice more. The youngsters now had the ball, but there was no way they were going to be able to hold the weight of the older men as the two lines of forwards crashed into each other. Bruno put one hand down to the pitch to make it easier to sprint up and catch their runner. But the ball carrier had his own ideas and darted like quicksilver. Bruno barely managed to catch the boy's ankle as he went past, sending the boy crashing onto his face. The ball bounced perfectly into Bruno's arms.

One sidestep and he was in the open field with only two players to beat. He heard Jacquot coming up to his right shoulder and sensed another dark blue shirt to his left. Bruno fended off one pursuer with a straight-arm to the face. Then as the other players dived low at his legs Bruno passed the ball to Jacquot, who darted over the goal line.

His hands on his knees, Bruno breathed hard as Jacquot converted the kick. That made it twenty-eight to zero.

"Didn't you see me?" came a crisp voice. It was Pons. "I was right at your shoulder waiting for that pass and it was clear in front of me. You should have passed the ball."

"I did pass the ball," said Bruno. "I passed it to Jacquot, who scored."

"I was better placed," Pons said. "Still, a good play, Bruno. Just remember there are other guys on this team."

Christ, thought Bruno, a prima donna. As Pons walked away, Bruno saw that there wasn't a speck of mud on him. His shirt and shorts were still immaculate. Bruno looked as if he'd been living underground for the past month. He shrugged and looked at the clock. Just over thirty minutes gone so far, still in the first half, and already Lespinasse was quietly being sick on the sideline, Stéphane was down on one knee, and Raoul was wheezing like an ancient locomotive going up a steep hill.

Bruno looked across at the youngsters with irritation. He'd trained these boys so they ought to be playing better than this. They were letting the old men use their advantages of weight and strength and relying too much on the speed of their running. That wasn't the smart tactic. Against a slower, heavier team, Bruno had drilled into them that the right strategy was to kick the ball down the field and force the heavier team to run and run until they dropped. And Bruno was fond enough of his pupils to want them to play the intelligent way, even if it meant exhaustion and defeat for his own team.

He lined up again to receive the kickoff, and this time the

ball came directly to him. But young Edouard was almost on him, so Bruno turned half sideways and punted the ball with a long, looping kick. As they lined up to take the throw-in, Bruno stood behind Stéphane, who turned to face him. Bruno kept his eye on the young player who was to throw the ball. As it left the youth's hands he shouted, "Now!" and ran forward, jumping into the air. Stéphane grabbed him around the thighs and boosted him upward so that Bruno towered above the line and plucked the ball from the air.

Still held upright in Stéphane's mighty grip, Bruno faked a pass to Pierrot, and the youngsters began to peel away. But then Stéphane dropped him gently, and with the rest of the pack at his heels Bruno broke through the opponent's line still holding the ball and pounded for the goalposts with nobody to stop him. But he was tiring now and slower than he had been, and as he dived for the goal line he felt the fullback crash into his side, rolling him over. But the ball was firm in his hands, and then the goalpost was smashing hard into his back as he planted the ball for another score.

Winded and bruised, Bruno lay on his back with his eyes closed and waited for Louis to come by with his magic sponge. He no longer felt the cold. His body was glowing with heat. But the strongest sensation was a deep tiredness until Jules the gendarme thumped down beside him, and the ice-cold sponge was in his face and then thrust down the back of his shirt.

"Nice run, Bruno," Jules said. "You okay?"

"I'll live," he said, rolling over and hauling himself to his feet. Louis gave the back of Bruno's neck a final wipe with the sponge, and Bruno trotted back to his team.

"Time to give us others a chance," Pons said curtly when

Bruno arrived. "A few of you are hogging the ball. You can't keep all the glory to yourselves."

Bruno stared at him in disbelief. Raoul spat angrily, and Lespinasse said, making a joke of it, "Glory? You're playing the wrong game, pal." Stéphane dropped a heavy arm onto Pons's shoulder and said softly, "Don't be a fool." Pons stomped off.

After halftime, with the rain coming down steadily, the game began to stall in the mud. It was a relief to the older men, for whom a slower game meant an easier game, but then the youngsters scored twice. They now did what they should have been doing all along, punting the ball into open space and using their speed to follow it. But this time the ball was bouncing unevenly, and they couldn't take it cleanly, and Bruno had the time to charge across and tackle their player just as he picked up the rolling ball from the ground, jolting the ball from the youngster's grip. Bruno grabbed it to his chest and rolled himself into a ball as the feet of a dozen players thundered around and over him.

Lespinasse looked sourly at Pons and called, loudly enough for spectators to hear, "Hey, beautiful. Where were you, pretty boy? Stopping that player was your job."

Pons colored, and his eyes flashed angrily. After the scrum, Pierrot darted around to the blind side, plucked the ball from the ground and passed it to Pons. He took off like a frightened gazelle, with just Bruno and a teammate trying to keep up with him.

Bruno was about five yards behind Pons, running flat-out, two opponents just coming into view and going full steam, when Pons shouted, "Bruno" and passed the ball to him. Completely surprised, Bruno just managed to catch the ball when the two defenders slammed into him, one at his ankles and the other at his chest, their weight and his own speed pile-driving him hard into the ground. In the millisecond before his face plowed into the earth he felt as if he'd been hit by a train, and then he felt nothing at all.

He didn't lose consciousness, but he was still dazed when the sponge came, and then suddenly it disappeared. Blinking and groggy he rolled and saw Jules had abandoned the sponge and was running to separate Pons and Lespinasse. Pons was down on his back and bleeding from his nose, and Lespinasse was standing over him and roaring, "You little prick, you did that on purpose. You were clear, you bastard, and you gave Bruno a suicide pass. What kind of shit are you?"

It certainly felt like a suicide pass to Bruno. Pons had deliberately passed him the ball just as the two young opponents were in range to hit him, and Pons had been in the open with only one player to beat and another team member outside him. Bruno felt too disoriented to think about blaming Pons or anybody else and felt only that the world had become a cruel and hurtful place. He coughed and spat out blood. His teeth still seemed to be in place. Gingerly, he moved his legs and arms, and they seemed to work. Jules came back with the sponge, and Bruno rolled to one side and was sick.

"You'll be okay," Jules said, looking carefully into his eyes. "Did you lose consciousness?"

"I don't think so," Bruno said. "Not really. I'm okay."

"We'd be down to thirteen men if you leave the pitch," Jules said. "The ref sent Lespinasse off. He should have sent that little shit Pons for pulling that trick."

"How much longer to play?" Bruno asked.

"About twelve, fifteen minutes, plus injury time. Mostly yours."

"Help me up." Bruno limped to his feet and stood, swaying. The ref came across and took Bruno's face between his hands and looked searchingly at Bruno's eyes.

"Have you been concussed?"

Bruno shook his head. It hurt. "No," he said. "I can play."

"Just as well because you're two men down already," the ref said. "Your teammate's taken himself off with that nosebleed."

He looked to the sideline where Lespinasse stood glowering beside the trainer as Pons limped off the pitch. Both men ignored him. A cheer came from the crowd as Bruno forced himself to trot back to his teammates. He heard a woman's voice calling his name. He turned, and Pamela was waving at him, and then beckoning him urgently to leave the pitch. He shook his head. Stéphane patted him gently on the back, and then lined up to restart the game. Bruno bent down not knowing whether he'd be able to get up again.

The mud was now so thick that there was no difference between the dark blue shirts of the oldsters and the light blue of the younger men. It was all mud, and the ball was a sodden, slippery mass, too elusive to hold. The mud sticking to their boots, the older men were almost too tired to move. The youngsters had taken charge.

Bruno glanced over and saw Pons at the sideline. He was fresh from the shower, with his Chinese chef, Minxin, beside him holding a tray with a bottle of champagne and four flutes. There was no sign of the nieces. Pons poured out the glasses and offered one to Pamela and the other to Fabiola. The two women waved the glasses away, their eyes intent on the pitch. Bruno barely heard the whistle as Pierrot kicked off and the old men lumbered grimly forward once again.

At last the final whistle went, the game ending in a draw, thirty-five all. As the players all lined up to shake hands,

Stéphane said, "Bruno, I'm going to ram that champagne bottle up Pons's ass. And if this town's crazy enough to elect him I'll shoot him before he sets foot in the *mairie*."

They limped off to the showers, the youngsters still fresh enough to trot ahead, whooping that they would take all the hot water. That suited Bruno fine. Cold water was probably what he needed. He ignored Pons and the glass of Pol Roger he offered and stopped in front of Pamela.

"Didn't you see me waving for you to come off?" she said, handing him her champagne, which she had now accepted. He nodded, almost too tired to speak, but he emptied the glass.

"The game was almost over," he said. "I was okay."

"You played well," she said, and leaned forward to kiss him. "I don't know the game, but I could see that."

"Hold on a moment," said Fabiola. She put her hands to his head, regardless of the mud, and lifted his eyelids. She looked searchingly into his eyes and told him to follow her finger with his gaze. Left and right, up and down.

"You'll do," she said. "I'm making a habit of this."

"She's a great doctor," said Pons. "Stopped my nosebleed in no time. She's making a habit of that, too."

Bruno looked coldly at him and turned back to the women. "Thanks," he said. "I'm off to the bath."

Ignoring the slaps on the back from other spectators, Bruno paused only to greet Dominique, who stood well back from the clinging mud that encased him to give him an air kiss.

"You and Dad were brilliant," she said.

"Tell him. It'll mean a lot to him, it does to me," he told her. He went into the locker room to find his teammates sitting with their shoes off and their tired bodies steaming. He slumped onto a bench and tried to undo his laces, but he couldn't bend. Pierrot limped across, knelt at Bruno's feet and eased the shoes off.

"You played a hell of a game," he said.

"Another one like that would kill me," Bruno replied.

Then the youngsters trooped in, carrying beers for all the players, and pride required that they stand up and drink before they went into the showers and stood a long time beneath the water as the mud slowly washed away. Finally feeling half human, Bruno dressed and left, and some of the stalwart supporters were still there to cheer. Pamela and Fabiola were waiting, but there was no sign of Pons. Just as well, thought Bruno. It would not be a good idea for the chief of police to punch his next mayor.

14

Bruno was not altogether surprised to see the hulking figure of J-J leaning against the side of the stall where grilled sausages were sold and holding a large plastic glass of beer. As he saw Bruno, he pointed to another full glass on the shelf beside him.

"Good game, you played well," he said.

"You haven't been here that long," Bruno replied. "I'd have seen you."

"Everybody said you played well. At least, the baron did. But that's not why I'm here. I've got the printouts from Hercule's phones, and some of my people have run them through their computers and done some cluster analysis. There are a lot of calls to your disappeared friend Vinh, who is no longer answering his phone. Several calls to you and the baron and some long ones to the Vietnamese embassy in Paris. And a lot of calls to prepaid cell phones that aren't registered to anybody. Meantime, I want to check some local names with you from other numbers he called."

J-J pulled a sheaf of computer printouts from a bulging briefcase and flourished them. "I was going to offer to buy you dinner tonight so you can tell me who they all are. Are you going to introduce me to these ladies?"

Laughing, Pamela said, "Lovely to meet you again, Commissioner. Are you going to the funeral feast tonight for Hercule?"

"Luckily, yes. Especially as Bruno's doing the cooking. Since I'm hunting Hercule's killer, the baron says I qualify. Maybe it was helped by my offer to bring a couple of decent bottles."

J-J's eyes followed the women with admiration as they left under the stone arch of the stadium entrance.

"Two fine women," said J-J. "And we're off to an all-male evening. We must be mad."

"If you're coming, you'll have to follow me home first. I've got to make the soup and pick up some supplies, and then we'll head over to the baron's place."

"A small château, they tell me."

"Very small. More of a *chartreuse* than a château. It looks imposing, but it's only one room wide. Leave your car here. You can start reading out those names as we drive."

"Let's start with buying the wine," said J-J. Bruno drove the short distance to the *cave* of Hubert de Montignac, a legendary place that sold individual bottles of wine for as much as three thousand euros but also dispensed local wine for little more than one euro a bottle from giant vats at the back of the store. Hubert himself came out from behind the counter to greet Bruno and usher the two men into his office that also served as a private tasting room.

"What's the matter with you?" asked Nathalie, rising from her desk and offering her cheeks to be kissed. "You're limping."

"Rugby," Bruno explained and made the introductions.

"You'll be seeing Hubert at dinner tonight, so you should take his advice on what to bring," he told J-J.

"Hercule loved his St. Emilion, and Château Angélus most of all," Hubert said. "But nobody can afford to drink much of that these days. I'm taking a bottle of the eighty-five because I really liked the old guy, and he bought a lot of wine from me. I'd thought of taking a ninety-nine because when we tasted it at the time he was right and I wrong. I thought it wouldn't last, and Hercule told me it would, and he bought a case. We drank a bottle the last time Nathalie and I saw him. I've got a couple left in the bin."

"Let's have them both, but I want to pay for them," said J-J. "I'm a last-minute guest tonight."

Hubert raised his eyebrows and exchanged glances with Nathalie. Bruno knew that as head of detectives, J-J's salary was at least double and maybe three times his own. But two bottles of Angélus would be more than a week's pay even for J-J. Nathalie shrugged, as if to say it was up to Hubert what he charged. Hubert said, "Give me two hundred and I'll open them now and bring them along to the baron's."

"Not often that I pay that much for a bottle of wine," said J-J as they settled back into Bruno's vehicle. "But I suspect that if I hadn't been coming to the dinner tonight I'd have paid a lot more."

Bruno nodded, thinking it would have been a great deal more and asked to hear the names from Hercule's phone list. Most of them were familiar to him, hunters or men from the truffle trade or the Ste. Alvère *mairie*. J-J ticked them off on his printout and stuffed it back into his briefcase as they rounded the bend at the top of the hill that led to Bruno's cottage. Gigi was sitting by the first of the row of young white oaks that bordered the track.

"He recognizes the sound of the engine," Bruno said proudly, greeting his dog. Pulling his sports bag from the rear seat, he led the way into his home.

"A policeman who doesn't lock his own front door," chided J-J. Bruno grinned to himself, and unlocked the one door in his house that was always firmly secured, the storage room where he kept his shotgun and the washing machine. He rinsed his mud-soaked rugby clothes in the old sink before stuffing them into the machine. He set it in motion and relocked the door.

"You have a choice," he said to J-J. "Have a Ricard with me now while I make the soup and then join me in walking the dog in the dark, or take him out into the woods while there's still some light and come back in half an hour."

J-J made two Ricards as Bruno went out to his *potager* with a garden fork and came back to the outdoor tap to rinse the dirt from the turnips, leeks and potatoes. In the kitchen, he began peeling and chopping the vegetables and lit the gas under a big iron saucepan. He tossed in some duck fat and began gently to fry them. From his refrigerator he pulled some of Stéphane's milk and a glass jar full of a dark brown liquid and set them down. Then he began to peel garlic cloves.

"What's the brown stuff?" asked J-J.

"Bouillon, made from the bones of the last wild boar Hercule shot. He gave me the bones for Gigi, but I made a stock first." He stirred the vegetables and sipped his Ricard. "I heard on the radio about the Asian supermarket. Was it arson?"

"Gasoline bombs again. Crude but effective," said J-J. He went on to describe the pattern that made Paris fear another gang war. There had been similar trouble between Vietnamese and Chinese in Marseilles two years earlier before they agreed to a truce, and more serious trouble in the thirteenth arrondissement in Paris before that. It always started with attacks on street vendors and restaurants. Local truces could be negotiated, agreements to divide sections of a city. In Marseilles the truce broke down because of a third party, the Corsicans, who wanted to keep the whores, the drugs and the docks. That left the Asians fighting over illegal immigrants, gambling, loan sharking and protection rackets. But the Chinese had the counterfeit goods that gave them a foothold in the street markets. Above all, the Chinese had more and more illegal immigrants. A decade earlier, the Vietnamese had outnumbered the Chinese. Now the balance had shifted.

"How many are you talking about?" Bruno asked. The vegetables were mashed, the stock on the fire but not yet simmering. He splashed in some water and then slowly added the milk, stirring carefully.

"Altogether, there's about a hundred and fifty thousand Viets and about two hundred thousand Chinese, probably more with the illegals. Then there are the Chi-Viets, the ones who got out as boat people. But the Viets have been here longer. That's why they're spread out more across France, and the trouble comes when the Chinese start to follow. And now the Chinese are muscling their way into the southwest, so we've been getting trouble in Bordeaux and Toulouse and Cahors, and it's spilled over here."

Bruno nodded and began grating nutmeg into the pot. He took a spoon from the drawer and sipped. The liquid at the center had begun to move, the signal that the simmering had begun.

"That's it," he said. "Now we walk Gigi, and you can tell

me the rest." He looked outside, where it was not yet dark, handed J-J a spare woolen cap, and they set off.

"Don't tell me," Bruno said when they had reached the top of the ridge. "When you got Vinh's citizenship papers, it was Hercule who was his sponsor. That wasn't hard to guess."

"In fact, it wasn't," gasped J-J. He wasn't used to walking in the dark woods. Nor was he accustomed to climbing even the modest slope they had taken through the trees to the ridge. Bruno stopped, waiting for J-J to get his breath back and feeling the soreness in his own legs from the rugby game. At least the stiffness had gone, and the cold night air had cleared the remaining fuzziness from his head and brought back his appetite. He breathed in deeply, relishing the deep quiet of the woods in winter when all the vegetation seemed asleep. The terrain was made for hunters, with only the game stirring and the knowledge that beneath the ground the finest of the truffles were reaching their ripeness. He heard Gigi rustling through the undergrowth and whistled softly.

Gigi gave a soft bark, almost a cough. Bruno signaled J-J to follow him and struck out down the slope. Gigi was waiting for him beneath a white oak, one front paw lifted and his nose to the earth. Bruno took a small trowel from his pocket and gave his flashlight to J-J, asking him to hold it. Bruno began to scrape away the earth just beneath Gigi's nose. The dog backed off slightly to give him room, making a noise that was almost a purr, deep in his throat. Trusting Gigi, Bruno loosened the earth around the spot, and then began to dig by hand, piling the loose earth to one side.

The unmistakable scent of a truffle began to rise, rich and fecund, as if the earth itself were ready to give birth, and he eased the trowel down around the sides of the hole he had made, levering gently. He used his hand again to touch the truffle, the feeling of it slightly warmer than the surrounding soil. It was big, perhaps the biggest he had ever found. Carefully, he loosened the soil around it and began picking out the soil a pinch at a time. The smell became almost overwhelming, and then the truffle was in his hand, a marvel of maybe half a pound.

"It looks perfect," he said as J-J shone the light on it.

"I never saw that done before," said J-J. "I can smell it from here. What would that be worth?"

"At least three hundred euros, maybe more," Bruno said. "But I'm not going to sell this one."

He put it into his pocket and then knelt again to push the pile of loose earth back into the hole.

"Very neat and tidy," said J-J, "but I don't think the woods will notice."

"That's not the point," said Bruno. "That soil contains spores. By putting it back, chances are this tree will produce more truffles in the same spot. That's why I'm marking this place in my mind, and why I'm going to imprint it into Gigi's memory."

Bruno caressed Gigi, murmuring to him and pushing his nose gently down to sniff the earth again and then the tree, stroking him all the time and telling him what a fine dog he was.

"That's why I prefer a dog to a pig for hunting truffles," said Bruno. "Some people will tell you it's because the pigs eat them and the dogs won't, but that can be fixed by putting a muzzle on the pig. The real reason is that a properly trained dog remembers the spot and remembers the trail back to it. Speaking of that, we'd better be heading back."

Bruno rose and brushed his hands together, then led the way toward his cottage, Gigi happy at his heels and J-J at the rear, following the flickering glow of the flashlight he shone on the earth before his feet.

"You were saying it wasn't Hercule who acted as Vinh's sponsor for the immigration."

"It surprised me, but no," J-J said. "Vinh's sponsor was a Capitaine Antoine Savani. My team's trying to find out what we can about him. Vinh's file also had a supporting letter from one Général Gambiez. But Vinh was just a baby when he came here. It was his parents who got the sponsorship, along with a few thousand others who decided that Vietnam without French protection wasn't a safe place to be."

"Like the Harkis who fought for us in Algeria and got slaughtered when we left."

"Exactly," said J-J. "It's a dangerous move to pick the wrong side in that kind of war."

"So you'll start putting all this together next week?" Bruno asked.

"We're going through channels. I'm not sure how frank the defense ministry will be with the files."

"You think I can do any better?"

"You have that friend in the military archives, the one who helped us out before with that dead Arab. He might be useful."

"I can try, but I think you'd have more luck with the brigadier."

"He's a last resort," said J-J. "He's not a cop, so he doesn't have our concerns about catching murderers. He'll only help if it suits his own agenda."

"I think you're being too hard on him," said Bruno. "He'll

help so long as it doesn't hurt his own agenda. There's a difference. I think his regard for Hercule means he'll go a long way to help us catch his killers, plus he owes us some favors."

Back at Bruno's house, they loaded the hay box into the back of the Land Rover, fixed a tight lid on the saucepan of soup and put that between J-J's feet. Bruno grabbed a couple of spare towels, a sleeping bag and an old rugby shirt and threw them into his sports bag. The wake would go on late, and they'd probably bed down at the baron's. He boosted Gigi into the back of the vehicle, and they set off down the hill toward town and the tiny hamlet beyond it that huddled around the baron's *chartreuse*. They parked in the small square that was named after the baron's grandfather.

The *chartreuse* covered more than a side of the square. It was almost two hundred feet long, built of stone that had stood for nearly four hundred years, and it soared three stories high with a tower at each wing. It was only one room wide, but each room was more than twenty feet deep, and each of the stone walls added another few feet. The rear wall facing the square was a long line of stone, marked by arrow slits in the towers and some small, shuttered windows in the upper levels. But the front of the house facing the lawn, with its long avenue of alternating apple and walnut trees leading up the slope of the hill, displayed an open face to the world. Its wide, tall windows and handsomely welcoming path of flagstones led up to an imposing iron-studded wooden door. The baron claimed it bore the original scorch marks of the attempt to burn out his ancestor after the revolution of 1789.

It led into a large hall that the baron had turned into a kitchen with an open fireplace, festooned in black iron hooks and large enough for a man to stand in. From one of them an age-blackened cauldron was suspended. Chains hung down that could raise and lower the hams that were hoisted there to smoke. On either side of the grate, where a couple of long logs flickered above a bed of red ashes, stood tall iron stands, notched to hold spits and roasting irons. To one of the thinnest of them were affixed a dozen pigeons, turning slowly through an alignment of cogs, each smaller than the next. They were moved by clockwork sturdy enough to rotate a sheep, as Bruno knew from experience.

Including J-J, they were twelve for dinner. Nicco from Ste. Alvère was accompanied by Roland, the president of Hercule's hunting club. Roland had brought his two sons, who claimed that their father had taught them to shoot, but Hercule had taught them how to hunt. From St. Denis were Stéphane, Hubert and Jo, Bruno's predecessor as chief of police, whose farm stood on the outskirts of the baron's hamlet. With them were the mayor and Sergeant Jules from the gendarmerie, each of whom had memories to share of hunting with their departed friend. They gave a chorus of welcome as Bruno carried his hay box into the big kitchen, took out the heavy pot and hung it unopened on one of the big hooks over the fire. J-J was carrying the soup, and Bruno directed him to put it on top of the modern six-burner stove. The ritual of handshakes followed, interrupted by a festive pop as the baron opened another bottle of champagne.

"Thank you for the wine," the baron said to J-J, nodding across to the sink where Hubert was decanting bottle after bottle. "It's very generous. We'll give Hercule a grand send-off."

"The real send-off will be when we catch his killers," said J-J. "But it looks as if they were professionals. It won't be easy. While you're all here, we've been going through Hercule's phone records, and there are some numbers Bruno didn't recognize that you may be able to help identify. Come and take a look at these printouts."

"You're assuming he knew his killers, or that they'd phoned him?" asked the mayor.

J-J shrugged. "Who knows? At this stage we're just looking for anything unusual. Hercule may have been doing something or making some inquiries that put his life in danger. Maybe his phone calls can lead us onto that trail."

A handful more numbers were identified as local friends from Ste. Alvère, Nicco winking as he explained that at least one of the unregistered cell phones was owned by a friend who was having an affair. Nervous that his wife might be keeping an eye on the bills for his usual cell phone, he kept a separate phone for his mistress. He must have confused the phones when he called Hercule.

"And this one is Didier, who manages the truffle market," Nicco added, putting a fat thumb beside one of the numbers on J-J's list. "He lost his old phone recently and got a new one but probably never got around to registering the number. And these two are *renifleurs* from the market who don't want the tax man looking into their phone records."

"That leaves me with just three unidentified numbers," said J-J. "That'll make life easier as we try to track them down. There's one more bit of business where you might be able to help, at least those of you from Ste. Alvère. Anybody see Hercule receiving any unusual visitors in the last week or so, or any strangers in town?"

"He had the son of an old army friend to stay for a weekend, maybe ten days ago," said Roland. "An Italian-sounding name or maybe Corsican. It began with an *S*. He was a middle-aged guy, a fancy dresser. Sanni or Salani or something like that."

"Savani?" asked J-J.

"That's it. Savani. I'd seen him before. It wasn't the first time he stayed at Hercule's place."

"The man who sponsored Vinh's citizenship papers," said Bruno, exchanging glances with J-J.

"I think it would have been the son of Capitaine Antoine Savani," the baron interjected. "He ran the Deuxième Bureau in Saigon back when Hercule was stationed in Vietnam. He'd have been Hercule's boss. I met the son, Pierre or Paul, a couple of times at Hercule's place."

"Hercule had a lot of Vietnamese visitors as well, from being stationed there in the fifties," Nicco said. "He had quite a social life, old Hercule. Anyway, let's drink to him, a great friend and a good hunter."

After the toast, Bruno turned to the soup, and the baron lifted the lid from the pot of venison hanging over the fire and began to stir, breathing in the rich smell of the wine sauce.

"Ah, that's good," he said. "You added some black pudding?"

Bruno nodded from his place by the soup. "But now comes something else," he said, and took from his pocket the truffle he had found in the woods, holding it up for all to see.

"*Putain,* but they'd give you a million centimes for that one up in Paris," said Nicco. "It's a real black diamond, black as night."

"Gigi found it this evening, just before we came here. And since it's Hercule's dinner, that makes it Hercule's truffle, and we'll enjoy it for him."

Bruno passed it around, and each man took a slow, reverent sniff. Then Bruno began to shave the black diamond into the soup, its scent expanding with the warmth of the pot and filling the room.

Hubert opened another bottle of champagne and refilled the glasses. The mayor washed two big lettuces that he had brought from his greenhouse, and Sergeant Jules began to make his special vinaigrette. Roland chopped garlic and parsley for the *pommes sarladaises,* and one son spooned duck fat into two giant frying pans, while the other dried off blanched potatoes. Bruno grated nutmeg into his simmering soup, tasted it and added salt before stirring in the pot of thick cream brought by Stéphane. Jo donned a thick glove to take the long spit from the fire and eased a pigeon onto each of the warming plates. From the stove he took the reduction of red wine and stock that he had made and poured it into a saucepan of cabbage and bacon he had prepared. Bruno never ceased to be amazed at how these cooking tasks were done almost automatically, the legacy of dozens of hunters' dinners such as this and feasts for family and neighbors after the annual slaughter of a pig.

At last all was ready, and they headed into the baron's adjoining dining room, where more logs were crackling in the stone fireplace. Reflections of the flickering lights of the candles on the long table of chestnut, darkened with age and decades of polishing, danced on the array of carafes, each with its cork beside it to identify the wine within. Bruno brought in his soup, and the baron took his place at the head of the table. The foot of the table was left empty, reserved for their absent friend. In his place stood a framed photograph of Hercule taken the previous year, standing beside a deer he had shot. The baron gestured J-J to sit at his left and Bruno at his right, and the others arranged themselves along each side.

The table, which the baron claimed had been in the same place since the *chartreuse* was built three centuries earlier, was more than three feet wide and could easily have sat half a dozen more. At a sign from the baron, Hubert served the first of the wines as they all remained standing, waiting for the customary toast. Hubert poured the last of the carafe of the Château Angélus into the glass that stood beside Hercule's place.

"To our lost friend and companion of many a memorable day, and a devoted son of France," the baron announced.

"Hercule," they chorused, raised the glasses to his photograph and drank and settled to their meal of truffle soup made of Hercule's stock, pâté that he had helped to make, roast pigeon that had been one of his favorite dishes and Bruno's venison stew from a deer that he had shot.

"This meal," the baron said, "is our friend's parting gift to us."

15

The next morning, Bruno was not at his best. He seldom suffered hangovers. He always drank mineral water along with his wine, and after heavy drinking forced himself to swallow a bottle of water before bed. But the morning after the feast for Hercule he felt dreadful. He wasn't the only one. The baron's kitchen had been full of morose men, all waiting for the coffee to be ready and gulping down the baron's sovereign remedy of a raw egg mixed with orange juice and *harissa,* the red chili paste from Morocco. Bruno took his medicine and left J-J nursing his second cup of coffee and waiting his turn in the baron's bathroom. Driving home to shower and change and walk his dog, he stopped briefly in his office to send a fax to his contact in the military archives for the details of Hercule's army record.

And that triggered a memory of perhaps the only other Vietnamese contact that he knew. Tran had been a colleague in the combat engineers unit with which Bruno had served in Bosnia, on what was supposed to have been a peacekeeping mission where there had been no peace to keep. He kept in touch with Tran as with other old comrades-in-arms through

Christmas cards and occasional letters to announce a marriage or the birth of a new child. He had Tran's address in Bordeaux, where he and his French wife ran a Vietnamese restaurant that Bruno kept promising to visit. He tracked down a phone number and called.

"I've heard of Vinh, but I don't know him personally. And I've heard about the troubles people have had—we've had some here in Bordeaux. It's a bad time," Tran had said when Bruno explained his reason for phoning. "I'll make some calls and get back to you."

Feeling better after a brisk jog in the morning woods with Gigi, Bruno ironed the uniform shirts he had left drying the previous day and headed for L'Auberge des Verts. Bill Pons had announced what he called a Green Fair, an exhibition of energy-saving products offered by local companies. When Bruno arrived, Pamela was already there, wrapped in a heavy black cloak and wearing a Russian-style fur hat and boots and chatting to Alphonse. It was even colder up here on the ridge than it had been in the shelter of Bruno's woods, and Bruno could see their breath steaming out in plumes in the chill air as they spoke.

Bruno stopped to observe Pamela from a distance, almost completely draped in black with only her face showing. For a moment he was reminded of an Islamic woman covered by a burka, but the flare of Pamela's cloak and the shape of her hat made the overall impression enticingly different. Perhaps it was her proud and upright stance, perhaps the animation of her face and gestures, but he felt a distinct erotic charge as he watched. He approached them and felt himself stir as he kissed her deliciously cold cheeks. He held her a moment, savoring her warm breath against his face, before turning to greet Alphonse.

"How was the boys' night out?" she said, smiling. "You're in better shape than I expected." She had been to one of the ladies' nights at the hunting club with him and knew how they tended to finish.

"I felt a lot better after my run with Gigi," he said. "Another coffee and I'll be as good as new. Is the restaurant open, or is it just the Green exhibition?"

"They have coffee and hot chocolate inside, and they're serving plates of toast topped with my cheese and honey," said Alphonse. "But it's full of schoolkids at the moment. Let's look around first. Here, I picked up a guide that Bill printed."

Armed with the map, they strolled through the gardens looking at the windmills, the arrays of solar panels and the drip-irrigation system Bill had installed to save water. Alphonse read out some figures from the guide on how much electricity the panels produced from light alone, even on a day as cloudy as this.

"I'm impressed, but all this must have cost a fortune," Pamela said. "I couldn't begin to afford to do this for my *gîtes*."

"Bill claims that it added about fifteen percent to his building costs, and he'll recoup that in energy savings in about five or six years," Alphonse said. He led them around to the rear of the restaurant to an open field that was half covered in campers and trailers displaying solar panels, double and triple glazing, woodstoves, and systems to heat swimming pools.

"What Alphonse didn't say was that you helped pay for this," Bruno told Pamela. "We all did. There are lots of grants and subsidies available for energy saving, and Bill used them all. I reckon he paid about half of the real cost, and taxpayers forked out the rest."

"But those grants would be available to me as well," Pamela replied. "Or anybody else with the wit to apply for them."

"Not for the rest of the financial year," said Bruno. "The money has run out, and there's already a long list of applications for next year's money."

They stopped at a trailer with a large tent attached, its plastic door closed but with a sign saying it was open and to come in. They pushed through into sudden heat from a blower. The tent was almost full of people enjoying the warmth and listening to a salesman talking about the merits of roof insulation.

"Forty percent of all the energy used in Europe is used in our buildings," he was saying. "If we adopted the current Swedish standards of roof insulation across Europe we'd save half of that, which means we'd save almost as much energy as we use in transport."

"Hear that?" whispered Alphonse. "That's the message we have to get across to the voters."

Pamela took some brochures, and they moved on, pausing at a strange-looking windmill. It was a central shaft that held at its top what looked like a hollow barrel, but instead of the wooden staves there were three thin spirals of metal acting as propeller blades that turned steadily and quietly in the light breeze.

"This is the future of wind power," said Alphonse, his voice eager. "This kind of vertical windmill is quieter and more efficient than traditional propellers. It works much better in lighter winds and in stronger ones. You can attach this to chimneys and roofs in towns, and you can't do that with the usual windmill. And it's from your country, Pamela. I'm saving to get one for our commune."

Alphonse greeted the salesman, whom he evidently knew, and Pamela began asking about prices and installation costs. As it looked like it would be a long conversation, Bruno excused himself, saying he'd better check in with the schoolteachers who were escorting the children.

He headed back toward the restaurant, but branched off to take a look at a large barn, newly restored, presumably where Bill and the staff lived. He could have kicked himself for forgetting about getting those nieces into school. He'd have to talk to Pons. The house had its own parking lot, and all the shutters were closed except for one set at a side window. Bruno looked in. A large sitting room was dimly lit by table lamps with heavy shades and decorated in an old-fashioned way that surprised him. He'd never have thought Bill would go for chaise longues in gilt and red plush and those overstuffed cushions. The room looked as if it had been designed as a whole, rather than filled haphazardly with furniture picked up at auctions.

There was a tap on his shoulder, and he turned to see Minxin, the chef. He looked cross. "Private here, you go now," he said, with none of the affability he'd shown in the restaurant.

"Ah, Minxin. I'm glad to see you," Bruno said. "I wanted to talk to you about your nieces. They have to be registered for school."

"No school. Chinese teacher," said Minxin, shaking his head. "You go now."

"Children in France go to school. It's the law," said Bruno firmly, but recognizing he'd get nowhere with the tall chef. He nodded in a friendly fashion, and as he turned to head back to the Green Fair, he added, "I'll have to talk to Pons about this."

Juliette, a plump and divorced primary-school teacher who always flirted with Bruno, waved as she saw him approach. Bill Pons, bare-headed and dressed as if for skiing at a fashionable resort, was standing beside a distinctly pungent hole in the ground. It was covered in thick black plastic with pipes leading into a small hut alongside. Pons was frowning as he tried to explain to the ten-year-olds the way in which cow manure could be turned into methane that could then produce hydrogen for fuel cells. Groans of disgust and much holding of noses greeted his efforts. Bill seemed irritated and impatient at this reaction. Had Bill never been ten years old? Bruno wondered. He deliberately walked into the boys' sight line and watched them take notice and stop their clowning. They all knew him from tennis and rugby lessons, and some saluted him cheerfully, which seemed to irritate Bill even more.

"As I was saying," Bill said crisply, "the methane gets turned into hydrogen . . ."

Bruno strolled off, leaving Bill to his explanations. Just then his mobile phone began to trill the "Marseillaise."

It was his old acquaintance at the army archives, calling to say he'd faxed Hercule's army records to Bruno's office. He explained that he'd known Hercule in Algeria and sat through a course he'd run on counterinsurgency operations. So he took Hercule's murder personally.

"I thought I'd tell you some detail you won't find in the official records," the man said. "He wrote a pamphlet on counterinsurgency, and I've still got a copy that I'll send you. He went back to Vietnam in sixty-seven and sixty-eight when the Americans were fighting there. They had asked him to come and give some lectures on the French experience. There was a big fuss behind the scenes when de Gaulle found out. And he was very opposed to the use of torture, said it did far more harm than good. I thought you might like to know."

"I didn't know that. Thanks."

"By the way, make a note of this number. It's my mobile and I'm calling you from a café outside the Invalides. If I can be of further help, use this phone rather than the official line."

Bruno thanked him and hung up. That was interesting, and he was looking forward to reading Hercule's pamphlet. From his own experience in Bosnia he'd learned that every counterinsurgency campaign was above all a political war, and every military action had to be weighed with regard to its political effects and vice versa.

Suddenly he stopped short. There was something else that he remembered that struck him as directly relevant to the campaign of intimidation being waged against the Vietnamese in the markets right here. People would end up supporting whichever side gave the best protection, whichever side threatened the most, and which of the two was seen as most likely to win.

Bruno looked around at the wintry scene, at the schoolchildren darting around the campers and trailers. He heard the sound of laughter as people came out from the restaurant full of food and hot drinks. It was a peaceful, happy landscape. But there was menace lurking on Bruno's turf, a threat of violence and subtle terror against hardworking and law-abiding people that Bruno knew and liked. Bizarre as it might seem to be thinking of counterinsurgency theory in the middle of the French countryside, Bruno knew it was his duty to defend the victims, to allay their fears and to bring the intimidators to justice. Another thought struck him, the irony that Hercule's war had started in Vietnam, and these Vietnamese were now French citizens and Bruno's neighbors. He had been to their homes, eaten their food, and their safety was his responsibility.

"Bruno!" he heard. There was urgency and alarm in the call. Jolted out of his thoughts he turned to see Juliette waving at him frantically and a small knot of children gathered around the plastic-covered manure pit. He jogged across.

"It's young Mathieu," Juliette cried. "He's fallen in."

As he approached, Bruno could see a corner of the black plastic sheeting had been loosened from its restraining pegs, and one whole side had sunk down into the reeking pit. He looked over the edge and saw a pitiful young face, the boy's body half submerged in the great pool of cow dung.

"I can't feel the bottom, Bruno," the boy wailed. He was clinging to a fold of plastic, but his grip was visibly slipping.

Bruno pulled off his greatcoat and jacket. Looking quickly around, he saw no other adult in sight. Filling his lungs he used his parade-ground voice.

"*Au secours.* Alphonse, Bill," he roared and turned to the aghast children, looking for the most sensible of the boys he knew.

"Laurent, run to the nearest tents and bring back the salesman and any other men in there. Tell them it's me, and it's urgent. Michel, you run to the restaurant and do the same. Tell people I need rope, rope and men."

He turned back to Juliette and gave her his greatcoat.

"Here, hold the collar of the coat tight and dig your feet hard into the ground," he told her. "Keep shouting for help."

He tugged off his shoes and with one hand on the hem of his coat he slid himself over the edge toward the boy.

"Mathieu, can you touch my foot?" he called. He turned, trying to see the boy, but he was out of his vision.

"It's too far," came the piping voice. "I'm sinking."

Bruno edged down farther, trying to get a grip with his stockinged feet on the side of the pit but slipping on the plastic.

"Lie down full length, Juliette," he called. "I need more length from the coat. Tell the children to hold on to you."

"I'm here, Bruno," came Alphonse's voice. "I'll hold the coat with Juliette."

Bruno let himself slide down to the limit of the coat's length and felt a small hand clutch at his ankle.

"I've got you, Bruno," called Mathieu.

"Hold on with both hands, Mathieu," Bruno told him. "Just hold tight, and we'll have you out in a moment." He looked up to the faces of Alphonse and Juliette peering over the rim. "Can you start to pull me up?"

"You're too heavy," said Alphonse. "We can hardly hold you as it is. But there are more people coming."

Bruno began lifting his right leg and Mathieu with it, feeling the strain in his knee and thigh. Gingerly, he took one hand from his coat and lowered it until he could feel the boy's hand on his ankle and then felt the sleeve of the boy's jacket. Despite the fumes, he took a deep breath, gripped and hauled the dripping boy up with a great heave until the two little arms were around his neck, the stinking slime smearing on his chin and collar.

"Climb up me, Mathieu, until you can stand on my shoulders, and they'll lift you out."

He felt Mathieu's shoes digging into his hip and his waist and then into his ribs as the boy clambered up Bruno's body. A dirty hand slid into his mouth, trying to get some leverage, and Bruno set his jaw firm to help the boy. Bruno felt his greatcoat collar start to tear, and he slid down a few inches.

His feet and lower legs were now in the slime, and he was surprised by its warmth. Then a knee was on his shoulder, the hand left his mouth and was in his hair, and the weight suddenly lifted as Mathieu was scooped out of the pit by eager hands.

"We've got him," called a woman's voice. Pamela's voice.

"Hold on, Bruno," called Alphonse. "Bill has a rope."

The collar of his greatcoat tore some more, and Bruno slid down up to his waist into the slime that was releasing an even worse stench as he broke more and more of the surface crust. But a rope was dangling beside his face, and he took hold of it.

"Take the strain on that rope," he shouted. "I'm about to put my weight on it."

"There's three of us on it," Bill called.

They hauled him out, black and reeking up to his waist, manure smeared all across his face, neck and hair. Mathieu was being bundled off toward the restaurant by Juliette. Bruno looked down to see his greatcoat floating on the black pool. Someone patted him on the back, despite the manure. He looked around and saw Pamela. As he smiled at her, a camera flashed twice in a row. Philippe Delaron was taking pictures for *Sud Ouest*. He had come to take photos of the schoolchildren at the Green Fair, but now he had a real news story, to be accompanied by another unflattering picture of the chief of police of St. Denis. Bruno grimaced and gestured into the pit.

"I'll need a hook to get my coat out. There are things in the pockets that I want to save," he said to Bill. "Then I'll need to go into your house for a shower, and I would be grateful for some spare clothes."

"Well done, Bruno," said Bill. "But not the house. There's

no hot water there today. We'll use the bathroom in the restaurant. There's a shower, and I'll bring some spare clothes and put yours in the wash."

"Oh Bruno," said Pamela. "You're a sight. But consider yourself kissed."

Looking down at himself, Bruno could not help but laugh. Half of it was relief that Mathieu was safe, but he had to admit she was right. He was a sight, and a stink. And he was cold. Then he started to become angry. To invite children onto the property and not take some elementary safety precautions infuriated him.

"You and I will be having a serious talk about safety procedures when you invite children onto your property," he said to Bill. "This very nearly ended in tragedy. I'll need to see your license for this large pool of manure and a statement of approval for its construction from the water authorities."

"It was just an accident, Bruno," Pamela said. "All's well that ends well."

"Yes, we were lucky this time," Bruno said, wondering why she was letting Pons off so lightly. "Now we have to make sure that all legal precautions are taken so we don't have to be lucky in the future."

He turned to Bill. "And we also have to talk about getting your chef's nieces into school. But first perhaps you could show me your shower."

16

As Bruno had expected, the archives of the *mairie* of Ste. Alvère were stuffed into a dark and chilly basement room next door to the wine cellar. It took him and the mayor's secretary twenty dust-filled minutes to locate the cardboard box that contained the records from the truffle market. She showed him to a vacant underground conference room lit by a single fluorescent light, brought him a weak coffee and left him to it.

He started on the logbook of weekly sales, looking for the two consignments that had triggered the complaints as a way to familiarize himself with the recording system. It was as Didier had explained. The date, weight, price and batch number were each recorded in the logbook, and they matched the identifying numbers on the labels that had been cited in the complaints. But something was odd. The batch numbers seemed out of sequence with the other sales recorded that day.

Bruno checked again, and indeed each of the suspect items seemed to have been packed and sealed at the end of the day, even after the items listed as having been sold in the special auction. And neither one carried the extra tick in the column marked "Chemist," which meant they had not been tested by Florence.

He began to look through the other sales lists and found that there were always some batches out of sequence at the end of the day. Perhaps there was an innocent explanation. But he could find no logbook of the sales in what Didier had called the special auctions of unsold stocks at the end of each market day. Bruno pulled everything out of the cardboard box and checked each file and item thoroughly. There was no such logbook, so he began going through the various file folders.

Mainly they contained bills for electricity and water, all of which seemed in order. Then there was a maintenance log for the monthly service of the photocopier and another for the vacuum-pack machine, with each visit signed for by the service technician. There was no payment sum listed, but Bruno found a note on the bottom of each bill that matched an annual service payment from the bank account. There was also a handwritten note on each service statement, evidently put there by the technician, that gave a number followed by the words "digital counter."

Bruno punched the telephone number on the servicing invoice into his mobile phone and went up to the ground floor to make the call to the technician. Yes, there was a digital counter on the packing machine that tallied how many times it had been used, and the technician always listed the number on his monthly visit. Bruno went back to the basement and checked the monthly totals. They went from zero in the spring and early summer to a maximum of more than five thousand in January. He looked at the figures for November, a relatively quiet month. The digital counter said the machine had been used 420 times that month. Bruno went back to the shipments log and found only 304 items that had been vacuum packed and shipped. That seemed like a sizable discrepancy, so he began to look at other months.

He took a notepad from his briefcase and began making monthly lists. It was tedious, repetitive work, but he felt it was worth it. In December, he found the machine had been used 1,974 times, but there were only 1,214 shipments listed as packed. In January, the machine was used 3,447 times, but the logbook showed only 2,689 items packed and shipped. He went back to the previous year, and this time the figures for the digital counter and the logbook matched almost precisely, with a discrepancy of only a dozen or so, which could be explained by a faulty seal or a package damaged and having to be resealed. But the discrepancy for the latest year was extraordinary. The packages must have been opened and then resealed, which would have triggered the counter a second time. That would have been the opportunity for cheap Chinese truffles to have been inserted instead of the genuine Périgord variety.

Bruno sat back, content. He had his evidence for the mayor that some kind of fraud was taking place at the market. But he also had a mystery in the absence of the separate logbooks for the auction sales. According to the account books, they contributed more than a hundred thousand euros a year to the market, about a fifth of its profit. That was serious money, and there should certainly be a logbook.

He closed up the cardboard box, sealed it with tape and scrawled his own signature across the seal to ensure it was not reopened. He took the box up to the mayor's secretary and asked her to lock it away. Then he walked across to the rear door of the truffle market, knocked and pushed the door open. Alain, the packer with a red nose from the glasses of *petit blanc* he sipped all day in the café across the street, jumped back in surprise.

"What the hell—oh, it's you. Not done yet?"

"No, I'm not. But you are, Alain," Bruno said. Alain was alone in the room. Bruno walked across to the inside door, and the next room and the market hall were both empty.

"Just you and me, Alain, and a nice quiet room for a chat. You're in big trouble. I've been checking the books, and I want you to tell me why you've been reopening and then resealing about one package in four. Suppose you start by telling me who's been giving you the cheap Chinese stuff to stick in the packages."

"What? I don't know about any Chinese stuff."

"You're lying. Let's go to the gendarmerie and get your fingerprints taken. Then we can match them to the packages with the Chinese truffles. Or maybe you'd like me to call in the mayor first and tell him about the scam you've been running."

"What scam?" Alain blustered.

Bruno turned to the vacuum-pack machine, studied the controls and pressed the catch that opened the service door. He pointed to the digital counter inside.

"Ever notice this, Alain? See how it counts every time the machine gets used? When I compared this count with the number of packages that you signed for as packed and shipped, I get some very different numbers. Want to explain to me why that should be? Or do you want to do your explaining down at the gendarmerie?"

Alain looked blankly at the digital counter, and then up at Bruno.

"*Putain*," he said.

"What did Didier pay you? A hundred euros a month extra?"

Alain shrugged. "I'm saying nothing."

"So you go down instead of him."

"You won't get him. He's related to the mayor."

"Have you got any idea how much he was skimming off this? If you got a hundred a month he was getting a thousand a week. The mayor couldn't hush that up even if he wanted to."

"A thousand a week?" Alain raised his eyebrows. "You're kidding me."

"I can show you the books. One of you is going down for this, him or you. Which would you prefer?"

"I just did what I was told."

"I know that. He was the boss. If Didier said open the packages up and seal them again, that's what you did."

Alain nodded.

"What happened to the logbooks for the auction? What did he do with them?"

Alain looked blank. Bruno let it go. Some things Didier would have done for himself.

"Alain, you have a choice to make right now. Either you sit down with me and make a statement and sign it, or I take you straight to the gendarmerie and charge you with theft and have you kept in jail under *garde à vue*. And then we go to your house and search everything with your wife and kids out on the pavement crying and all the neighbors watching in the street. And when you come out of prison, you never work again. It's your choice."

"If I make a statement, I'll lose the job anyway and still go to jail."

"Maybe. It's a risk. But you'll have me on your side. And you can say in the statement that you are speaking out of your own free will because you thought there was something funny going on. You did what you were told by Didier, but you became suspicious when you heard about the complaints."

"I would have spoken out, but who was I going to talk to—the mayor?" Alain said. "I'd have been fired on the spot."

"You make that statement with me as witness, and they can't fire you. The mayor would be voted out overnight by the council if he tried, relative or no relative."

"I'm no good at statements, don't know what to say."

"I'll help you, Alain. We'll do it question and answer, and then when we're done you can read it over before you sign anything. How's that sound?"

Bruno pulled up two chairs to the low table beside the vacuum machine and placed them side by side. He took a notepad from his briefcase, turned to a fresh page and wrote "Statement of Alain Bruneval" and the date at the top and said: "Tell me when you started resealing the packages."

Alain paused and looked at him with a half smile. "I saw you play rugby the other day. You're not as fast as you used to be."

"I remember when you used to play yourself," Bruno said, putting down the pen.

"I could have given you a run for your money."

"You still could, Alain. Maybe you should come out and start training again, get fit for next year."

Alain nodded contentedly, as if some scrap of pride had been satisfied, and Bruno started to write as he began to speak. "We'd always had a few resealings to do, when a package broke or we had the wrong label on it, but about a year ago, November last year, Didier began bringing package after package to be sealed again. . . ."

Twenty minutes later, Bruno had a signed statement that would stand up in court and send Didier to jail.

17

The mayor was chortling with delight as he looked at that day's edition of *Sud Ouest,* and not only because of the photo of a manure-drenched Bruno that graced the front page under the headline HERO COP OF ST. DENIS SAVES CHILD.

Inside, they had given it two pages. "Policeman Dives into Manure to Rescue Drowning Boy" topped one page. "Mayoral Candidate Apologizes for Dangerous Day Out" topped the other, with photos of Bill looking abashed, little Mathieu looking cheerful and Juliette the teacher looking angry, with a quote from her saying, "Bill the Green has lost my vote." At the bottom of the page was a story about Bill's use of manure to power his fuel cells, titled "Green Power's Pool of Death."

The mayor was quoted condemning Bill for "the height of irresponsibility" in bringing schoolchildren to a place without security precautions and promising an investigation that could lead to the suspension of the restaurant license for L'Auberge des Verts. Prodded by the mayor, the water department was threatening to close the restaurant as a health hazard.

"This is going to cost him a lot of votes," the mayor said to Bruno, not bothering to conceal his delight at Bill's embarrassment. "Mathieu comes from a big family, and every farmer in the valley knows his mother. And every pet owner."

Mathieu's mother was the receptionist for St. Denis's one veterinarian, a jolly woman and renowned local gossip who chattered away happily to everyone in the waiting room, even when she had nothing to say. Now she had a story that she could recount endlessly to all comers. Mathieu's father, who ran the meat counter at the local supermarket, was equally well known and doubtless every customer would ask after his son's health. Bruno could understand why the mayor was so happy.

"That was not exactly at the top of my mind at the time," Bruno said.

"I wouldn't think so," said the mayor. "But we'll have to increase your salary at this rate."

"Does this mean I get a new van?" he asked. Bruno decided to take advantage of the mayor's good mood.

"Certainly you'll get a new van. I don't see how you can do without it," said the mayor. "I've already put it on the agenda for the next council meeting. Plus we got the special insurance bonus since the old vehicle was destroyed in the line of duty. So we'll only have to pay an extra two thousand euros for the new van, police markings and blue light included."

"That's good news, thank you. And you saw the bill I put in for the new uniform?" Even two washings had been unable to save Bruno's shirt and trousers.

"Yes, yes, I already signed the approval for two full replacement uniforms, winter and summer. We'll make young Pons pay for them. And did you see this in the paper? Little Mathieu saying, 'Once I saw Bruno, I knew I would be safe.' "

"It looks as if Philippe Delaron is setting himself up to be your press agent," said Bruno, embarrassed. "He's certainly milked the story for everything it's worth, even a sidebar on how this damages Pons's election prospects."

"Philippe owes me a lot of favors," said the mayor. "I just had to encourage him to see what ramifications there were to this story. And it was a quiet news day."

"Not that quiet. Did you see the story on the next page about the fire at the Chinese restaurant in Bergerac? That's the third in a week."

"We don't have any Chinese restaurants in St. Denis. We don't even have any Chinese," said the mayor, waving his hand dismissively.

"We do now. The chef at Bill's restaurant is Chinese, and his nieces. That reminds me, I need to check about getting them into school," Bruno said. "But that's not the point. We have our Vietnamese being attacked by unknown Chinese, and now we have Chinese places of business being burned out across the region. This is what happened in Paris and Marseilles. It's a kind of gang war for control of territory."

"We only have Vinh, and he's disappeared," said the mayor.

"You mean that he's gone into hiding, but he was attacked here in our market, which makes it our business."

"It's a problem for the Police Nationale," said the mayor.

"But you already approved that request from the prefect asking for me to be seconded to the Police Nationale for Hercule's murder inquiry."

"And you're telling me that Hercule's murder is connected to this trouble between the Chinese and Vietnamese?"

"I'm sure of it and so is J-J, and our old friend the brigadier in Paris is showing interest," Bruno said. "Hercule was some kind of legend in the intelligence business and had a special connection to Vietnam after his time there in the war. He had a Vietnamese wife and child and helped a lot of our Vietnamese friends settle here when they had to leave the country in a hurry. There's a lot more to this than meets the eye."

"His funeral is at Ste. Alvère this afternoon?"

"Three o'clock. Shall I see you there, or do you want to drive over together? I'm going in the baron's car, but there's room for you."

Back in his office, Bruno had just finished booking the table at Ivan's bistro after learning with pleasure that the *plat du jour* would be calf's liver with sage leaves when his desk phone rang.

"Is that the police?"

"*Oui,* madame. Chief of Police Courrèges *à votre service.*"

"Oh, Bruno, you're in the paper today, saving that little boy."

"How can I help you?"

"It's Amélie Condorcet here, you know, from Laugérie."

"Yes, Madame Condorcet. We met at your neighbors' house, the Vinhs, and I know your husband from the rugby club." Bruno could place her now, a quiet, rather faded woman with a long nose and a bad leg. Her husband worked for France Télécom.

"Well, my husband says it's nothing and I'm dreaming things, but something suspicious has happened at the neighbor's place, at the Vinhs'. You know they've been away. It might be nothing and I don't want to waste your time."

"Go on, madame. What was suspicious?"

"Last night I was woken up by a car. I don't sleep too well.

Anyway, it stopped at the Vinhs' house, and thinking it might be them coming back I got up and looked through the window. It wasn't them. It was Asians, but not the Vinhs. But since they were Asian, I assumed they must be friends. Then I heard what sounded like breaking glass, and then they left so it wasn't a burglary."

"It certainly sounds suspicious."

"Well, it's been on my mind since, so I went over there just now, and in the kitchen window there's a small round hole cut in the glass and some kind of message pinned to the door in a foreign language. That's all I could see that was wrong. But the Vinhs gave me a key. They have one of ours, you know, like neighbors do, so I thought you might want to take a look, just to be on the safe side."

"I'll be right there, Madame Condorcet."

Vinh lived on the outskirts of the hamlet, and the Condorcets lived in an identical house, one of a group of four squeezed into what had been a small tobacco field. Madame Condorcet was already waiting on the front doorstep, a key in her hand, when Bruno pulled up in the Land Rover.

"That's not your police van," she said.

"I'm waiting for the new one to be delivered. The last one got wrecked by some criminals in a car chase," he said. "It sounds more exciting than it was. But let's go and see this hole in the window."

The hole was about eight inches in diameter and below it was an empty sack, one of the old-fashioned sort made of rough burlap. Although Bruno's first thought was that the hole had been cut so that gasoline could be poured into the house, there was no smell of it, and looking through the window Bruno could see nothing wrong and no sign of life. He bent to look more closely at the sack.

"One of them was carrying something," said Madame Condorcet. "It could have been that, but it looked full."

Bruno opened the sack. Inside there was a whiff of something feral, something animal. He stood up to look through the window again and saw something dart across the far corner of the room. One of the curtains had been torn, and an empty cereal package was on the floor.

A piece of cardboard had been pinned to the kitchen door, with what Bruno presumed was Vietnamese writing scrawled on it with a thick black marker. He pulled out his mobile and called Tran, his old army contact in Bordeaux.

"I need you to translate something. Remember I told you about Vinh disappearing? There's some writing I found nailed to the door of Vinh's house," he said. "It's in what I think is Vietnamese."

"Spell it out, or describe each letter to me."

Bruno did so, letter by letter, Madame Condorcet standing nervously at his side.

"It says 'Next time we set them on your children,' " Tran said. "It's bad Vietnamese, written by someone who's almost illiterate or not a native speaker."

"Next time we set what on your children?" Bruno asked.

"Not clear. It could mean 'these things' or 'this item' or even 'this shit'—it's a slang term. What is it about?"

"I don't know yet, but there's a hole cut in the window big enough to put a cat through. I'm here with a neighbor who has a key. Stay on the line. We're going inside now."

He handed the phone to Madame Condorcet, took the

key and opened the door carefully. He slipped inside, closing the door behind him, and his nostrils caught the same feral scent he had noticed in the sack. There was more darting from the far side of the room. As he moved into the sitting room beyond, he saw droppings on the carpet and sofa. Rats! A knot of four or five of them were huddling in a corner. In the bedroom, the coverlet had been pulled from the bed to make a nest, and more droppings were smeared on the bed. More rats were squeaking by the window. He checked the other rooms before he let himself out, depressed at the mess a dozen rats could make in what had been an impeccably neat home.

"Rats," he told Madame Condorcet, taking the phone as she put her hands to her face in horror. He spoke to Tran again. "They emptied a sackful of rats into the house. It's quite a mess."

"So the message is, 'Next time we let the rats loose on your kids,'" said Tran. "*Putain,* you know that was an old Chinese punishment. They tied you down and left you in a sealed room with some hungry rats. Some of the triads are supposed to do it still, exemplary punishment for traitors. Threatening to do this to kids is about as deadly an insult as you can get."

"Are you kidding me? This still happens? It's medieval," Bruno said, turning away lest Tran's voice reach Madame Condorcet. He didn't want word of this getting out in St. Denis.

"The Chinese were supposed to have done the same thing to some Viet prisoners of war in seventy-nine when they tried to invade and we stopped them at the border. I say 'we,' I mean the Vietnamese army. A short war but a nasty one. There were lots of rumors about atrocities against our POWs."

"I don't believe this is happening in France," Bruno said.

"I told you, bad times," Tran said. "This is very serious shit, Bruno. Remember how it was in Bosnia? That's how it's going. We're having to organize to defend ourselves."

"That includes burning down Chinese restaurants?"

"We have some real militants of our own, but this is getting beyond them. Look, I'm glad you called. I put the word out about your wanting to see Vinh and got the message back that there are some people you ought to meet. They very much want to see you. Maybe you should come here to Bordeaux and have that dinner we always talked about. The sooner, the better. And don't worry. We've got lots of protection."

"When's a good time?"

"How does tonight sound? You can stay with us overnight."

"I'll call you back and let you know," said Bruno. "How would you feel if I brought somebody else along who needs to know all this, another policeman. A good one."

"Anyone you vouch for would be fine," said Tran. "Call me."

Bruno closed his phone, wondering whether it would be a good idea to take J-J along. He sometimes took a rather literal view of the law, and if he thought he was meeting people involved in throwing gasoline bombs into Chinese restaurants, he might feel compelled to take official action. On the other hand, J-J needed to make some contacts in the Vietnamese community if he was going to stop this gang war from turning into something more sinister. He was smart enough to balance the short-term benefit of making quick arrests against the more important long-term benefit of getting to know what kind of people Tran wanted Bruno to meet. Tran had been a good soldier, one of the team who counterattacked the Serbian platoon and got Bruno to the medevac helicopter after he'd been shot. Bruno trusted him, and he trusted J-J. He'd take the risk of inviting J-J and make sure it worked.

"Who would want to put rats into a nice house like that?" asked Madame Condorcet.

"I don't know yet," said Bruno. "But I'll find out. You said you saw that the men who came were Asians. Do you think you might recognize any of them if you saw them again?"

"There was a very young one. I'd know him because his face was in the headlights."

Bruno nodded, called the fire station and told Albert, the fire chief, about the problem. He did not sound at all surprised, asking only how many rats there were.

Madame Condorcet made coffee as Bruno called J-J and explained Tran's proposal that they should go to Bordeaux that evening, right after Hercule's funeral.

"Who are these people who want to meet you?" J-J wanted to know.

"Leaders of the local Viet community, I assume. I trust Tran on this," he said. "Maybe even some people who know about the bombings, but at this stage it makes more sense to get to know them than to make any arrests."

"I wasn't born yesterday," said J-J. "And I've got news for you. Paris is getting involved. I just got a call from Isabelle. The brigadier is on his way down. He'll be in Bordeaux tonight, and he wants you and me at a meeting at the prefecture in Périgueux tomorrow morning."

"Should we bring him along to the meeting with the Viets tonight?" Bruno's mind was racing. If the brigadier were there, far more intent on gathering intelligence than on making arrests, J-J's legalistic instincts would be under control. That would suit Bruno.

"If Paris is sending him down here, this is getting above our pay grade, so he's probably the one the Viets really ought to meet," said J-J. "Why not invite him? Call your friend and see what he says. But I'll come with you anyway."

Tran said his people would be happy to be joined by "a top cop from Paris," and then asked Bruno if that meant what he thought it did.

"He's from the interior minister's special staff, *renseignements généraux,* and plugged into all the other intelligence groups. I've worked with this guy. He's okay, as far it goes. But these guys always have their own agenda."

"So do we," said Tran. "He sounds like just the guy we want to be in touch with. By the way, have you ever heard of the Binh Xuyen?"

"No," said Bruno. "I heard what you just said, but I'm not even sure I could pronounce it."

"I'll spell it," said Tran, and did so. "Look them up. From what I hear, you'll find lots of references to them in the books belonging to that old spook who was murdered, Vendrot."

"I'm going to his funeral this afternoon. That should finish about five, maybe five-thirty or six."

"Good, you can read up on them on the way. You coming by train? I can pick you up at the station."

"No, I'm driving with my police friend. He's the chief detective for this *département.*"

"Good. You have the address, it's just behind the Porte de la Monnaie. We'll expect you sometime around eight."

He rang J-J again. "It's set. Let the brigadier know he's welcome." He gave the address. "And you'll be driving, since I've been given some homework to read while we travel."

"In that case we can all go together," said J-J. "I had another call from the brigadier. He's coming here for Hercule's funeral this afternoon."

Bruno was sipping at a cup of Madame Condorcet's strong coffee sweetened with honey when Albert's small red van appeared up the hill, followed by Ahmed's battered Peugeot. Albert climbed out, shook hands, accepted the offer of a cup of coffee and began pulling rat traps from the back of his van. Ahmed joined them, the noise of dogs half barking and half yapping coming from the back of his car.

"The terriers first, then the rat traps," said Albert. "That'll clear them out. When it's this many, it's the only way."

Madame Condorcet came out with a tray carrying more coffee and some sweet lemon biscuits that she had made. Once they were finished, with many grunts of appreciation and the plate emptied, Ahmed put on some thick work gloves, and Albert took a large black plastic sack from his van and suggested that Madame Condorcet might want to go back inside. This would not be a pretty sight. To Bruno's surprise, with a glint in her eye she insisted on staying to watch. Ahmed released the two terriers, and they rushed to the Vinhs' kitchen door, yapping. Bruno opened it with Madame Condorcet's key, and the dogs jumped inside.

Albert and Ahmed led the way in after the terriers, and Bruno and Madame Condorcet followed, closing the door behind them. There were two rat corpses on the kitchen floor, blood on their heads and their backs broken. Ahmed casually shoved the dead rats into his plastic sack with his boot. The sound of moving furniture came from the sitting room, and as Bruno looked in he saw a terrier leap onto the back of the sofa to catch a scurrying rat by the neck. The terrier shook his head violently and tossed the dead rat aside before leaping down to growl at another hiding beneath a chair. Ahmed casually tilted the chair, and the terrier pounced as the rat tried to flee. Another shake of the head, another dead rat. In the bedroom, there were three more corpses on the bed, two on the floor and the sound of terrified squeaks from the other bedroom.

"I think that's all of them," said Albert. The terriers were prowling through the house, sniffing at cupboards and wardrobes and in corners for any rats that had escaped the slaughter.

"Twenty-two in the sack," Ahmed announced. "But we'll leave the rat traps here just in case. You're lucky we caught them early. Once they start to breed, it's terrible. The little ones can hide almost anywhere."

"This didn't happen by accident," Albert said. "And I saw that hole in the window. Somebody came here and tipped the rats in deliberately. What's all this about?"

"I'll tell you later," Bruno said, and turned to Madame Condorcet. "Thank you for calling me and alerting us to this, but it's now police business, and I'd be grateful if you could keep all this to yourself. Don't even tell your husband about it."

"But who would do such a thing to the Vinhs?" she asked. "They're such a nice, quiet family, and my husband likes those *nems* they make."

"I like them too," said Bruno. "And the sooner I can get to the bottom of this, the sooner we'll have them and their *nems* back. But I'll need you to keep quiet about all this while I'm working on this case. Will you do that for me? And I promise that when it's all over I'll come back here and have some more of your coffee and those lemon biscuits and tell you all about it. How's that?"

"I won't say a word," she said. "But you'd better call before you come. The biscuits are even better when they are warm."

"In that case," said Albert, "can we come too?"

18

It was, thought Bruno, a splendidly French compromise. On one side of the coffin, the state saluted a member of the Légion d'Honneur with an honor guard of six French soldiers in parade dress who pointed their modern rifles into the air and fired a volley of blanks. As the echoes died away, civil society paid its own tribute as six members of the Chasseurs de Ste. Alvère, two with tears in their eyes and all in their hunting gear, fired their own blanks in ragged timing from an unmatched assortment of shotguns.

The mayor in his tricolor sash and the brigadier in a uniform with a chest full of medals both made brief speeches of appreciation, and then the brigadier read out a letter of praise and condolence from the minister of the interior. Finally the priest spoke the final, ritual words, and they all lined up to scoop a handful of earth from the pile and toss it onto the lid of the coffin.

At the mayor's invitation, the mourners trooped off to a *vin d'honneur* at the *mairie*. Bruno drank one glass, made a swift circuit of the room and left for Hercule's house to scour the library in search of books on—he had to look up the spelling he had written down during the call with Tran—the Binh Xuyen. The bookcase beside the big desk ran from floor to ceiling and was organized into books on Vietnam, books on Algeria and books on recent French history. The first that he found that seemed relevant was written by Capitaine Savani, who he remembered was Hercule's boss in the Deux-ième Bureau in Saigon. Titled *Visage et images du Sud Viet-Nam,* it had been published in Paris in 1955 and had been inscribed to Hercule by its author. Bruno turned eagerly to a bookmark, a folded sheet of paper on which Hercule had written: "This section taken largely from Savani's secret DB report on Binh Xuyen." Bruno assumed the initials stood for Deuxième Bureau, military intelligence.

He put the book to one side and had just begun searching the shelves alongside, above and below, all devoted to Viet-nam, when his mobile rang. He did not recognize the number on the screen but flipped it open and said, *"Allo."*

"Bruno, it's Florence from the truffle market." Her voice was fast and excited, almost breathless. "I don't know how I can ever thank you. I got the job. Rollo wants me to start next month when school reopens."

"That's great news, Florence, congratulations. I'm really pleased it worked out. And since you'll be working in St. Denis, you can put your children into our nursery school."

"It's even better than that," Florence replied. "Rollo said I can have one of the apartments at the college. There's one empty, two bedrooms, and the rent's lower than what I'm pay-ing now for one bedroom. It's subsidized, Rollo says."

"In that case, the drinks are on you next time we meet," he said, laughing at the excitement in her voice and wondering what that rather stern face of hers would look like now that her happiness was almost spilling through the phone.

"I'll be delighted. In fact, I wanted to invite you to dinner to thank you properly. You've no idea how this changes everything."

"You don't have to do that, Florence," he said, thinking of how little money she had, but also remembering how impressed he had been at their only meeting by her intellect and her character, and how he had mused at the way she might look with different clothes, a different hairstyle.

"But there is something you could do for me," he said. "Well, not just for me but also for the truffle market, I suppose. That logbook you mentioned, recording all the sales of the extra truffles after the market closed. Didier said it would be with the papers stored in the *mairie*. It isn't. I searched all through the box of files. If you could track it down, I'll buy you dinner, or maybe make a lunch for you and the children together. That would be even better, since they'll get to know me when they start school and come to my tennis lessons. And they'll like my dog."

"Are you sure you know what you're letting yourself in for?" she said gaily. "It will be a very chaotic lunch with two boisterous three-year-olds and a very harassed mother. Not many single men would put up with that. But certainly I'll look out for the logbook. If anyone can find it, I can."

"And that reminds me," Bruno added. "Since you're about to become a citizen of St. Denis, there's a children's party we're planning. It was originally going to be for the kids of the people who lost their jobs at the sawmill, but it's sort of grown into a party for all the children, and it's going to be at the old folks' home, opposite the post office."

When he closed his phone, Bruno was feeling in a much better mood and turned back to Hercule's books. There were hundreds of them. He concentrated on the books with an index, thumbing through to find references to the Binh Xuyen, and those that contained Hercule's own bookmarks with notes on them. After nearly an hour of searching and skimming the texts, he had chosen three books in addition to Savani's. The newest was *Le Viêt Nam depuis 1945: États, marges et constructions du passé,* with half a dozen bookmarks. There were even more bookmarks in a book called *Le maître de Cholon,* about a Binh Xuyen leader called Bay Vien. But the most bookmarks of all were tucked into page after page of a fat paperback in English, *The Pentagon Papers.* Perhaps he could get Pamela to help him translate the marked passages, he thought, but then caught himself and felt the good mood that Florence's call had stirred start to evaporate. Pamela did not seem inclined to see much of him these days, far less to be helpful. Beside the paperback he found a photocopy of a master's thesis from the University of Paris VII, titled "Les Binh Xuyen, étude d'un groupement politico-militaire au Sud Vietnam (1925–1955)."

He checked his watch. It was time to join J-J and the brigadier for the drive to Bordeaux. Swiftly he changed from his uniform into the civilian clothes he had brought in his shoulder bag. The blue trousers and blue shirt stayed. It meant only removing his tie, cap and jacket and donning a casual black windbreaker jacket. But that left no room for the books, so he scoured the kitchen for a plastic bag, locked the house and left. When he got back to the *mairie* he spotted an anonymous black car with two radio aerials and a grim-faced driver. It had to be the brigadier's car.

"I know who you are, monsieur," the driver said. "You can leave your bags with me. I'll put them in the back."

"I'll need to work on the books in the plastic bag while we drive," Bruno said.

The driver nodded and looked at his watch as Bruno went inside the *mairie* and took a glass of wine from the table at the door. The crowd seemed even bigger than it had been when he left it. He saw J-J looming above the sea of heads and edged across to say he was ready to go.

"The brigadier was looking for you," J-J said. "Someone he wanted you to meet. He's over by the big window."

Bruno struggled through the crowd again, holding his glass of wine above his head to prevent it from being jostled, and found himself squeezed against the burly shape of Pons the sawmill owner who was talking business with the baron.

"There you are, Bruno," said the baron. "I think I preferred our private send-off for Hercule to this zoo."

"You know the *mairie,* Bruno," said Pons in his brusque way. "How long will it take me to get a construction permit to turn my sawmill into residences?"

"A very long time," said Bruno. "This mayor won't be helpful while you're running against him. And because you're running against him he could well lose and be replaced by your son. From what I've seen of him, your son is not likely to be very helpful."

"But what if I apply to build green housing?" Pons said. "What if I were to make it an ecological project, with solar panels, geothermal heating, full insulation, carbon neutral— all the fashionable bells and whistles."

"Then you'd probably get your permit," Bruno replied, "along with a corruption scandal in the press that will say you have a deal that could make you rich, and he's your heir. At that point, the rest of the council would turn very hostile very fast. There's already some grumbling in town about the tax breaks you're getting for opening a new sawmill in St. Félix after you closed ours."

"That's exactly what I told him. What would make it work would be the subsidies we could get for a project like that," said the baron. "But the moment you apply for public funds, there'd be trouble. That's why I told Pons that he should sell the land to me."

"Even then you could have trouble," Bruno said. "Industrial land that's going to be rezoned for housing needs an environmental damage survey. Those cost a lot, and a cleanup can cost even more. And no mayor could get around that regulation, even if he wanted to."

"You wait till the elections, Bruno," grunted Pons. "Then you'll see what mayors can and can't do."

"Since you raise the topic, why in hell are you running when you know you'll just take votes from the mayor and probably make your son the winner?" the baron asked.

"What makes you say that? I'm going to win, not my damned son and not that wimp Mangin, who spends all his time trying to appease the Reds and the Greens and doesn't really know which side he's on."

"You haven't got a chance, but you'll take a few hundred votes from the mayor," the baron said. "Anyone would have to say objectively that you're trying to put your son's Red-Green coalition into power."

"*Va te faire enculer,* Baron. I've got a lot of support and I'm going to win this thing and if people like you come to their senses, I'll win by a landslide. Anyway, I thought you'd become a friend of my son, Bruno. I hear you've been getting free dinners at that fancy restaurant," Pons said with a sneer.

Bruno's mouth fell open in disbelief, but his jaw clenched. If there had been room to move his arm, Bruno would have been tempted to punch the sneer off Pons's face, but the baron's hand was on his arm.

"You're out of line," the baron snapped at Pons. "I was there. Your son wanted to pick up the check, but Bruno insisted on paying."

"Okay, maybe I was misinformed," Pons said with a shrug. "I suppose you're pissed off with him because he's stealing your lady friend."

Bruno took a deep breath. "Were you born such a miserable old bastard, Pons, or do you practice this stuff every day?"

"Hey, no offense," said Pons, his meaty face suddenly creasing into a grin as if it were all a joke between friends. "Plenty more where she came from for a rugby star like you. And one thing about the ladies, what it is that they've got, it doesn't wear out."

Bruno turned away in disgust. Pons caught his arm. "I didn't mean anything by it. So what if he is a ladies' man, that damned son of mine? He gets it from me. And it's about all I see of me in the jerk."

Bruno ignored him and turned to the baron. "I've had enough."

"The baron understands me," Pons insisted. "I was just telling him about a *maison de passe* I know in Bergerac, very discreet, very well run. I've known the madam since she was working herself. She's always got some fresh young things on offer who are eager to please. The younger the flesh the better, I always say. We ought to organize a party, make a night of it. My treat, Bruno. What do you say?"

Bruno squeezed back into the crowd behind him to make room and grabbed Pons's belt buckle. He pulled just enough to make a gap and poured his glass of wine down into the man's crotch.

"I say you ought to cool down," he said, pushing the

empty glass down behind Pons's belt and squirming away through the crowd. He was steaming with the effort of suppressing his anger but knowing that phrase "stealing your lady friend" would stick in his brain. There could be a kernel of truth to it, an unpleasant little voice whined in his head. She was seeing a lot of him, and he was luring her onto his council list. And he was handsome. And rich. Bruno slammed a mental door shut on the nasty seed that Pons had planted, knowing it would open again, probably in the small hours of the morning.

19

"There you are," said the brigadier, grabbing his arm. "Here, you look as though you need a drink." As if by magic in this crowded room full of mourners, he conjured a clean glass from the windowsill beside him, poured a large scotch from a bottle at his side and handed it to Bruno.

"Here's someone I want you to meet," he said, putting his arm around the shoulders of a short and very expensively dressed man in his fifties with a tiny mouth in the shape of a perfect cupid's bow and a strong smell of cologne. He was wearing a tie of woven black silk, and his hair had the cut and sheen of an expensive weekly barber. "Meet Paul Savani, son of the legendary Capitaine Savani, and a good friend of the man we buried today."

"I'm just about to read your father's book on Vietnam," Bruno said, shaking hands. "Hercule left a note in there saying bits of it came from some confidential Deuxième Bureau report your father wrote."

"It's no great work of literature, that's for sure," said Savani in a strong Corsican accent. "Hercule thought highly of you, so any friend of his . . ." He pulled out a slim leather wallet, removed a business card and slipped it into Bruno's shirt pocket. "My private number's on there."

"Paul has a lot of friends in strange places, and you never know when they might come in handy," said the brigadier. "He wants to help you find Hercule's murderer."

"We know it's the Fujian Dragons," Savani went on. "We just don't know exactly who."

"What dragons?" Bruno asked, not sure he'd heard correctly through the noise of the crowd.

Savani explained that the Fujian Dragons were a Chinese triad, an old one. It had started as a sect of Buddhist monks fighting the Manchus in the seventeenth century, trying to restore the Ming dynasty. Now the triad's focus was organized crime, specializing in smuggling and illegal immigration.

"But your father's expertise was Vietnam. Isn't that different?"

"Fujian and Binh Xuyen, they both started out as river pirates. There's a centuries-old feud, but sometimes they cooperate. It's a bit like France and Germany, or France and England—hundreds of years as enemies, then allies. Vietnam and China are old enemies, but Binh Xuyen and the Dragons were never very obedient to government. They always had their own deals."

"So the trouble we're seeing is not some Chinese-Viet ethnic conflict but something between criminal gangs?" Bruno asked. He had trouble thinking of Vinh as any kind of criminal, far less a gang member. "And why would they want to kill Hercule?"

"Hercule was killed because he was a symbol. He was an important friend to the Vietnamese. And then he's French, a top man in intelligence. They wanted to intimidate, to show how far their arm could stretch. And when you say 'gangs' you can miss the point. These are old organizations, more like clans. Membership has to do with family and heritage. Sometimes you don't have a choice."

Bruno got the impression Savani was talking about himself. He looked quizzically at the brigadier.

"Family traditions work in different ways," the brigadier said, trying to refill Bruno's glass. But he put his hand over it, knowing he'd had enough. "The Savanis have always been helpful to the French state. Or at least, there has always been one wing of the family that played that role."

"It goes back to Napoléon," Savani explained. It had taken a while, but Bruno began to suspect that he was in the presence of a leading figure in the Union Corse, the oldest network of organized crime in France. "We were cousins with the Bonapartes."

"I think I'm out of my depth here," Bruno said.

"It's very simple," Savani said. "We Corsicans ran the French empire in Indochina. Hotels and casinos, rubber plantations, the civil service and the colonial police and military. Hercule worked for my father in Vietnam. They were friends. So when Hercule started recruiting *barbouzes* to go after the OAS killers, he turned to my father, who knew where to recruit even better killers. Most of the real *barbouzes* were Corsicans."

"And very grateful we were too," the brigadier said. "So was de Gaulle, after they saved his life a couple of times."

"Where do the Fujian Dragons get involved?"

"For their own reasons, the Dragons killed Hercule. He was a good friend to us and the Vietnamese, so there's a feud. And the Chinese are attacking the Vietnamese here in France, which means they're attacking the Binh Xuyen, with whom we have an old alliance. We help our friends. It's tradition."

"One of the reasons why the Viets are seeing us this evening is that Paul here smoothed the way," the brigadier said.

"It would have happened anyway," Savani said. He took a thin cigarillo from his breast pocket and began to light it, ignoring the DÉFENSE DE FUMER signs all over the *mairie*. Without a word, the brigadier leaned across to unlatch the window and threw it open. Savani spoke again. "Your old army friend Tran is well respected, and right now the Viets need all the help they can get. They called me last week, when all this trouble began. So I called the brigadier."

Bruno studied the two men. Every time he met the brigadier, he had a sense of some looming secret government of France, operating behind the façade of politicians and media. It troubled him.

"Paul also helped broker the truce last year between the gangs in Marseilles," the brigadier said. "You know about that?"

"Only what I read in an old *Paris Match* while waiting at the dentist," said Bruno, looking sideways at Savani. "They said it was a war over drugs."

"*Paris Match* had it mostly right, even though they kept Paul's name out of it," said the brigadier. "They had twenty killings in less than a month. Chinese against Viets, Viets against Corsicans, Corsicans against Chinese. But it wasn't just about drugs; it was about who got to control the port. Paul brought the leaders together and helped broker a deal. We're going to do the same thing here."

"Does that mean you'll be joining us in Bordeaux?" Bruno asked Savani.

"Not this time. And I have to get back to Ajaccio."

"Paul kindly flew me down from Paris in his plane," the

brigadier said. "It's at Bergerac, and he'll take it on to Corsica tonight. And now I think we'd better head for Bordeaux."

The three of them shook hands, and the brigadier picked up the whiskey bottle by its neck and shepherded them out, collecting J-J on the way. By the time Bruno looked around for Savani, he was gone. Bruno touched his shirt pocket. Savani's card was there.

"Would Savani be the kind of guy we might want to investigate one day?" asked Bruno, wondering just how discreetly he should put it as they sped toward Bordeaux in the brigadier's car.

"What's to investigate? Savani is part of the establishment," said the brigadier, turning from the front seat to address Bruno and J-J. "Paul is a prominent businessman with a construction company and property interests in Marseilles and Corsica and hotels on the Côte d'Azur. You'll probably see him elected to the Assemblée Nationale someday. That's not to say that he hasn't got cousins who're involved in shady business. But not Paul. He figured out long ago that there's more money to be made legitimately. His current big project is an industrial park he's building in Vietnam with a lot of support from the French government. Naturally he's been reviving his family's old contacts there. Not everyone in Vietnam was a Communist. Governments come and go. Families and clans go on forever. Like the Binh Xuyen."

Bruno had learned from his hurried reading that the Binh Xuyen pirates ran the river trade to Saigon, which meant they controlled the opium trade. They expanded from that lucrative base into casinos, property and politics. They fought for the French against the Communist Viet Minh in return for a free hand for their business activities in Saigon. Savani's father and Hercule had arranged that. In the final years of

French rule, the Binh Xuyen had the world's most profitable casino, the Grand Monde, and the world's biggest brothel, the Hall of Mirrors, twelve hundred girls. Their leader, General Bay Vinh, ran the army. Another of the Binh Xuyen leaders became director-general of police. France was broke at the time, and Binh Xuyen's opium trade financed French intelligence.

When the war ended in 1954, Vietnam was partitioned between the Communist-run North and the supposedly independent South. The French backed their local puppet emperor, Bao Dai, but the Americans wanted a republic ruled by a pro-American strong man, Ngo Dinh Diem. With French backing, the Binh Xuyen launched a coup against Diem. It failed, and the Binh Xuyen leaders had to flee to France in a hurry, along with the emperor and his courtiers. Hercule and Savani arranged it.

"So the people we're going to see are a bunch of refugee drug smugglers living under the protection of the secret service?" asked Bruno.

"No," said the brigadier. "Maybe it was like that fifty years ago, but not now. We are meeting some of the leaders of a loyal and French-born community of Vietnamese origin, made up of hardworking businesspeople who have recently been subject to violent criminal attack."

"There are over a hundred and fifty thousand Vietnamese living here. Where did they all come from?"

"There were waves of refugees," the brigadier replied. "When Diem was assassinated in the military coup in 1963, a lot of his people fled. Then when Saigon fell to the Communists in 1975, another wave got out. Then there were the boat people, and since the Binh Xuyen had the best-established community organization in France, they became more influential. I'm not saying they were all entirely law-abiding, but like Savani they learned it was better to make money the legitimate way."

"I've heard this lecture before," J-J said gloomily. "You're going to tell us it's like the American Mafia. The old gangsters built Las Vegas, and then sent their sons to Harvard Law School, and the sons made a lot more turning it into a legitimate tourist playground. Crime as just another step on the ladder of social mobility."

"But that's the way it's always been," said the brigadier. "It's not just Las Vegas. Remember Balzac, who said that behind every great fortune there lies a great crime. The grandson of yesterday's crime lord is today a pillar of the state."

"The state and its custodians may think in those grand terms of decades and generations," said J-J. "But I'm a policeman on the ground, and the ones I see are the victims of crime today. They're the ones I'm supposed to protect."

"That's why the French state in her genius has always had different arms of the law, operating by subtly different rules," said the brigadier. "You do your job, and I'll do mine, and Bruno protects the interests of St. Denis. And France is grateful to us all. What that means today is that we want a truce between the Viets and the Chinese."

"So we're not trying to stop organized crime," said Bruno. "We're just trying to organize it better."

"Precisely," said the brigadier. "We're never going to stop it, so we have to control it and make it play by our rules as much as we can. You may not like it, but that's just as much policing as catching bank robbers."

"Or dressing up as Father Christmas in St. Denis," said J-J, elbowing Bruno in the ribs.

"I'm glad you reminded me," said Bruno, handing J-J a

copy of Alain's signed statement. "The man in the red suit and white beard has been out there solving crimes. It's not bank robbery, but finding out who was cheating the truffle market is important for the Périgord people who pay our wages. Consider it an early present from the Father Christmas of St. Denis."

20

The twin spires of Bordeaux's ancient cathedral of St. André glowed in their floodlights as the car approached the Pont de Pierre across the wide Garonne River. Bruno called Tran to check that they were still meeting at his restaurant as planned. He closed the phone and directed the driver into the warren of narrow streets that surrounded the Basilica of St. Michael. Halfway to the Porte de la Monnaie the brigadier spotted the multiple aerials of the unmarked police car blocking an alleyway. As their car slowed, two men came from the shadow of the alley and flagged them down. The brigadier opened his window and showed an identity card. At a signal from one of the guards, the unmarked police car quickly reversed to make room for them to pass. The alley was perhaps a hundred yards long and unlit, but the car's headlamps picked out a small knot of people standing at an open door from which a dim light spilled. The driver headed toward them at a crawl.

"*Salut, chef,*" Isabelle greeted the brigadier and warmly shook the hand of J-J, her boss before she had been promoted to the minister's staff in Paris. Bruno knew she was in Bordeaux. He was not entirely surprised that she was there to check security for her boss. But he still felt that sudden, familiar jolt at the sight of her. She gave him a brisk smile and a friendly "Bruno, *ça va?*" before she gestured to them to move quickly inside the back door to Tran's restaurant. She was holding an automatic pistol down by her thigh.

Behind her, Tran waited beside the door, two burly security men flanking him. To Bruno's eyes, he hadn't changed much since Sarajevo, still tall and pencil thin and looking completely French until his face broke into a wide smile at the sight of his old comrade-in-arms, and as the eyes narrowed the Asian genes shone through.

"Bruno, it's been too long," Tran said, hugging him as Isabelle fretted to get them indoors. The two men broke off their embrace and, arms around each other's shoulders, tried to squeeze through the narrow doorway.

"The place is secure," Isabelle said once they were all in the cramped hall and the door closed behind them. There was barely room for one person to pass at a time with the stack of cases of soft drinks and beer piled against the grimy wall. On top of them, Bruno noted with appreciation, stood four shiny new industrial-sized fire extinguishers, a precaution against further gasoline bombs, he suspected. Two poker-faced Vietnamese stood by a door at the far end of the passage that led to a kitchen. Steam and cooking smells and the sound of clanging pots leaked from the opening.

"We had the dogs in earlier to check for explosives," she said. "The Viets have their own security upstairs and next door and in the kitchen. Tran here is the liaison for that. The entrance to the restaurant is at the front of the building on the next street, but it's been closed for the evening, and we have another unmarked car outside."

"Who are these two?" asked the brigadier, looking at the two burly security men who stood by the door.

"Fusiliers Marins from the naval base at Lorient," she said. "The same unit we'll be using for the mission. I've been training with them." The brigadier nodded, and Bruno was impressed. What mission? The marine commandos were the elite of French special forces. Knowing that she was liaising with the British navy on a joint operation against illegal immigrants, he was now pretty sure it would involve boarding a ship at sea.

"Is there a specific reason for all this security?" the brigadier asked.

"The Viets insisted on coming armed," she said, shrugging. "But there are no threats on our radar."

"The meeting will be upstairs in the banquet room," said Tran, leading the way up a narrow staircase. The brigadier followed him, and Isabelle hung back, insisting on taking the rear, her gun still in her hand. It was all turning out very differently from the amicable reunion of old soldiers that Bruno had expected.

The banquet room occupied the full width of two houses, and with its dark wood paneling, louvered shutters and dragon lamps it looked as if it had been imported direct from one of the old French colonial mansions in Hanoi. The big oval table and chairs were in heavily carved rosewood, and places were set for eight people. Three Vietnamese men were already seated, and the first of them to rise was Vinh. He greeted Bruno with an apologetic grin. The second Vietnamese bowed and came around the table to shake hands with the new arrivals. He was in early middle age, as tall as Bruno, and looked as tough as the two marine commandos downstairs. The last of the Vietnamese remained seated, smoking a *kretek* cigarette held between thumb and forefinger. It filled the room with the scent of cloves. His hair was white, and the veins on the back of his hands were thick and twisted, making his age much greater than his almost unlined face suggested. A bottle of Rémy Martin stood before him.

"A pleasure to see you again, Vien," said the brigadier, leaning across the table to shake the hand of the still-seated old man. "Let us hope our discussions this evening can prove as fruitful as they were in Marseilles."

The old man nodded and studied J-J and Bruno with a piercing eye. Bruno had absorbed enough of the history of the Binh Xuyen to know that "Vien" was the honorary title of the sect's leader. The post was named after the legendary Le Van Vien, who had risen from being an illiterate river pirate to control the city of Saigon as police chief, army general and drug lord.

"How's your wife?" Bruno asked Vinh. "I haven't seen either of you since the attack in the market. We've been worried about you."

"She is recovered, and we are very grateful," Vinh said, rising from a deep bow with his eyes downcast and glancing across to the seated Vien as if for approval. All the Vietnamese seemed to defer to Vien. "Perhaps we'll come back one day. Tran told me you took care of our house when those Fujian animals put rats inside."

"It's still quite a mess," Bruno said. He turned to the tough-looking Vietnamese and held out his hand.

"Bruno Courrèges, chief of police of St. Denis," he said. "And you are?"

Almost reluctantly, the Vietnamese returned Bruno's handshake and murmured, "Bao Le." The edge of his hand and the knuckles were thick with calluses Bruno could feel in the handshake. The only other hand he had shaken like that had belonged to an army karate champion.

"From Paris?" Bruno asked amiably.

"Sometimes," Bao Le replied. "My family is from Hue."

The elderly Vietnamese muttered an aside to Tran, who opened the ornately carved door of a low sideboard and brought out a bottle of Macallan.

"Please, our honored guests will sit and take some refreshment before we dine. I know the general likes his Scottish drink, and there is also champagne," said Vien, gesturing to a tall silver chalice on the sideboard in which two bottles of Dom Pérignon were chilling. At each of the places set for dinner were glasses for champagne, white wine, red wine, dessert wine and cognac, alongside thick crystal tumblers for the scotch. Bruno exchanged glances with Isabelle at the door, who gave him the merest ghost of a wink.

Vien put down his smoldering cigarette, opened the bottle of Macallan and poured a large tumbler for the brigadier. Tran's eyes rose, as if this act of Vien pouring a drink for someone with his own hands was an extraordinary honor. Bruno felt adrift, as if in a strange country where the laws and customs were wholly foreign to him.

"You see, I remember. No ice," Vien said to the brigadier, and then clinked his cognac glass against the tumbler. "Chin-chin," he said, and Bruno fought to suppress a smile.

Tran steered Bruno and J-J to the chairs on either side of the brigadier and then began pouring champagne. Isabelle declined a seat and remained standing by the door, her gun now in a shoulder holster beneath her loosely cut jacket. Bao Le, Bruno noted, was drinking water.

"You are Sergeant Bruno, who defended my friend Vinh and his wife when you were dressed as le Père Noël," said

Vien. "We are most grateful, and I would like you to take a drink with me. But first let me convey our condolences for the death of your friend Hercule Vendrot. We mourn with you. He was a great friend to our people, a fine Frenchman and a good man. I knew him for over fifty years, and I shall miss him."

He put one hand on the table to help push himself slowly to his feet and raised his cognac glass to Bruno, who stood and raised his glass in return. All the Vietnamese were now standing, and the brigadier joined them. The last man still seated, J-J grabbed a glass and hastily got to his feet.

"Hercule Vendrot, in respectful memory," said the old Vietnamese, and drank his glass to the end. He refilled it and then leaned across to clink his glass against Bruno's champagne.

"We never forget those friends who fight for us," he said, putting his hand on the table once more for support as he sat down. He looked at the brigadier. "We have been under attack again, but only now do you seek me out. You have left it late, monsieur."

"Like you, we were taken by surprise by these latest attacks. We're trying to establish whether this is something local that blew up and got out of hand or whether the *treiz-ième* is behind it, in which case they'd be breaking the truce."

"The *treizième* is always behind it, but they'll lie through their teeth when they talk to you French. They're just giving the Fujian Dragons their head, letting them act as scouts to see how much we resist," Vien said. "Where is Savani? Is he not with you?"

"If we can organize a meeting with the *treizième*, Savani will come for that. He sends you his respects, but said that he'd want to know his Binh Xuyen friends sought his help before he intervened. I saw him today, but he is back in Corsica by now."

Vien grunted and waved a hand at Tran, who went across to a dumbwaiter in the wall and began pulling out plates of Vietnamese delicacies, *banh bao* fern cakes, *nem lui* pork dumplings rolled as thinly as a cigarette, and *banh bot loc tom* smelling of fish sauce and sugared vinegar.

"These are my favorites," Vien said, pushing a plate of sticky rice and baby shrimp toward Bruno. "*Banh ram it,* from my mother's hometown of Hue."

"A lot of this is new to me," said Bruno. "What's this *treizième* you mention?"

"It's slang for the main triad council, from the *treizième* arrondissement in Paris," the brigadier explained. "Sometimes they claim a loose authority over all the triad groups; sometimes they deny having any influence. This time they claim this outbreak has nothing to do with them."

"The Chinese are fighting among themselves, you know that," said Vien. "They blame us for these bombings when they're doing it to themselves."

"You trying to tell me that you aren't defending yourselves?" the brigadier asked.

"Do we have a choice?" countered Vien. "But defending is one thing. Attacking, using gasoline bombs, that's something else."

Vien smiled and poured the brigadier more whiskey. Bruno glanced at Vinh, who kept his eyes downcast and sat with his chair some distance from the table, as if he were not really part of this.

Bruno looked around the table, confused. The two Vietnamese that he knew, Vinh and Tran, were law-abiding small businessmen, and yet this discussion seemed predicated on the assumption that a war was under way between two rival groups of organized crime. Any intervention he made would probably be unwelcome, but so be it. This meeting had only taken place because he'd gotten in touch with Tran, and now it seemed to be another kind of meeting altogether. He cleared his throat.

"When you talk about defending their turf, I think we might be missing the point," he said to the brigadier. "You're probably thinking of the big picture, but I only see the small one, and that's Vinh here, who has no more to do with organized crime than the man on the moon. He sells *nems,* not drugs. He doesn't run whores or protection rackets. Believe me, I'd know if he did. The Vinhs work hard, pay their taxes and are respected neighbors. They're entitled to our protection. Protection by the French police, not by some shadowy organization called the Binh Xuyen."

Vinh raised his eyes to Bruno's and nodded his head very firmly, just once. Bruno looked across at Tran, seeing something of the young soldier he had known in Bosnia. Why on earth was he playing some kind of scene from *The Godfather,* a Mafia boss surrounded by his underlings?

"Tran, you run a restaurant, and you're no crook. Can you explain to me what's going on here?"

Tran looked nervously at Vien, who was smiling indulgently at Bruno. "Go ahead, Tran, explain it to your friend," the old man said.

Tran shrugged. "It's tradition. We turn to our own for protection. And to be frank, we haven't had much help from the French authorities over the years." Tran looked across at Vinh, whose eyes were looking down at the table once more. "When Vinh and his wife were attacked, they turned to the one organization they could count on, the Binh Xuyen. But you're right about one thing. We aren't gangsters anymore. Only the very old men remember what the Binh Xuyen used to be back in Saigon under French rule. I haven't handled a gun since I left the army, not until this week when I felt the need to get one for protection against these Chinese bastards. And where did I have to turn to get one? To the Binh Xuyen. It's the only organization we've got. But it's not what it was. It can't defend us. The best it can do is help us defend ourselves, and maybe get to sit at a table with people from Paris and ask just what we get for our taxes."

"So who's running the Burmese heroin into Marseilles, if not the Binh Xuyen?" the brigadier asked.

"I don't know anything about Marseilles, just like I don't know anything about heroin or opium or the old days," said Tran angrily. "This is Bordeaux and Aquitaine, where we run restaurants and market stalls and teach school and work in banks."

"And sometimes help run boatloads of illegal immigrants," the brigadier said drily.

"One moment," came a new voice. For the first time Bao Le spoke, and Bruno was struck by the way the other Vietnamese, even the elderly Vinh, turned attentively, even respectfully, toward him.

"I wouldn't wish our French friends to get the impression that the Binh Xuyen is primarily an organization involved in illegal pursuits," he said in a voice of great authority. "Historically, that was the case. But now here in France the Binh Xuyen has evolved over the decades since so many of us were driven into exile. It's a leading part of our community, a support network, even a welfare system. And of course it has the means and the will to defend us when we are attacked. That is why I am here, to show my family's support."

Bao Le looked around the table, holding each gaze for a moment before moving to the next, and Bruno noted that the other Vietnamese bowed their heads in respect. What had Bao Le meant by referring to his family? No sooner had he asked himself the question than the answer came to him. The Vietnamese family name always came first, so Bao Le came from the same royal family as Bao Dai, the last king of Vietnam under the French until the Americans installed the republic under President Diem in 1955. Bruno looked at the young man more closely, pondering the combination of royalty with the hands of a karate champion.

The brigadier looked across the table at Vien, who was slowly sipping his cognac. "You can still put a hundred gunmen on the streets of Marseilles if you have to."

"So why aren't the Chinese going after the gunmen in Marseilles with the drugs and money?" asked Bruno. "Why are they going after little men in villages, like Vinh in St. Denis and the Duongs in Ste. Alvère? I don't understand this."

Bruno stopped at the sound of a spoon tapping firmly against a cognac glass.

"Our young friend from St. Denis is at least asking the right question," said Vien, putting the spoon down. "The answer is simple. There are too many Chinese. They are coming in such numbers that there would never be enough jobs for them in the *milieu,* even if they took over all the narcotics trade in Europe. They bring in the illegals by the boatload, and then they have to find them work. They want the restaurants, the market stalls, the hairdressers, the supermarkets, because the real problem the *treizième* has to face is economics. It's all driven by numbers."

"So even if you can arrange another truce now with the

treizième, it won't last. Is that what you're saying?" Bruno asked.

"I suppose it is," said Vien. "That doesn't mean a truce that lasts even for a few years won't be worthwhile, if our old friend here can help us achieve that." He nodded at the brigadier.

"If I may contribute something," said Isabelle from the door. "If numbers are the problem, the priority must be to stop the illegal immigration. That's our job. But it might also be where you Viets may be able to help us."

"You want us to act as your spies?" asked Vien, his voice icy. Tran made as if to speak but then with a visible effort clamped his mouth shut. Vinh drew in his breath in a long, worried hiss.

"That's one way to put it," said the brigadier. "Another way would be to say that the inspector has just defined an important area of common interest between us."

"I agree with that," said Bao Le quietly.

Vien nodded slowly in acknowledgment and lit another *kretek* cigarette, his eyes half closed. After a long pause, he turned to Tran, who was almost quivering to control some emotion. Bruno guessed it was impatience.

"This might be an excellent moment to serve dinner," Vien said.

"Not until you give them an answer to what impresses me as an excellent suggestion," said Tran, the words almost exploding from his mouth as he ignored the menacing look the old man was giving him. "I respect you as an elder and as an old friend of my father," Tran went on urgently. "But my father has passed on and I'm part of another generation, which has no interest in whatever the Binh Xuyen may do in Marseilles. My interest is in making sure that I don't have to carry a gun or worry about a bomb hitting my restaurant or seeing one of my kids kidnapped."

"This is not a decision I should take alone. There are others to be consulted," Vien said, turning to give a polite nod of his head to Bao Le. "But I understand the importance of cooperation with the French authorities. In fact, I came to this meeting prepared to share some information that they should find useful."

He reached down to a slim briefcase that rested against the side of his chair and took out a clear plastic folder with some papers inside.

"As you know, we have experience in this field of immigration," Vien said. "We know how the system works. For large-scale movements coming by ship, you need an onshore base and a fast distribution system to get the arrivals away from the coast. We developed a technique that involved renting or buying beachfront trailer sites and camping grounds with campers waiting to move them on. We could move a hundred people across France within twelve hours of their coming ashore."

He pushed the plastic folder across the table to the brigadier. "The same *treizième* holding company that organized the bankruptcy and takeover of the supermarket here in Bordeaux has recently bought a large campsite south of Arcachon. Last month they also took over a company in Lille that buys and sells used campers. Over the last week, forty of these vehicles have been driven down to this region, converging on the campsite. The implications of that should be obvious." He looked up at Tran. "Now may we have dinner?"

Bruno looked across at Isabelle, who'd nodded at the brigadier and picked up Vien's folder. She leafed through the documents, pulled out her mobile phone and opened a program that brought up maps. Bruno leaned over to watch her thumb in the coordinates for the Arcachon region, a vast lagoon of a bay south of Bordeaux, famous for its mussels and for a giant sand dune, two miles long and fifteen hundred feet high. She checked the address on Vien's dossier against her map and nodded again. Then she looked up, her eyes shining.

"I think we're in business," she said.

21

"Tamarind tree soup and lily blossom fish and coconut prawns," said Tran, taking dishes from the hatch where the dumbwaiter had just arrived from the kitchen. "*Gio thu*—that's pig's head pie—and *kim long,* minced pork with sugar-cane. And here's the *com hen,* rice cooked in mussel juice, and *tom chua,* sour shrimp from Hue."

"And *banh chung,* there must be *banh chung,*" said Vien, rubbing his hands together.

"Of course, the dish that won the kingdom for the young prince who was wise enough to know his father would insist on rice for his favorite dish," said Tran, grinning as he brought dishes to the table, evidently proud of the food his restaurant was serving. "*Banh chung* is sticky rice with pork, cooked in banana leaves," he explained to Bruno.

Bruno had eaten Vietnamese food in the occasional restaurant in Paris and in Vinh's home, but never like this. He had thought of it as a variation on Chinese food, but these flavors and textures were quite distinct, and the green coloring of the rice and subtle taste of the *banh chung* surprised him. He looked around to see the others intent on their food. Isabelle was still standing by the door. He stood and offered to take her place while she ate.

"Finish your own meal first," she said, smiling. It was a real smile this time, with affection and a suggestion of happy memories in her eyes, not the automatic greeting she had given him in the alley. She looked tired and a little drawn.

"I'm fine," he said. "You didn't even take a drink. Go and eat. If I want more, I can always go back."

"Are you armed?" she asked. Bruno shook his head. Isabelle handed him her Sauer automatic, squeezed his hand in thanks and moved across to the table. Bruno felt Bao Le's eyes on him as the Vietnamese stood up and held the chair for Isabelle. Tran served her a bowl of soup, and Vien poured her a glass of champagne despite her polite refusal. She ate quickly, exchanging brief words with the brigadier.

Isabelle had barely begun on a new plate of fish and *banh chung* when there was the sound of shouts, swiftly overtaken by a high-revving engine roaring up the street outside and a sudden flare of light through the louvered shutters of a window. Then came two shots in quick succession, and then a third, more distant.

J-J was close to the window, but Bao Le beat him to it, a heavy automatic in one hand and a cell phone in the other.

"Gasoline bomb," Bao Le said, standing to one side of the window and looking down. He punched a number into his phone.

Isabelle was suddenly at Bruno's side, retrieving her weapon and darting through the door and down the first flight of stairs, calling to the Fusiliers Marins below.

"Wait," Isabelle called up. Bruno looked down to see her on the lower landing, half hidden by the balustrade post, her knees bent and both hands on the gun.

"The fire's out," called J-J from the window. "They used a couple of extinguishers, and it looks like the street's clear."

"Front and rear secure," Bruno heard one of the Fusiliers shout up the stairwell. The brigadier was at the door beside Bruno, his gun in his hand.

"You watch the door," said Bruno. "I'll find out what happened."

Aware that Bao Le was on his heels, Bruno followed Isabelle down the stairs and out through the empty ground floor of the restaurant to the street. The bomb had been aimed at the front window but had missed and hit the brick wall to one side and part of the front door, now covered in foam from the extinguisher. Beside him, Bao Le was talking into the phone in Vietnamese. One of the Bordeaux police from the unmarked car that had been blocking the street entrance approached cursing, his clothes spattered with white paint.

"Three motorbikes, coordinated so they hit at the same time, two men on each bike," he said. "One bike for each of the cars, a paint bomb on the windshield, then a third bike swerved around our car and into this street, and the guy on the back tossed the bomb."

Bruno could feel the broken glass from the bottle that had held the gasoline grinding under his feet.

"They've gone," the policeman added, looking down in dismay at his paint-smeared coat. "Too fast for us to react. We need some paper towels or something to clear the windshields, or the cars are useless."

"Towels will just smear it," said Bruno. "You'll need turpentine. Better call in and ask for another car to bring some."

Bao Le grabbed Bruno's arm, his phone at his ear. "I think

we've got one," he said. "I had men around the corner in case of something like this."

Bruno pulled out his own phone, called J-J's mobile and reported what he had heard. Then he followed Bao Le around the corner where the hood and windshields of the police cars were drenched with paint. Along the street a trail bike lay sprawled on its side beside a garbage bin, spilling empty tins and plastic bottles. Three figures were struggling on the pavement and front doors were opening, more people looking out windows.

Bao Le shouted an order in Vietnamese, and the struggle suddenly became orderly, two Asians in black raincoats holding between them a man in a motorbike helmet. Bao Le spoke again. It sounded like a question. One of the men in raincoats replied, and Bruno could see that his nose was bleeding.

"I asked them what happened to the second man on the bike," Bao Le explained. "They said he ran away while they were struggling with this one. They did well to stop the bike. They threw the garbage can at it and knocked the bike over."

"Let's take this one back to Tran's place and find out what we've got," said Bruno. "But first, I need a number where I can reach you. It's about something else. I need to find Hercule Vendrot's daughter, and I think with your connections you should be able to help me."

Bao Le made as if to speak but then stopped. He took an embossed card from a card case and slipped it into Bruno's hand.

Siren howling and blue lights flashing, a fire engine appeared at the far end of the street and headed toward them. Bao Le took a plastic cord from one of his men and roughly bound the elbows of the prisoner together behind his back.

The two Vietnamese in raincoats stayed on watch, one of them picking up the motorbike and wheeling it to the side of the street. Bruno scribbled down the registration number and then steered their stumbling prisoner back to the corner where the police in their unmarked but paint-smeared car were arguing with the firemen and refusing to move.

Ignoring them, Bruno marched his charge to the foam-smeared door and into the restaurant. Isabelle, J-J and the brigadier were already there, each talking on a different phone.

"Bao Le's men caught one," Bruno announced, and pushed the slim figure down into a chair. Three telephone conversations were hurriedly ended. "I got the license plate of the bike." He read it out, and J-J punched a new number into his cell.

Bao Le removed the helmet from the prisoner and stood back. Bruno gave a start of recognition.

"I know him," he said. "It's the guy we arrested in St. Denis for the assault on Vinh's stall. He's supposed to have paid his fine and left the country by now."

"The one who had that bastard Poincevin as a lawyer?" asked J-J, turning away from his new phone call.

"The very one." Bruno looked again at his notebook, thumbing back through the pages. "Yiren Guo, age twenty-two, Chinese nationality, claiming to be a student but on an overstayed tourist visa. Pleaded guilty and agreed to self-deportation."

"So this time it's a prison term for sure," said J-J. He turned back to his phone and read out the motorbike's license number. "There's more," he continued into the phone. "I want the court record for the case of Yiren Guo, pleaded guilty to charges of assault and immigration offenses in

Périgueux. Poincevin was his lawyer. I need to know how much the fine was and who paid it and the terms of his deportation order, and I don't care what you have to do to get it."

"There's no paint on this one's hands," said Bruno. He walked behind the chair where Guo sat and bent down to sniff the bound hands. "Gasoline."

"And I want a forensics guy down here," J-J said into his phone. "It looks like we've got one of the petrol bombers."

"Why not run a DNA check on him?" suggested Bruno. "See if you get a match to those tissues you found in that abandoned Mercedes after Hercule's murder."

"Worth a try," said J-J.

Isabelle was searching the pockets of the young Chinese. They were empty, except for a thin wad of euros, a mobile phone and a telephone charge card and a slip of paper with a telephone number. Bruno checked his notebook. It was the number for the law offices of Poincevin in Périgueux.

"Maître Poincevin will have some explaining to do," Bruno said. "And I have a fine witness in St. Denis who saw some Asians putting rats into Vinh's home. I want to put this guy into a lineup for her."

"Wait," said Isabelle, pulling off Guo's shoes and frisking his ankles. "I've been lucky like this before." She pulled out a BNP bank card from the young man's sock, held it up triumphantly and read out a different name. The prisoner closed his eyes.

"Chan Kang-ying," she said. "It doesn't sound at all like Guo. But with the bank account, we'll get an address and an ID card number along with a paper trail. And that should give us enough to get a whole lot more information from this lawyer of his, starting with who paid the legal fees."

"I imagine that whoever hired this guy isn't going to be

happy that he got caught, and even more angry that he was foolish enough to be carrying the bank card," said J-J. "So we're going to have an interesting conversation about what he should tell us in his own self-interest." He ruffled the prisoner's hair, almost affectionately.

"What happens now?" asked Bao Le.

"We wait for the forensics team, get this man formally booked and charged and locked up overnight, take his bike to the police garage and start looking into his bank account," said J-J. "But most of that can be handled by the Bordeaux police, who are on the way."

"Three motorbikes and six men," said Isabelle. "And somebody had to reconnoiter this place so they knew about the cars blocking the street, and they brought paint to blind them so they couldn't be followed. It's quite an organization that can put all that together with a couple of hours' notice."

"I can't work out what they were trying to do, beyond send us a message that they knew we were meeting," said the brigadier. "It was a lot of effort just to toss one Molotov cocktail at the door."

"It could have been more serious if it had gone through the front window," said Isabelle. "But I see what you mean."

"What worries me is how they knew we were meeting here," said Bruno. He turned to Vien and Tran and Bao Le. "Could there be a leak on your side?"

Vien shrugged. "It's always possible, but I doubt it."

"Or could they be tapping some of our phones?" suggested Bao Le. Like Bruno, he was watching Guo for any sign of reaction. "Perhaps we should change them all, just in case."

"If they're tapping mine, they've broken the best encryption system in France," the brigadier said. "And I don't think they're that good—yet." He picked up Guo's mobile phone and opened the phone log, and then scanned through the text messages. From a distance came the sound of a police siren.

"It's in pinyin, Chinese with Roman letters, and I can't read it. But it looks like somebody was sending him this address. The message came at 7:42, that's not long after we got here. It's possible that we were simply followed."

"All the way from Ste. Alvère?" said Bruno. "We'd have spotted anyone following us, even a motorbike."

"Maybe you were followed," the brigadier said to Vien and Bao Le. The police siren was getting louder.

"Almost certainly not," said Bao Le. "I had my own people watching our tail."

"In that case, they're tapping Bruno's phone," said the brigadier, and held out his hand for Bruno's mobile. Reluctantly, Bruno surrendered it. "I'll make sure you get one of ours."

"What about the prisoner?" asked Bruno. "The other guy on his bike knows he went down. If they think we've got him under arrest, they'll clear out in a hurry."

"Good thinking," said J-J. "We'll put out a release saying an unidentified Asian was found dead in the street after a hit-and-run. I'll see to that now."

Police, firemen and the forensics team all seemed to arrive at the doorway together. Leaving Tran and J-J to sort out the procedure, the brigadier steered Bruno and Isabelle, Vien and Bao Le through the back door, past the two Fusiliers and into the alley.

"I'm sorry we're missing the meal, but I don't think we need to be part of that mess back there, and I have to go and brief the prefect. I'm staying with him, but I'll drop you off at your hotel on the way," he said to Isabelle. He hit a speed-dial button on his mobile to call up his car and gave Bao Le and

Vien each a card. "My e-mail address is on there, so send me your new phone numbers as soon as you get them. The e-mail's secure."

He bundled Bruno and Isabelle into the backseat as soon as his car arrived. Then with a curt "I'm sure you have your own arrangements" to the two Vietnamese, he climbed into the front passenger seat and told the driver to head for the place des Quinconces.

"You're at the Hôtel des Quatre Soeurs?" he asked Isabelle. She nodded, and he turned to the driver. "Drop them off at the corner of Trente Juillet and Esprit des Lois." He pulled out another phone from the car's dashboard and began scanning e-mails.

Bruno and Isabelle looked at each other, and then at the same moment each looked away. They drove on in silence.

"My bag is in the back of the car," Bruno told the driver as the car pulled up. A button was pressed and the trunk opened.

He and Isabelle were left standing on the pavement. She lit a cigarette and drew in the smoke hungrily. She had stopped smoking when they had been together. He made no comment.

"Where were you planning to stay?" Isabelle asked, not looking him in the eye. There were few areas of etiquette more difficult to handle than an evening with an old flame, Bruno thought. If you don't suggest a burning desire to rekindle the ashes, any woman would be offended. But if you do, her pride would require refusal. Bruno avoided even contemplating the possibility that Isabelle might invite him to her bed, knowing that the more he thought about it the more the prospect would entice him.

"I'd originally planned to stay with Tran. But I think he's

in for a long night with J-J and police statements. So it's best that I get a hotel."

"I need a drink," she said. "Get yourself a room here and tell them to put it on my bill, room three-three-four. I imagine we get better expenses than St. Denis might offer. I'll be in the bar. What shall I order you?"

"Armagnac, please," he said, and followed her into the hotel, suddenly remembering for some reason the weight of her gun in his hand and the casual way she held it, as if she used it daily. His own weapon lived in his safe at the *mairie* and was usually only ever taken out for his compulsory refresher course each year at the gendarmerie range in Périgueux. He drew a clear distinction between weapons, which he had used all too often in the military and which included his police firearm, and guns, which for Bruno meant the shotguns he took when hunting. These he saw as essentially civilian companions.

He checked in, taking the cheapest room available, a single on the top floor. It was still eighty-five euros, and he knew he could have had two nights in a St. Denis hotel for the same price. He took the elevator to the top floor, tossed his bag and coat on the bed, washed his hands and brushed his teeth and headed down to the half-full bar. Isabelle was sitting at a small table in a corner, two glasses on the table before her.

"Well, here we are," she said brightly, pushing his glass of Armagnac toward him as he sat.

"Leaving a nice mess behind us for J-J to clear up and wondering if our phones are tapped," he said. He felt a strange need to laugh. It was probably caused by the tension of the evening, and now the added tension of Isabelle's presence.

"Mine will be fine. They have some technology that

secures it automatically, or so they tell me," she said, carefully not quite looking at him.

"I don't think we're quite at that technical level in St. Denis," he said. "I got my phone at Intermarché. I saw yours had maps on it."

"And GPS," she said. "God, I want another cigarette. This isn't how I expected this conversation to go."

"They never work out as you expect," he said.

"Sometimes I think that's a good thing. Not that I had any particular plans," she said. Bruno nodded, waiting. She raised her eyes to his. "Funny how fate keeps throwing us together."

"Fate or perhaps duty," he said, and paused before speaking again. "Talking of duty, Hercule had a safety-deposit box and as his executor I'm responsible for it. The key seems to have disappeared with your archives people. Is there anything you can tell me about it, or anything left that I should see?"

"I know there were some papers the office took. You'll have to ask the brigadier about them. Or get the *notaire* to write to him formally, then he'd have to respond."

"Any idea what the papers were about?"

"Algerian War, that's all I know. Memoirs, but sometimes the old stuff is the most sensitive."

"Was there anything else?"

"I heard there were some fake passports for Hercule, different nationalities, a few blanks," she said. "The usual spook cache. I didn't hear anything about money, but a man usually keeps some ready cash where he stashes his passports."

"And I'm still looking for that journal of Hercule's, his truffle diary. Could that have been in the safe deposit?"

"No, I'd have heard if they'd found that," she said with a small smile. "It's the kind of thing people gossip about in the canteen. Truffles in Périgord."

"Are you enjoying this new work?"

"Sometimes. Like this evening, when somebody remembers that I need to eat too. That was sweet of you, Bruno, always the gentleman."

"Your new assignment on illegal immigrants, liaising with the navy and the British, I presume it's dangerous."

"Why on earth would you think that?" she asked, studying him.

"I presume you'll be boarding the ship."

She raised her eyebrows. "You're not supposed to know that."

"It wasn't hard to work out. You told me you were liaising with the British navy on illegal immigrants, and then you show up with Fusiliers Marins."

"Worried about me, Bruno?" Her laughter was a little forced. "Surely we're beyond that. Anyway, I'll be the last one up the ladder or down from the helicopter, whichever it is."

"I don't think you ever stop caring for someone you've loved."

"No," she said slowly. "I don't think you do. So what are your plans tomorrow?" With the speed that only a woman can manage, she had thrown off one mood and assumed another. Voice, carriage, gesture, tilt of head and the look in her eye had all been transformed. For Bruno, it was one of the fascinating marvels of her sex.

"I'll have to check in with J-J, and I'll want to see Tran before I catch the train back to St. Denis. I've got a busy day. There's a Christmas party for the children that I've got to arrange," he said, starting to grin as her smile widened. "And that reminds me that I'm supposed to have a new Father Christmas costume waiting for me at the *mairie*. And at some point I have to pick up my new police van and then drive it up to Périgueux to pick up my new uniforms, since the old ones were damaged in the line of duty."

She laughed, a genuine one this time. "This is real police work. Do explain, Father Christmas."

So he told her everything that had happened, from the attack on Vinh's stall and the theft and crash of his police van to the ruin of his uniform in the manure pit.

"I saw that in the paper, when you pulled that little boy out."

"They made too much of it. Just that fool Pons, who invited all the schoolkids but didn't secure his pool of dung . . ." He sipped at his drink. "What are your plans tomorrow?"

"We both have a meeting with the brigadier and the prefect at nine, and then I have to be at Merignac airport at eleven for another liaison session with the navy and the British. You're right, there's a ship we're monitoring. And then in the afternoon I thought I'd better take a discreet look at this campsite near Arcachon the Viets told us about."

"Be careful," he said.

"We might not be boarding the ship at all, if the campsite is where they're planning to bring them ashore. We could seal the place off and round them up there. I suppose that's what tomorrow's meetings will be about."

"Sounds like an early start for both of us." He began to push back his chair.

"Give me a minute to go up first, Bruno," she said. "It would be too embarrassing to stand with you in the elevator, wondering if you were going to escort me to my door and pounce."

"I'm not the pouncing type." He grinned at her.

"No, but sometimes I am," she said, rising, and leaned forward to kiss him on the mouth. "Good night, dear Bruno."

Isabelle left with that proud and straight-backed stride of hers, and Bruno sighed and turned to the bar to pay for the drinks. As he headed through the foyer, he saw she hadn't taken the elevator at all. She was standing on the pavement outside the revolving door, smoking another cigarette. He paused, tempted to go out to her.

He pressed the UP button and rose alone to his room, telling himself he should have joined her on the pavement and held her close. He shook his head. It would simply have forced them to decide all over again whether to revive an affair that had run its course. But he went to bed asking himself just what it was about his relationship with Pamela that he was being faithful to. With her new interest in politics she seemed to be spending as much time with Bill Pons as with him. He drifted off to sleep until the hotel phone woke him just after 4:00 a.m. It was J-J, telling him to get dressed fast because he was coming to pick him up.

22

"It's the breakthrough we need," said J-J as the unmarked car from the Bordeaux police pool raced up the deserted rue de Pessac. J-J had turned down the volume on the radio, but Bruno could still hear the constant chatter of the dispatchers and other cars reporting in. "Thanks to the bank card, and a security man who became unusually cooperative once we said this was about a terrorist bombing, we got the little bastard's address. Apparently it's a small apartment house above a cinema and another of their Chinese restaurants, owned by one of the holding companies linked to the *treizième*."

"Bordeaux police are running the show?" asked Bruno, looking at his watch. It was not yet four-thirty. Dawn was more than three hours away.

"They'll make any arrests, but the brigadier runs the show."

"Does Bordeaux know that?" Bruno asked.

"The brigadier's in the ops center, and he's cleared it with the prefect. For once, Bordeaux will do what they're told," J-J said.

"How many cars are they sending?"

"We're promised four, and they're supposed to wait for my order before moving in. They're led by an Inspector Verneuil. He's supposed to be good. He'd better be. This has all been set up at the last minute."

J-J slowed as the cinema and restaurant came into view. At the next side street, Bruno saw two police cars, displaying only parking lights, stopped with their engines running. An unmarked police car waited at the corner, a tall man wearing a Russian fur hat stood beside it, a radio in his hand. J-J pulled up alongside him.

"Inspector Verneuil?" Bruno asked. The fur hat nodded.

"You got my message?" asked J-J, leaning across Bruno to speak through the open window. The fur hat nodded again.

"Can we get a dedicated channel on these things?" J-J asked, gesturing at Verneuil's radio.

"Not without setting it up earlier," Verneuil replied.

"Well, if you hear me refer to Operation Deutschland, that's you. If I say Operation Deutschland Now, bring your guys at the double. If I don't, sit tight."

"Got it," said Verneuil. "Why Deutschland?"

"Because nothing else sounds like it, and it has no obvious connection to the target. I wouldn't put it past these bastards to be monitoring our radio. Understand?"

Verneuil nodded again, the fur hat exaggerating the gesture.

"We're going to take a quick look around on foot," J-J went on.

"The radio is attached to the car," Bruno said.

"*Putain de merde.* We'll get closer in the car, then Bruno here will take a look on foot, and I'll stay close to him."

"And I'll wait for the words Operation Deutschland Now," said Verneuil.

All lights switched off, J-J crept ahead slowly, cruising past the target building at just under the speed limit. All the lights were off. J-J turned left at the second corner and then left again, to find the way ahead blocked by a high wire fence surrounding a parking lot.

"You take a quick look around," said J-J. "I'll go back to the main road so there'll be no interference if I have to use the radio. If there's an emergency, whistle and I'll call in the troops. Otherwise I'll wait till you get back, and I'll keep the window open so I can hear you."

Bruno reached up to turn off the master switch for the overhead light. The last thing he needed now was a flare of a courtesy light as he opened the door. He got out of the car, leaning against the door to close it with minimum noise, and headed for the fence. There was little light, but the parking lot seemed huge, probably for the cinema patrons, and now mainly empty. He turned right, following the fence for another ninety feet, and then turned left until he recognized the looming hulk of the target building.

Two large commercial trucks were parked at strange angles close to the building's rear. Bruno followed the fence farther until he came to a double gate, chained and padlocked. He moved on, trying to get closer to the trucks. They seemed to have been positioned in a way that hid something else. He crept on, trying to make out what lay behind them. It was too tall for a car, too small for a truck, in a pale color, perhaps white. Then Bruno saw the dark shape of a large window and the outline of a narrow stepladder, and he realized it was a camper. Now that his eyes were attuned to the shape, he saw that there were three, no, four of the campers parked closely against the rear wall of the building.

Campers, Isabelle, the campsite by the beach at Arcachon and the company recently bought in the north; the connections snapped together in his brain. He began jogging toward the main street, taking the risk of running past the front of the building to alert J-J that Operation Deutschland would have to be aborted.

"Cancel it. Close it down," he gasped into J-J's window when he reached the car. He made an effort to calm his breathing. "Four campers are parked at the back. It's the connection to Isabelle's operation, the illegal immigrants and the campsite at Arcachon. If we raid them now, they'll abort the landing."

"I get you," said J-J, reaching back for the radio. Then he stopped. "On second thought, I won't transmit. It could be misunderstood. I'll drive back quietly, and we'll tell Verneuil in person."

"Bordeaux won't like it. They want the arrests."

"They'll have to live with it," J-J said. Bruno slipped into the passenger seat of the car, holding the door closed rather than slamming it.

"Do you think you'd better call the brigadier?" Bruno asked. "If they have the campers assembled here already, it's my guess they'll be bringing the people ashore tonight. It must be pretty close."

"We wouldn't want to ruin Isabelle's big operation," said J-J. Then he turned and grinned and elbowed Bruno in the ribs. "Mind you, if it does go wrong, she'll probably be booted out of the minister's office and sent back here to us. That wouldn't be so bad."

"A humiliated Isabelle kicked back down here in disgrace wouldn't be the same Isabelle," said Bruno, wondering how

J-J could have been married for so many years and not understand the first thing about women. "She probably wouldn't even want to see us."

An unmarked police car was parked along the street, and a cheerful Vietnamese was humming to himself in the weak December sunlight as he repainted the door to Tran's restaurant. Bruno saw no other sign of the previous evening's attack as he stepped inside and saw waiters laying the tables for lunch and a trail of deliveries of chickens and vegetables coming from the rear alley. Tran was receiving the goods, squeezing the cabbages and poking the breasts of the chickens as he ticked off the deliveries on the invoices. He signaled to one of the chefs to take over when he saw Bruno.

"Did you get any sleep?" Bruno asked.

"They let me go about two with Bao Le, after giving our statements. J-J was helpful. How about you?"

"I gave my statement this morning," Bruno said. "I just wanted to say hello before heading back to St. Denis and see if you needed anything. I can't be here to help with security, but I have some advice, starting with those deliveries."

"Don't worry. I have a guy in the alley checking every box before it comes in the back door. Come up to the office. Bao Le is there, and he said he needed to talk to you." Tran turned to the kitchen and called for coffee before he led Bruno upstairs.

Bao Le was working on a laptop at the wrong side of the desk. A pleasant courtesy, thought Bruno, to leave the main chair for Tran. He looked up, quickly closed a program and rose to shake Bruno's hand.

"Sorry," he said. "But I have to keep up with my real job."

"What's that?" Bruno asked.

"I'm a partner in an international consultancy, but I wanted to follow up on your question about Hercule's daughter. You know Hercule had been pressing us for information on this for years?"

"I'd be surprised if he hadn't," Bruno said. "Is she still alive?"

"No, and Hercule knew it, but it gets complicated. You know she ran away from home as a teenager?"

"I know nothing, not about his wife, his daughter, anything. In this area he was a very private man."

"Maybe I should start by saying I'm involved in this too. Hercule's wife was my aunt, so his daughter was my cousin."

"Both members of the royal family."

"Very distant and junior members. My great-grandfather was a cousin of the father of Emperor Bao Dai. Our family was never rich but they were courtiers, mostly living and working in the palace. When Bao Dai fled to France, almost the entire family left with him. By then my aunt had married Hercule, but she died giving birth to Linh. Because Hercule was in Algeria, Linh lived with us. She and I grew up together in Paris, with her as my big sister. I adored her—I say this to let you know that I was as committed to finding her as Hercule was."

"She must have been considerably older than you," said Bruno.

"Eleven years older, so she was my babysitter," said Bao Le. He pulled a wallet from his jacket and withdrew a small, passport-sized black-and-white photograph of a pretty teenager with a Western face and Asian eyes and hair that fell in curling waves to her shoulders. He passed it to Bruno. "I always carry this. In a way, she brought me up. She always spoke Vietnamese to me, taught me to read and to swim and how to ride a bike. But this was the end of the sixties, with the Vietnam War raging and the so-called peace talks under way in Paris. You probably remember, Kissinger and Le Duc Tho eventually got the Nobel Peace Prize. To his credit Le Duc Tho declined it."

"I can't say I remember, but I've read the history," Bruno said.

"As you can imagine, the whole émigré community in Paris was obsessed with the war, and none more than Linh," Bao Le said. "We were all Vietnamese patriots, but we despised the Saigon regime and hated the way the Americans fought the war. But we also detested the Communists in Hanoi. Except for Linh. She became committed to the Vietcong. She wasn't a Communist, but she felt going back to the war was the only practical way to be a patriot."

"She could have been right, looking back," said Tran. "If I'd have been born then, I might have made the same decision."

Bao Le looked at Tran thoughtfully. "Who knows?" he said. "History takes a long time to work out who was right and who was wrong. We make the best choices we can at the time. And she was very young."

"When did she run away?" Bruno asked.

"In seventy-four, when she turned eighteen and was able to get a passport. She flew to Warsaw and then to Hanoi to volunteer for the war. The embassy in Paris had given her a visa. But when she arrived, they didn't know what to do with her. She was a distant member of the royal family, half French and with French citizenship. They sent her to train as a nurse. We know from the handful of letters we received that she was with an army unit when they took Saigon the following year.

And she was with the same unit when they were ordered into Laos and later into Cambodia. She was an outspoken critic of both those forgotten little wars, so she got into trouble and was sent to a reeducation camp."

"A concentration camp, more like," said Tran.

"It was a terrible place, but we, or rather our friends in Vietnam, managed to track down two people who had known her there. One was another woman, another prisoner, who told us that Linh had been raped by the guards and become pregnant and had the baby in the camp. The other, an army medic who was also a prisoner but worked in the hospital, said there was no baby, and he was sure he would have known. That's all we have, except that Linh was released at the beginning of 1979 and sent back to the army and was killed later that year when the Chinese invaded in the border war."

"A tragic story," said Bruno. He didn't know what else to say. "A nightmare for Hercule. And for you."

"We don't know if she had a baby, but they were all given new revolutionary names, with no indication of the mother, or the father, come to that. It was part of the way the Communists tried to abolish history. The records show that over twelve thousand babies were born in that camp, and we've been trying to trace them. But many of them have changed their names. I can't say I blame them. If my name was 'October Revolution' or 'Patriot Vengeance' I'd change it too. But it's the only plan we have, to trace as many as we can and check their DNA."

"How many have you been able to test so far?" Bruno asked.

"Just over three hundred."

"Perhaps the child would have had some of its grandfather's genes," Bruno offered. "It might stand out."

"Can you imagine how many Vietnamese orphans of that period had American fathers? Tens of thousands of them look Western."

Bruno slumped into a chair, thoroughly frustrated. "Is there anything we can do?"

"We just have to keep trying. We're even advertising. You can put notices in the Vietnamese newspapers now, and they have whole sections of people searching for family members who got separated. There are information brokers, private investigators," said Bao Le.

He looked at his watch and then at Bruno. "You said something about catching a train. I have a car and a driver outside. We'll get you to the station."

23

Nicco, Bruno's counterpart in Ste. Alvère, was waiting at Le Buisson station and looking grumpy.

"You lost your phone?" he asked. "I've been trying to reach you."

Bruno dropped his hand to the familiar pouch at his waist to find it empty and then remembered the brigadier taking it from him. He had spent the journey dozing, half waking as the little train stopped at St. Emilion and Ste. Foy la Grande and chugged on its way through the vineyards of Castillon and Pomerol. Wine lovers would take this train as an act of pilgrimage. For Bruno, the endless rows of vines were comforting images of the homeland he loved, more felt than seen as he tried to catch up on his sleep.

"Sorry," he said. "My phone's being replaced by some fancy model that can't be wiretapped. We've had some trouble that way."

"Florence from the truffle market has been trying to reach you. Good news, she says. Something about a logbook."

"How well do you know Didier, Nicco?"

"The market manager? Well enough. Can't say I like him much. Is he the one behind this fraud business?"

"The logbook'll tell us. It's been missing."

"So it's an inside job, no great surprise. But how big is it? I just heard about a couple of complaints. It didn't sound like much."

"I won't know until I've gone through all the books, but it looks pretty serious."

"You mean there could be criminal charges?"

"That'll be up to your mayor." Bruno wanted to change the subject. "When did Florence call?"

"She called me a couple of times, said she couldn't reach you. She also said she'd see you at the children's party today, unless you want to see her sooner. I could take you to her place once we've picked up your car."

"Thanks—but I've no idea where she lives."

"She's got a little place above a hairdresser's, just a couple of rooms. Must be cramped with the kids, but she said she'd be moving to St. Denis."

"That's right. She's got a new job there, teaching science at the *collège*."

Back in his Land Rover, Bruno followed Nicco to the small hairdresser's shop that served the public housing project on the outskirts of town. Nicco pointed, waved and drove off, and Bruno pressed the cheap plastic button that flanked the narrow door to the upstairs apartment. He heard the sound of a distant buzzer and then steps coming down a staircase.

"Bruno!" Florence said with surprise as she opened the door, at once putting one hand to her hair, another smoothing her apron. Animated, her face had softened and become more . . . Bruno searched for the word. He could never call her pretty. It made her more attractive, and much less remote. "I hadn't expected . . ."

"Nicco picked me up at the station and told me you'd called, about the logbook. But if this is a bad time . . ."

"I was just getting the children ready for a walk." She gestured vaguely at the folding double stroller that almost blocked the narrow stairs.

"Then I'll walk with you," he said. "Let me get the stroller ready, and you bring the kids down." He reached in and took the folded stroller from the hall, and with a hurried smile she nodded and went back up the stairs.

Bruno smiled to himself as he looked at his watch. Perhaps two minutes to dress the kids, another two minutes to bring them down, and the rest would be spent changing her clothes and fixing her face. Some women would keep him waiting half an hour. He suspected that Florence would be down more quickly than that. She made it, changed and hair brushed, and with the kids in overcoats and gloves and little woolen hats, in less than five minutes.

"Dora and Daniel," said Florence. " 'Dora' is short for 'Dorothée.' "

Bruno knelt down to the height of the children and solemnly greeted each of them before lifting them into their seats and fastening the little seatbelts. The children were clean and cheerful and glowing with health.

"I found the logbook," she said as he rose. "I know how Didier's mind works. He's careful. He likes to have proper excuses when things go wrong. I didn't think he'd destroy the logbook or even hide it somewhere that had no reasonable explanation."

"As if it had been accidentally misfiled?"

"Exactly," she said. Somehow, Bruno had automatically taken the helm of the stroller as they walked, Florence striding briskly as she explained her thinking. Rather than search Didier's office, she'd gone down to the basement storeroom, telling the secretary who gave her the key that she needed to check some of last year's figures. She'd found the logbook in the third box she looked in, tucked beside a pile of *taxe d'habitation* returns. She pointed to a red leather accounts book with a black spine peeking from the bag attached to the stroller.

"I guess you'll need to compare it with the main set of accounts," she added. "I saw you had sealed that box so I couldn't examine it. But I checked it against my own records, and two things struck me. The first was that the prices paid at these end-of-day auctions were consistently much lower than prices at the market itself."

"That suggests a ring," said Bruno. Florence looked blank. "It means an agreement among the bidders in order to keep the prices low. It can only work over time if the auctioneer, which means Didier, is prepared to go along and sell at the lower price rather than withhold his stock. What's the second thing?"

"The main buyer almost every time was someone called Pons, and he seemed to be paying less than his official winning bids. And he always paid cash."

"Was there an initial? There's a Boniface Pons and a Guillaume."

Florence shook her head. Bruno cast his mind back to a conversation with Hercule. The old man had said Didier once worked for Boniface Pons, running a truffle plantation before Pons gave up and sold the trees as timber. So Pons would know something of the truffle trade. It was possible that Pons's name was being used without his knowledge, but either way Bruno reckoned that Florence had come across something far more serious than some cheap Chinese truffles stuffed into a vacuum pack.

"It seems you've done my work for me," he said, turning his head to smile at her. She looked at him directly, her gray-blue eyes suddenly seeming less cold than he remembered.

"Watch out!" she grabbed his arm, as he was about to run the stroller into a lamppost.

"Sorry, I'm not used to this," he said.

"I do it myself, once I start thinking and I'm suddenly miles away." She looked down at the children. "They usually warn me when I'm about to run into something."

"I'm going to have to check this logbook against accounts at the *mairie*," Bruno said. "But I expect I'll see you at the children's party. There'll be lots to eat and drink there, so you needn't bother feeding them beforehand."

She looked down. "I'm not sure we'll be able to come. The other mother who usually gives me a lift has gone shopping in Périgueux. I don't have a car."

"Mine is parked at your place. I'll come back from the *mairie* and pick you up and take you all to St. Denis," he said, thinking what kind of life it must be, stuck in a small country town with no car, little money and the supermarket at the other end of town.

"And I can bring you back, if you don't mind waiting while I change out of Father Christmas clothes." He looked down at the children, now squabbling amicably over a picture book. "I'd hate the kids to lose their illusions too early."

"If it's not too much trouble . . ."

"Not at all." Bruno checked his watch. "I'll be back at your place at about four-fifteen because the party starts at five and I'll need some time to change into my Christmas gear."

"You can find your way back?"

"I think I can manage that." He said good-bye to the children and went off down the rue République toward the *mairie,* the logbook tucked inside his jacket.

With Florence's advice to guide him, Bruno began to list the difference in prices paid at the morning market and the much lower prices at the later auction. Florence was right. One name kept recurring in the lists of buyers in the final auctions. Pons seemed to be buying every time there was an auction, although it wasn't clear from the logbook whether it was father or son. Leafing back to the previous year, it was still Pons, still buying at every opportunity. It must have been Boniface, since Bill had not yet arrived in the district. Bruno began to list Pons's purchases, whistling in surprise as he totaled the amounts that the man was buying. There were several days when Pons was spending more on truffles than Bruno's monthly salary.

He turned back to the spidery writing in the logbooks. Not only was Pons the biggest single buyer, but as Florence had noted he was consistently paying less per gram than others were paying for their batches of truffles, no matter what he bid at the auction. And they in turn were paying about two-thirds of what the customers in Paris and elsewhere were being charged when they bought direct from the market. This was like giving them a license to print money, a guaranteed profit. Was it possible that Pons was getting a discount because of the volume of his purchases?

Bruno checked his figures again. Not only was Pons getting a consistent discount, but because he was invariably listed as paying in cash, that presumably meant Pons would have attended each auction. Bruno found that very hard to believe. But could he prove it? Then he remembered. He opened his own pocket diary and turned back to January, when he and Pons and the baron and others from the St. Denis rugby club had gone to Marseilles for three days to support the town's team in a tournament there. Pons had been hundreds of miles away with Bruno when he was listed in the market logbook as present and buying truffles cheaply with cash.

So if Pons was not present, then someone—presumably Didier—had been buying on his behalf. And Pons and Didier had worked together before at Pons's truffle plantation. And what was Pons doing with all the truffles he bought? By Bruno's calculation, he had spent half a million euros the previous year buying hundreds of kilos. He had to be selling them somewhere. And all that cash, tens of thousands of euros a week, had to come from somewhere. This stank of money laundering, and Bruno began to feel that this inquiry was getting far too big and complex for him. He'd have to call in J-J and the specialist accountants from the fraud squad. The national tax authorities would want to get involved.

As he gathered his notes and logbooks and climbed up the stairs to the photocopying machine, another thought struck Bruno. If the investigation into Pons was launched within the next three months before the election, that would be the end of Pons's campaign to become mayor. Those votes would drift back to their usual recipient, Gérard Mangin, the veteran mayor who had given Bruno his job and been something of a father figure to him since Bruno's arrival in St. Denis. Copy-

ing page after page of the two logbooks, Bruno pondered the
political consequences. The election would be a straight fight
between young Bill Pons and his Red-Green coalition and the
mayor. There would be no Oedipal battle between father and
son to bring the TV cameras to excite the politics of St. Denis
out of their usual placid ways.

His copies of the logbooks tucked safely into his briefcase,
Bruno headed for the mayor's office in Ste. Alvère. He greeted
the secretary and politely refused her offer of coffee. He
paused at the mayor's door, knowing as he looked down at his
notes and logbooks that he was probably holding the political
future of St. Denis in his hands. He collected himself, looked
once more at his notes and at Alain's statement as he worked
out how to explain the double fraud. He'd start with the tampered vacuum packs and the evidence from the digital
counter, and then he'd explain about the auction ring and
Pons's manipulations. It was an odd way, Bruno reflected, to
spend the time before he had to become Father Christmas.
He knocked, opened the door and went in to greet the ener-
getic and doubtless ambitious young politician, no older than
himself, who ran the affairs of Ste. Alvère.

After the usual handshakes and preliminaries, Bruno
launched in. "Monsieur le Maire," he began. "I've come up
with some troubling information. You're being doubly
cheated. The truffles from your market are being tampered
with after the vacuum packs are sealed. This is the source of
the complaints you've received. Didier, your market manager,
is responsible."

The mayor stood up, his fists clenched. He was wearing a
black turtleneck sweater over black jeans and looked fit.
Bruno recalled seeing him play rugby for his town only a few
years before, and he'd been pretty good. The cigarettes didn't

seem to have slowed him down. "Didier?" the mayor asked. "You sure about this?"

"Here is a copy of a sworn statement from one of the market staff explaining how the sealed packages were reopened." Bruno handed Alain's document across the wide desk. "Alain gave this statement to me voluntarily. I don't think we should try charging him. We're better off having him as a cooperative witness."

"Didier, what a damn fool," said the mayor, scanning Alain's statement. He took a Disque Bleu from the pack on his desk. Bruno thought of the DÉFENSE DE FUMER signs all over every *mairie* in France. But a mayor could make his own rules.

Bruno went on to explain how the town was being cheated out of tens of thousands of euros each month. "The prices paid at the auctions held at the end of the day are much lower than they should be. And it's getting worse. More and more of the truffles, particularly the high-grade ones, are being sold at these special auctions where the town makes very little profit. By my calculation, if these items were sold at the proper price, the town would be at least half a million euros better off."

"*Putain,*" said the mayor, blowing out a stream of smoke. "This could cost me the election. Who else knows of this?"

Bruno decided to ignore the question. When politicians asked who else knew about an embarrassment, it usually meant they were tempted to hush things up. "There is also strong evidence that this final auction is being used to launder cash. The records say that it comes from Boniface Pons, although I can prove that on some occasions he wasn't present when the cash was supposedly paid. As you know, Pons started a truffle plantation that was managed by Didier."

The mayor nodded slowly. Bruno noticed that his healthy pallor had taken on a grayish tinge.

"Since Pons always paid cash this was probably lost on your accountants and may not have come to your attention. I have to recommend that you bring in the Police Nationale at this point. At any rate, I have to report my findings."

"Half a million euros," said the mayor, slumping down into his chair.

24

To Bruno's surprise, all three mayoral candidates awaited him around the Christmas tree in the dining room of the retirement home, the largest indoor hall in St. Denis. Mathilde, the magnificently bosomed former nurse who ran the home, was engaging all three in stilted conversation while elderly ladies scurried back and forth with plates of sandwiches and cakes from the kitchens. They had clearly been baking all week, vying to outdo one another with their *sacristains* and *madeleines, tartes aux noix* and *galettes* for the children. There were bowls of raw baby carrots and tangerine segments, apples in bowls for bobbing and long rows of plastic glasses filled with orange juice and milk. Everything to fill with delight the soul of a healthy five-year-old, thought Bruno, and healthy forty-year-olds as well, even when clad in red velvet and a false white beard.

"Ah, our Father Christmas has arrived," said Mathilde. "You look splendid, Bruno. It is you under all that?"

"Ho, ho, ho, it is indeed, Mathilde," he said, leaning forward to kiss her thickly powdered cheeks and shaking hands with the three men. Pons senior, evidently still smarting from having Bruno's wine poured down the front of his trousers, gave him a cold nod.

"I'm very glad we were able to combine all the parties this way and leave politics out of it," said Bill with a brittle and unconvincing brightness. His features were drawn and strained. He stood to the left of the mayor and his father to the right. Neither one looked at the other or seemed ready to acknowledge his presence in any way. "After all, it's for the children."

"And after that incident with the manure pond, you wouldn't have been allowed to hold it at your place anyway," said the mayor drily.

"You certainly took care of that," said Bill, sourly. He began to speak again, but the mayor interrupted and spoke over him.

"And, Bruno, we have to thank Boniface here for a most generous donation of a thousand euros to buy presents for the children. We just about cleaned out the toy department at the supermarket, and Mathilde's dear ladies here have been wrapping them all day while you were in Bordeaux. How did that go, by the way?"

"I'll give you a full report tomorrow," Bruno said, adjusting the hook that attached the white beard to his ears. Mention of Bordeaux reminded him with a jolt of Isabelle and the ambush at Arcachon later that night. He felt a flash of memory of his own days in the military, the rush of adrenaline before an operation, coming to terms with the fear, mouth dry and unable to eat. And then he remembered the sniper's bullet that caught him in the hip and had spun him bleeding into the snow. He hoped she stayed well behind the Fusiliers Marins, as she'd said she would.

He turned to young Pons. "Bill, I'm having trouble here, could you help with this hook for my beard? It seems to be tangled in my collar." As Pons began fiddling with the hook, standing so close that the scent of his cologne was almost offensively strong, Bruno asked, "Where are your chef's nieces? This party's for all the children."

"They're not well," Pons replied. "Got the flu. Besides, they only speak Chinese."

"Kids learn languages fast, they'll be bilingual by summer. You should have a letter from the *mairie* by now about getting them into school."

"Not much point. They'll be going home to their parents after Christmas. There, that hook should hold now."

Parents? Bruno had read somewhere that China limited families to a single child. The excited sound of childish voices was swelling beyond the double doors that led to the hallway. Mathilde looked at her watch, cast an appraising glance over the array of food and drink and rolled her eyes.

"Brace yourselves, *messieurs,*" she said, heading to open the doors. "The barbarians are at the gate."

The noise grew into a high-pitched roar, the doors opened and the sound redoubled. Wriggling, pushing and squeezing to be first into the hall, the horde erupted into the vast room, which was suddenly filled with shrieking children, heading like so many locusts toward the food on the tables. Anxious mothers followed them in.

"Silence," roared Bruno in his best parade-ground voice. The place was suddenly still.

"Ho, ho, ho, is this any way to greet Father Christmas," he went on in an almost normal voice. "We have to arrange ourselves so I can say hello to everybody properly." He asked all those age six and over please to go to the right of the hall and all the under-sixes to the left. Mothers with babies and toddlers were instructed to keep their children at the back of the hall.

From the corner of his eye, Bruno saw a new figure hurrying through the doors, slipping off her coat. It was Pamela, coming late to volunteer, and heading toward Bill, holding up her cheeks to be kissed. He had no time for that now.

"Alain, Régine, Mireille, Simon, Dominique, Jean-Louis, Philippe and Colette, come over here to me please," he called. He knew them from his tennis classes, and they came forward eagerly. He explained how he wanted them to organize the under-sixes into groups of four and take them to the tables.

"They are allowed one sandwich each, and one of each of the cakes. Otherwise we might run out. If you have a brother or sister among them, pick them first. Off you go."

He heard Simon muttering, "I'm sure that's Bruno" as they left, so he raised his voice again, gave a few more Ho, ho, hos and walked across to the mothers with the toddlers.

"*Mesdames,* I count on you not to let your little ones grab too much or make a mess. Perhaps you would go after the under-sixes have been fed."

Then Bruno turned to the over-sixes, who were almost dancing with impatience, and he told them to go to the CD player and decide which of the Christmas music discs they wanted to hear. He waved Bill over and asked him to supervise the music. The elder Pons had disappeared, and the mayor was being political, kissing the cheeks of each of the venerable ladies who were watching proudly from behind the tables as their cakes and biscuits were eagerly devoured.

"Where are the presents, and when do you want to give them out?" Bruno asked Mathilde.

"I think Monsieur Pons wants to hand out the presents," she said crisply. "That's what he said, and he added very firmly that since he'd paid for them, he was the one to do it."

"Ah," said Bruno. "Well, just so long as he doesn't dress up as Père Nöel to do it. The kids would get awfully confused if they saw two of us."

"You're right," she said. "I'd better go and find out what he's planning."

Bill had gotten the CD player to work. Pamela stood close beside him. Bruno could discern the gentle tones of "Silent Night" being drowned by the low roar of children's voices. Ah well, time for some more Ho, ho, hos, and perhaps a sandwich or two. He headed over to the tables, ruffling the hair on little heads along the way and lifting toddlers for a Christmas kiss until one of them became alarmed and started to bawl. He quickly handed the infant back to a clucking mother and moved on.

"I think these two want a kiss from Père Nöel," said Florence, pushing her children toward him, their cheeks round with food and their mouths smeared with chocolate.

"Happy Christmas, Dora," he said, swinging her up. "And you, Daniel," he said, scooping up the boy with the other arm. He received a smacking kiss from each, and then their mother leaned forward and kissed him on each cheek.

"Merry Christmas to you, Père Nöel, and thanks for everything. You've got a bit of chocolate on your beard." Florence pulled a tiny handkerchief from her sleeve, popped a corner into her mouth to wet it and began to scrub his cheek. He felt himself blushing, convinced that Pamela was watching.

"Ho, ho, ho. Thank you, Florence. I'd better get some food before it all goes."

He had time to devour a ham-and-cheese sandwich, a *madeleine* and a *galette,* and was washing them down with a glass of orange juice when the mayor approached with an urgent look on his face and holding out a mobile phone.

"It's Nicco from Ste. Alvère," he said. "There's been a tragedy and they want you over there."

Bruno took the phone, but couldn't hear. He turned away toward the door to the kitchens, fumbling to unhook his beard from his ear as he tried to make out what Nicco was saying.

"It's Bruno, it's Bruno," called out one of the older children as his beard swung down to one side of his face and Nicco's voice said, "It's Didier—he's dead. He shot himself."

Then the kitchen door swung open and another Father Christmas emerged, flanked by two elves dressed in green and carrying large sacks. Bruno had just begun to register this when Pamela appeared before him, her face tight with anger.

"I'm not going to make a fuss here, but I think you're a bastard."

He stared at her in bafflement, and one of the elves brushed against his arm with a sack of presents, knocking the mobile phone from his hand. He bent down to grope for the phone on the floor. People were turning to look at the appearance of the second Father Christmas as Pons strode majestically to the center of the hall.

"I suppose you didn't know Dominique was doing her Christmas shopping in Bordeaux and saw you and your Isabelle together in your hotel last night," Pamela snapped as his hand found the phone. "She just told me. Well, good luck with your policewoman. But that's it for me."

He had the phone, rose and in one fluid movement took

Pamela firmly by the arm and frog-marched her out bodily through the kitchen door before letting her go in front of three very startled old ladies.

"Listen to me," he said urgently. "I've just been told somebody has killed himself, and I have to get to Ste. Alvère. Second, yes, I was in Bordeaux and Isabelle was there because we were working on the same case. We slept in separate rooms."

"I don't believe you. Dominique saw you huddled together in the bar."

"That's all she saw. I slept alone. Third, I had to get out of that room because there are hundreds of kids who want to believe in Father Christmas, one Father Christmas, not two. I'm sorry I hauled you out here, but that's why. And I'm even more sorry it has to end this way, but I have to go."

"I suppose you'll try and pin all this on Bill as well," she said. "You've been out to get him ever since he challenged that precious mayor of yours. It was you who got his restaurant closed down, and it's all your damn politics, Bruno, and I've had enough."

"Closed his restaurant? When?"

"This morning. A *huissier* came with a court order to close the only hopeful Green place in the region. They even closed the campsite and made people leave. Some made-up claim about water supplies, but I know that you were behind it, you and the damn mayor. You'll do anything to win this election and stay in power."

"This damn mayor had nothing to do with the arrival of the bailiffs, madame," came a voice from behind Bruno. The mayor had slipped into the kitchen. "On my word of honor, Bruno and I weren't responsible for this. I only just heard about it."

An odd time of year to have campers, thought Bruno as he began pulling off his red jacket and red trousers. But he had to get to Ste. Alvère. The old ladies were rapt with attention, as if this scene was almost worth growing old for.

"Damn the pair of you," Pamela said, and turned to walk past them. "You might as well be one person, the two of you. Your harassment of Bill has been unforgivable."

The kitchen door swung closed behind her. The mayor came up and put a hand on Bruno's shoulder.

"I'm sorry," he said. "She'll calm down. But what's happened in Ste. Alvère?"

"That investigation you asked me to make into the truffle market," Bruno said, taking off his false beard. He turned to the kitchen tap and splashed cold water onto his face and looked in the mirror. He was still wearing the Father Christmas hat. He pulled it off and turned back. "I gave their mayor my report this afternoon. It was the market manager, stealing them blind, and I advised him to call in the Police Nationale. Now the manager's killed himself, and they want me over there."

"You did not hear that, *mesdames*," the mayor said to the old ladies. "This is police business."

"That means it will be all over town within the hour," said Bruno, steering the mayor out of the kitchen to the bathroom where he had left his clothes. "There's something else you need to know. It looks as if Boniface Pons is up to his neck in this truffle business."

"It wouldn't surprise me," said the mayor. "I've always seen him as a bit of a crook, ever since he came back from Algeria with enough money to build his new sawmill. How's he involved?"

"Money laundering, hundreds of thousands in cash, and

making some special auction arrangement with the manager, who used to work for him."

"Do you think he will be charged?"

"Probably. Certainly he'll be hauled in and questioned, and the tax people will be all over him about the cash. But without Didier to testify, he might be able to squirm out of it for lack of evidence."

"Will the scandal break before the election?"

"Now you sound like the politician Pamela accuses us both of being," said Bruno.

"Like life itself, politics goes on," the mayor replied. "I thought I'd taught you that."

Bruno paused and looked at the mayor somberly, thinking of the mixture of admiration and affection that he felt, with a thread of cynicism running through it. "You taught me every-thing else," he said, already at the door that led out to the parking lot. "I have to go."

"And I have to stay, and make a speech of thanks to Pons. That's politics, too."

Bruno put his head around the door. "The new science teacher at the college, her name's Florence and she has two toddlers. I brought her over from Ste. Alvère but she'll need a ride back."

"Is she the blonde who was wiping chocolate off your face?"

"That's her."

"Consider it done. If she's moving here she's a new voter, so I'll drive her myself."

"She might represent a vote for the other side. She's teach-ing environmental science, so I guess she's a Green."

"So am I," said the mayor. "When I have to be."

25

Didier was sprawled on the floor behind his desk, his legs still entangled in the chair. Inspecteur Jofflin from Bergerac was bending over the body. He squinted at the inside of the ring he had removed from Didier's hand. "Didier—Annette" was engraved upon it.

"Is that a Rolex he's wearing?" Bruno asked. "They cost a fortune."

"Rolex Oyster Perpetual," said Jofflin. "About five thousand euros. And his name's engraved on the back."

"The bastard," said the mayor of Ste. Alvère, his eyes squinting against the smoke from the Disque Bleu hanging from his lip. "That was the town's money."

"He left no note?" asked Bruno.

Jofflin went to the desk and handed him a piece of notepaper inside a plastic bag. "Just this."

Bruno glanced at the three words, and read them out: *"Je regrette tout."* The mayor snorted.

"And these were in the wastebasket." Jofflin pointed to a not-yet-crumbled mass of burned paper inside another evidence bag. It looked as if it had been glossy. "I think they were photos. Maybe the forensics boys can get something from them. They're on their way."

"Has his wife been told?" Bruno asked.

"My wife is with her," said the mayor. "She knows."

"About the fraud?" Bruno asked. He felt a great weight of responsibility creeping over him.

"Not yet," said the mayor. "Just the suicide."

"The mayor showed me your findings," said Jofflin. "Would that be enough to make him blow his head off?"

"He'd have been going to prison," said the mayor, about to stub out his cigarette in the wastebasket. Jofflin put out an arm to stop him, took the stub from the mayor's fingers, opened the window and tossed it outside.

"Mustn't pollute a crime scene, sir," Jofflin said with a polite smile. This young man would go far, thought Bruno.

"Sorry," said the mayor, lighting another cigarette. "I wasn't thinking. But yes, we'd have made sure he went to prison, and I made that clear when I spoke to him. I called him in soon after you left, Bruno, once I'd looked at the log-books and verified the notes you gave me. I kept Nicco here as a witness."

"It was Alain's statement that got to him," Nicco said. "He broke down, said he'd been waiting for this to happen and was very sorry. I took some notes because it sounded to me like a confession. Then he said something about being under a lot of pressure and wanting to call a lawyer. We let him go, and about ten minutes later we heard the shot. I'm pretty sure I recognize it as Didier's shotgun, a Manufrance."

"It seems strange that he would have kept it in his office," Bruno said. "And the ammo as well."

"Probably kept it locked in the trunk of his car," said Nicco. "A lot of people do."

"Have you searched his car, and the desk?" Bruno asked, as the front bell sounded and a SUV could be heard pulling up outside.

"We'll leave that for the forensics team. That's probably them now," said Jofflin.

But it was Bruno's boss, the mayor of St. Denis, coming to offer condolences and ask for a word with Bruno. Behind him the forensics team began to clamber out of their vehicle.

"I'd better take a statement from each of you, but I'd rather not do it here," said Jofflin.

"We can use my office," said the mayor of Ste. Alvère, crumpling an empty cigarette packet and casting a last glance at Didier's body. "I've got some more smokes in there."

"Our new science teacher and her children are home safe and sound, but she gave me a real interrogation about you and Pamela on the way back," Mayor Mangin said as they stood in the corridor, waiting for Bruno to make his statement. "I barely had the chance to ask for her vote."

"And what did you tell her?" Bruno asked.

"I explained that you had a broken heart. Women like that sort of thing. But the real reason I wanted a word was to give you my phone. J-J called me, very frustrated because you had to hand your phone to the brigadier, and so J-J can't reach you. He says mine will be safe enough and says to tell you that the operation will go ahead tonight."

"Thank you, I'll take care of it," Bruno replied, taking the phone. "What did you say about my broken heart?"

"What everybody in town knows, that you were in love with Isabelle, and she wanted you to join her in Paris, but to our great relief you insisted on staying in St. Denis. And then along came Pamela and caught you on the rebound, but that was never going to work."

"Why is that?" Bruno asked, intrigued to hear this view of his love life. "Because she's British?"

"Not at all. They make excellent lovers because they always think we Frenchmen are a little exotic. Of course, our own womenfolk know better," said the mayor. "It's because Pamela told Fabiola she didn't want children and didn't want to settle down. One look at you teaching the kids to play tennis is all it takes to see you want kids of your own."

"And you told all this to Florence, with her children all ears in the back of your car?" Bruno did not know whether to be amused or furious. He felt both.

"Well, not in so many words," the mayor replied.

"So having realized that she was too Green to vote for you as a politician, you decided to win her sympathy by explaining what a sensitive and thoughtful soul you are and get her vote that way."

"Now you're sounding like Pamela, not that she isn't a very sound woman in many ways. In fact, if I win the next election I'll bring her into the council somehow, probably as liaison with the foreigners."

Nicco emerged from the thick oak door and pointed his thumb back into the room. "Your turn," he said to Bruno.

"Just one thing, Nicco. Is Gaby Duchot still the bailiff around here?"

"That's right, he's been the *huissier* for everybody since his old man died. Still lives above the office in the old house on the road to Lalinde. Anything I can help with?"

"While I'm giving my statement, can you find out whether

he was the one who served the closure notice on L'Auberge des Verts this morning?"

"I'd be surprised if it wasn't him, but I'll check for you."

Bruno's statement took fifteen minutes to complete, and when he left the room Nicco was waiting for him, to confirm that it had been Duchot who served the closure notice on Bill's restaurant. Bruno used Nicco's phone to call the *huissier* and ask the question that had been nagging at him since the children's party.

"Sorry to bother you at home, Gaby, but it's about L'Auberge des Verts, where you served the closure today. Somebody said you also had to close a camping site and move some campers off. Is that right?"

"Not really a camping site, Bruno, more a trailer park. There were four campers there, the kind you can sleep in. And yes, we had to tell them to go elsewhere. In fact one of them asked me where he could fill up with diesel. I showed him the way to Lespinasse's garage."

"You wouldn't have made a note of the license plates, would you?"

"Sorry, no. But if they filled up at Lespinasse's place, he'll have a note of their credit card. And since that break-in he's got one of those security cameras. That would have the numbers."

"Thanks, Gaby. By the way, were they foreign?"

"Yes, Asian, maybe Chinese. All four drivers."

"Did they seem to know the owner, Guillaume Pons?"

"Oh yes, but the guy they were really talking with was a tall Chinese who said he was the cook. He was the one who was angry with me. At one point I thought he was coming for me with that big cleaver of his. The French owner—he said to call him Bill—he calmed the cook down once I'd explained about the water department."

"I'm glad it ended quietly, Gaby, and thanks again."

Bruno rang off, his mind racing. Trailers and Chinese parked in a place within two hours of Arcachon where they'd attract no suspicion, and Pons had Chinese connections and a Chinese cook. He told himself to slow down and cover all the details. He gave Nicco back his phone and used the mayor's mobile to ring Lespinasse at home. He reached his son.

"*Salut,* Edouard, it's Bruno. That was a quite a game you played the other day."

"Not too bad yourself, old man. What's up?"

"Those campers that filled up at your place today, did they pay by credit card?"

"Part of the bill; they had to. Didn't have enough cash, not for all four campers. They weren't happy about it."

"And the card went through all right?"

"Sure."

"And were your security cameras working?"

"As far as I know. Want me to spool them back and get the license plates on all eight campers?"

"Eight? I thought there were four."

"Four came first, then four more came down the back road behind the cemetery and joined them."

"The back road? There's nothing up there except a couple of old barns and that cave the tourists go to, but it's closed this time of year."

"Right. I assumed they just spent the night at a quiet place where they wouldn't be disturbed and where they wouldn't have to pay parking fees."

"Did you see where they were heading?"

"They took the road to Périgueux. That would get them onto the autoroute for Bordeaux or Brive and then up to Paris."

"Could you check the film and get me the numbers of the campers and the credit card, and I'll call you back."

"I can give you one registration number now—I always write it down on the credit card slip, and I've brought all the slips back home to enter them in the books. Hang on. . . . Here you are." He read the number out, and Bruno scribbled it down. The license plate ended in 59—that meant it came from Lille.

"Thanks a lot. There's no hurry on the other plates from the security film, but if you could get them for me tomorrow, that would be great. I'll just read the numbers back to check."

Bruno's next call was to J-J, to give him the numbers, but as soon as he answered J-J said, "Monsieur le Maire?"

"No, it's Bruno."

"You're supposed to be under arrest. I warned Jofflin about you and told him to give you a hard time. Stealing the mayor's phone now?"

"Stop it, J-J, I've got something important. Remember those campers we saw at the Chinese place in Bordeaux? I've just had eight more of them here in St. Denis, Chinese drivers and a Lille license plate."

"You have the number?"

"Yes, and better still, I've got the credit card they used to buy diesel."

"Let's have it. We might be able to roll up the whole operation with this, maybe even some of the big boys of the *treizième*."

"What time are you going in?"

"That's up to them. The air force has the ship on radar

closing in on the coast. We've got the roads sealed from the campsite and a couple of patrol boats and choppers ready to take the ship. We'll wait till they bring all the bodies ashore, catch them in the act."

"Where are you now?"

"In the operations room at Mérignac. The brigadier sends his regards, says he has that fancy new phone for you."

"Where's Isabelle?"

"With the assault team at Arcachon. Don't worry, they're wearing flak vests."

"One more thing, the place the campers stayed is called L'Auberge des Verts in St. Denis. It's owned by Guillaume Pons, who just came back home with a sackful of money he made in China. He moved all over Asia, and he's got a big, tough-looking Chinese, Minxin, who he calls his chef."

"The Chinese connection?"

"Exactly. Could you tell the brigadier about this and ask him to check if anything is known about Guillaume Pons, calls himself Bill. The Brits might have something on him from Hong Kong. I remember he told us he'd been a cognac salesman in Shanghai, sold wine in Vientiane, taught French in Bangkok and then worked in a casino in Macau—"

"Hold on, I'm writing this down," J-J interrupted. "Casino in Macau, that sounds interesting."

"I think he was a croupier. Put all that together, and the brigadier should be able to get something from his own networks. Maybe our Corsican friend Savani knows about him."

"Right, I've got all that. Hang on, the brigadier wants a word."

Bruno waited no more than a couple of heartbeats, and the familiar gruff voice came onto the line. As always, he got straight to the point, no small talk.

"This Pons guy, how old is he?"

"Mid- to late thirties, I'd say. Looks a bit younger."

"What about his father?"

"Boniface Pons, at least seventy, a big local businessman, involved in timber, sawmills, truffles. We're onto him for money laundering at the local truffle market, hundreds of thousands of euros. Not much liked locally, and he's said to have been a wife beater. He and his son hate each other. They had a public fight not long ago. Oh yes, and he's an ex-soldier, Algeria."

"Boniface Pons," said the brigadier, as though thinking aloud. "So that's what happened to him."

"Did you know him?"

"I knew of him. Dirty work in Algeria. That's for tomorrow, when we get tonight's business finished. Thanks as always, Bruno."

26

J-J's call woke Bruno just after five in the morning. He felt as if he had not slept long, lying awake and thinking about Isabelle waiting in the sand dunes by the Arcachon campsite as a darkened ship crept close to shore.

"It's over, we got them, but there's some bad news," J-J said.

"Isabelle? What happened?" He shot up in bed, his heart pounding. He closed his eyes.

"She's been wounded. She took two on the bulletproof vest and one high on the leg. It's a bad wound but she'll recover. She's in the operating room now at the *hôpital militaire*. We had a medevac chopper on hand, thanks to the brigadier."

"Have you seen her?" His voice sounded thick and slurred.

"I saw her loaded into the chopper. She'll be okay, Bruno. The brigadier spoke to the chief surgeon."

"Anyone else hurt?"

"Just the bad guys. Isabelle got one of them when they opened up with AK-47s, and the marines got three more. But it's all under control. We've got the ship, the campers, the site, and we're still counting the migrants. It was over two hundred last I heard. No kids, but some of them look pretty young."

"Do you know if the bullet hit the bone? Can I see her?"

"I don't see why not. It hit her high on the leg, close to the hip, but it didn't get the joint. That's all I know. And she lost a lot of blood. They were giving her transfusions as they loaded her into the chopper. She'll still be under anesthetic for a while. Maybe better to wait till the afternoon. I think the hospital's called Robert Piquet, or was that the old one? I'll get you the address and see you there about three. The brigadier wants to see you first."

"Any idea why?"

"That Guillaume Pons you were asking about, we just arrested him at the campsite. He was the only non-Asian there except for a couple dozen Iraqis and Afghanis who were paying their way. And there's a lot about him in the brigadier's files. He may have started as a croupier in Macau, but he rose fast. He took a bullet in the shoulder, and he's probably going to lose an arm."

"Is he in the same hospital as Isabelle?" Bruno was surprised that Pons had been at the scene. He'd have thought Pons either too important to the organization to risk his presence at the landing of the illegals, or too peripheral to be so deeply involved. If he hadn't been at the scene, the only count against him was allowing the campers to stay on his premises. He wouldn't even have been charged.

"He's in a prison hospital," said J-J. "He was armed and shooting back. He'll be going down for a long time."

"What was he armed with?" It was hard to imagine Pons with a weapon.

"A cheap handgun. A Norinco nine millimeter, Chinese

military issue. You find them all over Asia, they tell me. More and more of them here in Europe."

"What happens now?"

"The brigadier says it's time to play peacemaker between the *treizième* and the Vietnamese. Now that he's rolled up this operation, he reckons he's dealing from strength, and the *treizième* is on the defensive, so it's time for the truce meeting. And that credit card you gave us—it's leading right back to the big boys. There's a whole network of connected accounts, and we've frozen all of them."

Bruno hung up and lay back on the tangled sheets, thinking of Isabelle and her wound and the fascination with which she had explored his own scar in this very bed, tracing it with her fingers. And now her perfect body would carry its own mark of violence received. Would she be as lithe, as skilled and fast at her karate, after her release from the hospital? Would she feel the dampness and the coming of winter somewhere deep in the wound, as Bruno did?

Why did it matter so much to him? Their affair was over, the weeks of magic she had brought to his life would never return. But why had he not taken his chance for a final night with her in Bordeaux, to follow her into the elevator and down the hall to her room and into the welcoming darkness where the only light would be from the whiteness of her body and the sparkle of her eyes?

He turned onto his side. He had to try to stop thinking about her. It was finished. He had to find some way to repair his relationship with Pamela. But he'd have to start by explaining that Pons had been shot and arrested. Surely she couldn't still take Pons's side after that, even though she'd blamed him and the mayor for the closure of the Auberge. Even if she admits that she's been wrong about Pons, she'll feel like a fool, which probably means she'll resent me, Bruno thought. He'd probably lost her already. And when she learned that Pons would probably lose an arm, she might even blame Bruno. At least her political career wasn't over, if the mayor went ahead and brought her onto the council. And now there was no chance of his losing the election.

This time it was the siren that woke him, the rising and falling whine from the roof of the *mairie* that always made him think of war and invasion. He sat up in bed. At this hour, it had to be a fire. He fumbled for the light switch, knocking over the book he'd been reading, and looked for the phone. It was on the chair, recharging. He was about to hit the familiar single number for the *pompiers* but remembered it was the mayor's phone. He scrolled through the directory and found it under *P*.

"It's Bruno. Where's the fire?"

"I just tried to call you but there was no answer. It's Ahmed here."

"I'm on another number. Where is it?"

"That new restaurant out on the road to Les Eyzies, L'Auberge des Verts, and it sounds like a big one. We've got everything out there, and all of the engines from Les Eyzies and Le Bugue as well. Albert's in charge and he's been asking where you were."

"Tell him I'm on my way."

He washed his face and neck, brushed his teeth and dressed quickly. He swigged at a bottle of milk and remembered to pocket the phone. He fed his dog and his chickens and grabbed the remnant of an old baguette and a hunk of Stéphane's Tomme d'Audrix and raced for the Land Rover. There would be a bottle of water in the car, and knowing

Albert, he'd have arranged to have coffee available at the fire.

So the Vietnamese had taken their revenge. He had no doubt that this fire was deliberate. Tran might have been oblique, but his message had been clear: the Vietnamese would have to fight back. How they had identified Bill as an enemy was beyond Bruno. Perhaps they had followed the campers from Lille and seen them seek safe harbor at Bill's Auberge. Perhaps they were tapping phones as well. It wouldn't surprise him. A big fire, Ahmed had said. That probably meant that more than just the main building had been hit. Christ, those Chinese girls were living there. He pressed the accelerator against the floor. An old Land Rover would take him anywhere, but it wasn't built for speed.

He raced through St. Denis, chewing stale bread and cheese, noting all the lights on in the gendarmerie and in the medical center. They'd have been alerted by the siren. There was probably not much need for him to be there, if he were honest. But he had standing instructions at the fire station to call him for every fire in the commune. This was his town and his responsibility. The townsfolk had to know that he'd always be there.

Once past the railway crossing and the bend over the bridge, Bruno could see the red glow up on the ridge against the cold night sky. He dropped a gear, raced into the turn onto the side road and powered up the hill to the pretentious stone pillars that Pons had erected. As he slowed to enter the big compound, he could see three separate fires raging—one in the Auberge itself and two in the outer buildings. As he watched, the glass of the solar panels cracked in a series of small explosions that sounded almost like gunfire. The roof of the restaurant crumpled and fell, and one of the windmills beside it began to topple slowly onto its side. He parked out of the way of the fire engines, went looking for Albert and found him shouting into a mobile phone.

"I don't care if the silly bastards turned the water off because of a court order. I need it back on again now. We're running out of water here, and I've got three fires." He waved to acknowledge Bruno's presence. "At least can you tell me where it was turned off so I can get it back on again? You don't know? *Putain de merde,* how am I supposed to fight this fire?"

Albert slammed his phone into his pocket and shouted, "Fabien, get over here." One of his men came running. "Take my van and head up to the water tower and see if it's turned off there. If so turn it on. If not, then follow the line and check every valve. If you see a water department seal, ignore it and turn it back on. Understood?"

"Where are the children?" Bruno asked.

"What children?"

"Two young Chinese girls, nieces of the cook."

"The main building was empty, and we got four adults out of the staff building. Nobody said anything about children. Where would they sleep? *Merde,* we were told that third building was empty. Let's go. *Merde en croûte,* Fabien has my van."

"We'll take my car," said Bruno, and they raced back to the Land Rover, pulling out just as a huge new fire engine heaved through the stone gates. Albert climbed half out of the Land Rover, waving at the new arrival and shouting, "Follow me."

Bruno raced around knots of firemen shifting hoses from their engines to their water tenders. Unless Fabien found the right valve, there would be no more water once the tenders were empty. He went past the staff house, fire now leaping om every window, and on to the farthest building, trying to remember where the manure pool had been so he could avoid it. In his mirror, he could see the fire engine following him, heaving over the bumps in the ground, its headlights half blinding him in the mirror as they rose and fell with the terrain. He pushed the mirror to one side and concentrated on the ground ahead.

"Where's that damn ambulance?" Albert was shouting into his phone. "I want it at the farthest building. That's where you'll find me, with the engine from Les Eyzies that's just arrived. And send any more new arrivals to the same place. There may be kids in there."

Bruno recognized the far building as the one where he had peered into the window and seen the curiously old-fashioned furniture. The fire was concentrated at the front, and the west side and the roof had yet to catch. He swung the Land Rover around to the eastern side of the building and parked, leaving the engine running. There was movement at an upper window, and he pointed it out to Albert. Bruno darted across to the side of the engine from Les Eyzies and clambered up to the locker where they kept the protective gear, at least they did if it was the familiar model from St. Denis.

"Hey, what d'you think you're doing?" came a shout as Bruno jumped down with a protective jacket and helmet in his hand. He ignored it, scrambled into the jacket, put the helmet on and grabbed a hand ax from its bracket on the door. Albert was already breaking into the rear door with his crowbar as Bruno arrived. Bruno breathed deeply, fighting down the old fear that fire provoked ever since it had first reached out to hurt him. The scar on his arm seemed to prickle in anticipation as he remembered the burning armored car on the airfield at Sarajevo and the sound of soldiers screaming inside as he fought to widen the flaming door and pull them out. Grimly, he used his ax to make another hole for more leverage for Albert, and between them they hauled the door open.

Albert eyed him doubtfully and pulled a scarf from his pocket. "Tie this around your face. It's fire retardant." He pulled down his own protective mask. He plucked a flashlight from the Velcro on the chest of his jacket and led the way into the smoke. The bright yellow of his jacket seemed to disappear at once. Bruno could follow him only by the swirls Albert's movement left in the smoke.

The flashlight was almost useless, but at least it picked out the first of the stairs. Albert leaned down to touch them and shouted, "Not too hot, but it could catch anytime. You look around the ground floor, I'll get the ladder to that upper window." He handed his flashlight to Bruno and retraced his steps to the door.

The first two ground-floor rooms were empty, and the third had a door so hot that Bruno did not dare open it. He went back to the stairs and began to climb slowly, controlling the threads of panic that seemed to run like electricity from the scar on his arm into his brain by counting and testing the heat of each tread.

He reached a landing where the wall was hot, but the stairs then turned away from it and seemed cooler. He climbed on, and the smoke was thinner. His flashlight picked out two doors straight ahead, neither of them warm. He opened the first, and smoke seemed to be pouring from the ceiling. He clamped his mouth shut against the smoke and the fear, but the room seemed unoccupied. He stubbed his foot against a bed, felt along its empty length and turned back to the other door.

Something was blocking it. He used his ax to lever the

door open. His brain was shrieking at him to run, to leave, to save himself in flight. He knelt down to feel the blockage. It was a piece of rolled-up cloth that he was able to tug away. More smoke was coming from the ceiling, and Bruno knew he had better be fast. He couldn't breathe in this much longer. He felt himself going dizzy, and his self-control was ebbing.

The screams had kept him going in Sarajevo, an appeal for help from men he knew whose flesh was burning that had made him plunge again and again into the flames to haul them out. But there were no screams here. They're dead already, a part of his brain was insisting. It's wasted effort. They're corpses. The smoke got them. They suffocated. Get out and save yourself.

Bruno fought the fear and made himself think of water. Cool water. He was swimming, swimming in the river with Isabelle. No, it was colder than that, he told himself. It was snowing. He was in the mountains, and the snow was all around.

He groped along the wall and reached a bed, and then his hand met a very thin leg. He felt along the length of the unconscious child, picked up the limp body and staggered to the window. Holding the child against his chest with his left arm, he used his right to break the window open with his ax, almost tripping as his feet encountered another body crumpled beneath the window. He leaned out and gulped at the clean night air.

"This way," he shouted as the ladder swerved toward him from the adjoining window. A fireman began clambering up as Bruno stuffed his ax into a pocket and held out the child in his arms. Smoke billowed thickly around him.

"There's another child," Bruno shouted down to Albert, standing by the controls of the ladder.

The first fireman took the child from Bruno's arms and handed the small figure down to a second man who had clambered up below him. Bruno pulled his head and body back into the thickening smoke and held his breath as he hauled up the second child at his feet and passed it through the window.

"Get out now," Albert was shouting, and Bruno leaned out to grab the ladder with his right hand. He hauled a leg over the windowsill and then felt his ax tumble from his pocket, and he gripped the ladder tightly as he sensed it begin to swivel away from the window, and the room seemed to explode behind him. Hugging the metal step with both arms, his legs swaying in the breeze, Bruno felt a scalding heat on the back of his legs, and a great rush of flame roared past him into the night.

"You damn fool," Albert was saying from a great distance. "I told you to stay on the ground floor."

There was white foam all over him, and then a familiar face was looking into his eyes. It was Fabiola, pulling open his jacket to put a stethoscope against his heart.

"The kids will be all right, Bruno," he heard her say. "You got them out in time."

27

Fabiola stood beside him with a glass of milk, saying it would soothe his throat and nourish him. He felt his chest burn with every breath. He was in a strange bed, lying on his back, but he could see his feet. Both his legs were suspended in the air, a light gauze dressing on them. Dr. Gelletreau was at the foot of the bed, looking up from a chart to smile at him. Fabiola raised her head and eased a straw into his mouth. Bruno drank, realizing with relief that he was at the medical center in St. Denis. If he'd been badly hurt, they'd have moved him to the big hospital in Périgueux.

"You're a lucky man," Gelletreau said. "Mainly second-degree burns, including some bad ones on the back of your calves. The smoke inhalation doesn't seem too bad. A few days rest and you'll be fine."

"I have to be in Bordeaux at three this afternoon," Bruno said.

"Too late," Gelletreau said. "It's almost three already."

Bruno looked out the window. It was bright daylight, and he could see the sun on the stone of the *mairie* across the river.

"Don't worry," said Fabiola. "J-J knows all about it. Everything is taken care of."

"The Chinese girls?" he asked. His voice sounded hoarse and it hurt to talk.

"A boy and a girl," Fabiola said, but her face was grim. "They'll be okay."

"A boy? I'm sure I saw two girls when we were there."

"You did. We both did. One of the girls didn't make it."

"Did I leave her in the room?" he asked, dreading the answer.

"No, she was in the front of the house. She'd have been dead before you arrived. You saved what there was to save, but Albert says he's never letting you near a fire again."

"Fine with me," Bruno said, waving away the milk and sinking back onto the bed.

"There's something else," Fabiola said. "Those Chinese children, when I examined them, they'd been abused, sexually abused, not once but repeatedly and over a considerable time. We're waiting for a Chinese translator and a child psychiatrist to try and find out what happened to them."

Bruno closed his eyes. That meant they can't have been Minxin's nieces. If only he'd gotten the children registered and into school he might have prevented all this. He'd been meaning to do that ever since he saw the girls at the restaurant.

"The girl who died," Fabiola went on. "She wasn't alone. There was a big adult male with her. They died in bed together from the smoke."

"Do we know who he was?"

"They're checking the teeth with local dentists. It's the only way he'll be identified."

Arson and a double murder, thought Bruno. The Vietnamese were in trouble. He hoped Tran and Bao Le had not been part of it.

"You've got some visitors," Gelletreau said. "I think you're well enough to see them."

Fabiola opened the door and the mayor came in, then stood to one side and held the door wide open. A camera flashed from the outer room. Philippe Delaron again, thought Bruno wearily; he's making a living out of me.

"Look at these, Bruno," said the mayor, coming to the bed and leafing through some prints. "By the way, I fed your chickens and dog and gave him a walk. In fact he's in the back of my car."

He thrust one of the photos close to Bruno's face. It showed him leaning out of the window, handing one of the children to a waiting fireman while fires leaped from a lower window. There was another, with Bruno swinging on the firemen's ladder and silhouetted against a ball of flame erupting from the room behind him.

"Tomorrow's front page, and Philippe says he's also sold them to *Paris Match*. That's why he wanted the picture of you in the hospital, to round out the story."

"Did you know that young Pons has been arrested?" Bruno said.

"J-J called to tell me. That means I win the election, as Pamela might say. She's waiting outside, wants to know if you'd like to see her."

Of course he wanted to see her. "Does she know about Pons?"

"I just told her."

"How did she take it?"

The mayor shrugged as only a Frenchman can, a gesture

that carried with it all the weight of the world's imponderables and prime among them the glorious mystery of women.

"Have you heard anything from J-J about Isabelle? You know she was shot?"

"J-J said to tell you she's fine."

"What have you heard about the bodies they found at the fire?" Bruno asked.

"No identification as yet. There's a young *inspecteur* from Bergerac waiting to see you who wants to talk about that, when you're ready."

"That'll be Jofflin. Bring him in first, there's things that have to be cleared up."

Jofflin too came into the room brandishing some photos, but his were gray and fuzzy.

"The forensics people used infrared and then computer enhancement on those charred prints in Didier's wastebasket. This is what they got. I think he was being blackmailed."

Bruno tried with little success to control the revulsion he felt at the images of Didier with a naked young Chinese boy. It somehow made it worse that Didier had kept his socks on. Bruno looked more closely at the chaise longue on which Didier was lying.

"I think I recognize the furniture from Pons's Auberge, the house where the children were." He felt sick. If only he'd pressed the issue sooner about getting the kids into school, this would never have happened. He hadn't even known there was a boy as well as the nieces.

"There's no doubt it's the same Chinese boy as the one here, the one you pulled out of the house," Jofflin said.

Bruno handed the photos to the mayor. "A hell of a cop I am. Didn't even know someone was running a pedophile brothel in my backyard. That's another crime we'll be charging young Pons with, and to think he might have been your successor."

"I tried to call his father, to let him know his son was arrested and in the hospital, but I haven't tracked him down yet," said the mayor. "I know they were badly estranged, but still, a son is a son. The tie of blood is strong."

Bruno nodded, feeling very tired, and wondering just what Pons might feel. He turned to Jofflin. "Do you have enough to arrest Boniface Pons for the truffle fraud?"

"More than enough," the young *inspecteur* replied. "We've already been in touch with the tax authorities about the money laundering. He's not at home, not in the new office he set up in St. Félix, not answering his phones. I was going to ask you where that plantation of his was, we might find him there."

"It's on that back road behind the cemetery," said the mayor. "The one that leads down past the Lespinasse garage."

"Of course," said Bruno, suddenly making the one connection that threw everything in a different light. "I've been a fool. They conned us all, the two of them."

He tried to sit up, but his legs were immobilized.

"Get my feet out of these damn straps and bring one of those doctors in here. I've got work to do."

The mayor protested, but Jofflin unhooked Bruno's ankles from the supporting straps and helped Bruno to his feet.

"Pass me those trousers on the chair," he said, clinging to the bedpost as he sat gingerly, his burned legs stretched out before him.

Jofflin held up the trousers with a smile. They were in tatters. Another new uniform to go on his expense account, thought Bruno.

"Pass them over and hand me those scissors on the

counter." He snipped off the legs and was left with a pair of serviceable shorts. Jofflin helped him ease them over the gauze bandages, looked in the closet and held out the shirt and jacket that were hanging there. They stank of smoke and were still smeared with foam, but they would do. There were no socks, but Bruno jammed his feet into his boots and stood, swaying as the dizziness hit him, just as Fabiola reentered the room.

"You're mad," she said. "You're in no condition to be up."

The faces of Pamela and the baron peered around the door, and in the distance Bruno could hear the clattering sound of a helicopter. He tore his eyes away from Pamela's worried face.

"Which dentist did Boniface Pons use?" he asked the mayor, who shook his head.

"Same one as me," said the baron from the door. "Piguin in Siorac; I've met Pons in the waiting room there."

"Get Piguin to look at the teeth of that corpse in the Auberge," Bruno said to Jofflin. "I'll bet you a fortune it's old Pons."

"Are you going to lie down?" Fabiola asked harshly.

"No. I'm going with the *inspecteur* here to Pons's place. All the answers will be there."

"You're going nowhere," Fabiola snapped. "Get back into bed."

"It struck me when you reminded me about Pons's planta-tion," he said to the mayor, but sitting back on the bed. "That's where some of the campers were parked overnight before heading on to Arcachon, where Pons's son was direct-ing the landing of a shipload of illegal immigrants. They fooled us into thinking that they were estranged, but the two of them were in league all along. They were in it together, father and son, the truffles and the Chinese market, the alliance with the Chinese, the pedophile brothel and above all the election."

"But they were opposing each other in the election," the mayor objected.

"No, they weren't," said Bruno, remembering that book on British intelligence that had been on Hercule's desk, the passage about a British agent becoming mayor of some small village in order to issue ID cards and ration books for other agents.

"Old Pons was only running to take enough votes from you so that he'd get his son elected. And guess why? Who issues identity cards and birth and marriage certificates? You do, at the *mairie*. What better place to give a bunch of illegal immigrants good French identity papers than a *mairie* under your own control?"

"But what about that fight over closing the sawmill?" the mayor said, speaking loudly above the sound of the helicopter. It sounded as if it were almost overhead.

"That was how they conned us, don't you see?" Bruno replied. "Pons wasn't going to lose a damn thing by it. He already had another sawmill site lined up, and he told me and the baron about his plans to develop the sawmill site here in St. Denis for housing. With his son in the *mairie* granting development approval, he'd have made a fortune."

"And on top of all that, the son was providing little Chinese girls," said Jofflin. "And little boys to blackmail Didier with at the truffle market." Jofflin was thumbing through a notebook, found the page he wanted and looked up. "Piguin in Siorac is on the list of the dentists we're checking for the teeth. By the way, we found this in Boniface Pons's Mercedes. It seems like some sort of local diary."

"Give me some gloves," Bruno said. The mayor handed him a pair of medical gloves from a box on a side table. Bruno slipped them on, took the bag from Jofflin and pulled out what he was sure would be Hercule's truffle journal. There was no name on the inside cover, but the first page was dated December 1982, and it began: "Three fine *brumales* from the oak behind the hunters' hide just off the Vergt road, total weight 340 grams."

Bruno turned to the last entry, stopping when he saw one of Hercule's tidy sketches. A lump came into his throat when there was one of Gigi, front paw and tail raised, nose high and sniffing, his eyes fixed on something off the page. There was a gentle caricature of the baron and an account of the wines the three of them had shared at dinner. Beneath that was evidence of a new technology, a GPS reference for a site deep in the woods where Hercule had found truffles. The last entry listed the sale that Bruno had made in Ste. Alvère and a final phrase, "If anyone can get to the bottom of this fraud, it will be Bruno."

"This is it," said Bruno. "Hercule's journal, the one he left to me in his will."

"What was it doing in Pons's car?" the mayor asked.

Bruno could hardly hear him for the sound of the helicopter landing on the sports field behind the medical center. He looked out the window as the noise of the engines died, and J-J and the brigadier emerged, stooping under the slowing rotor blades.

"By being in Pons's car, it provides the evidence we need that Pons was connected to Hercule's murder," Bruno said. "That's why I have to get to Pons's house. More evidence will be there. There'll be a will, with his son as beneficiary. There'll be paperwork on the truffles trade, and I'll bet the cash he used at the truffle market came from his Chinese friends. But what I'm really looking for . . ." Bruno broke off as J-J and the brigadier eased past the baron and Pamela at the door and came into the room.

"What I'm really looking for," Bruno repeated, "is evidence that Pons was directly responsible for the murder of Hercule."

"I think I can help you there. We've established a motive," said the brigadier. "But should you be up and about?"

"No, he shouldn't," said Fabiola. "But you try stopping him."

"What's the motive?" Bruno asked.

"Clear the room, J-J," the brigadier said, and stood silent at the foot of the bed while J-J escorted Fabiola, Jofflin and the others into the hallway outside. He closed the door and leaned against it. The brigadier turned to check the room and nodded his thanks.

"It's Hercule's memoirs, from the safety-deposit box," he began. "Hercule incriminates Pons not just as a torturer in the Algerian War, but as a crook. Hercule says it all happened at a detention camp called Ameziane, and it was hushed up at the time. He says Pons took bribes from their families to ease up on the torture. He claims Pons would specialize in rounding up children, and then taking money to free them after he'd had his fun with them."

"Why did he leave it so long to make this public?" From the back of his mind, Bruno recalled the baron talking of Pons coming back from Algeria with enough money to build a new sawmill. Now he knew where the cash had come from.

"The typescript was in a sealed envelope in the safety-deposit box, addressed to his *notaire* and marked not to be opened until after his death. The manuscript wasn't complete," the brigadier said. "There were rumors among the old *barbouzes* that Hercule was up to something like this. He'd been asking questions of some old comrades. I guess Pons heard those rumors too."

"Are you going to release it for publication?" Bruno asked.

"That's not my decision, and there's a lot of other stuff in there that we wouldn't want to see made public. But if you subpoena parts of the manuscript for evidence in a murder trial, the memoirs would have to be made available to the court. Just remember you didn't hear that from me."

"But if Pons is dead, there'll be no murder trial."

"He's dead?" asked the brigadier. "Are you sure?"

"No, but we think he died in the fire, in bed with a little Chinese girl," said Bruno.

"There will be a murder trial," said J-J. "That young Chinese thug you arrested in Bordeaux gave us a DNA match on the tissues and the cigarettes in the abandoned Mercedes that was at the murder scene."

There was one more question Bruno had to ask before the others came back into the room. "How's Isabelle?"

"Still not awake when we left, but the doctors say she'll be as good as new. They have to put a titanium brace onto her thighbone. After a few months, she won't know it's there, but she's in for a long convalescent leave."

"Can the others come back in now?" Bruno asked. The brigadier nodded, and J-J opened the door and beckoned them in.

"Here," said the brigadier, handing Bruno a new mobile phone. "It's got your old number, and you've got dozens of messages already, half of them from the media."

"The other half are from me, calling to apologize," said Pamela. She didn't look in the least apologetic, perhaps a little embarrassed. Mainly she looked her usual self, and Bruno felt a rush of affection.

"No need," said Bruno, smiling at her. "Pons fooled all of us. I didn't even know he was running a child brothel. And I agreed with a lot of what he said that night at the public meeting."

"Have you any idea how funny you look in those filthy shorts?" she asked him.

"I don't think he cares," said Fabiola, and Bruno tried to work out which of the two meanings of the phrase Fabiola had meant. One of them was wrong. He still cared for Pamela. But he also knew that as soon as he could he'd be heading for Bordeaux to visit Isabelle.

"Could you fetch Gigi for me from your car, please?" he asked the mayor. His room was so crowded that a dog wouldn't make much difference. The mayor squeezed his way out.

"Do you want to come with me to Pons's place?" Bruno asked J-J and the brigadier.

"I can't," said the brigadier. "The helicopter is taking me to Marseilles, where we'll have the truce meeting. Vien sends you his regards, and Bao Le says he'll let you know if they learn anything about the girl. The Vinhs will be home in St. Denis tomorrow and back in the market next week."

"I'll gladly come with you," said J-J. "But I don't think there's much hurry."

Then came the sound of running paws and Gigi darted into the room and made a flying leap to join Bruno on his bed.

"For God's sake," said Fabiola, with an exasperated laugh. "This is supposed to be a hospital."

She and Pamela sat down beside Bruno on the bed and joined him in stroking Gigi's long velvet ears.

"I'll be off," said the brigadier. "My offer still stands, Bruno. I want you on my team. Think about it."

Raising his face to escape Gigi's tongue, Bruno looked around the room at his friends, the mayor and the baron and J-J, Pamela and Fabiola. Through the window behind them the wintry sun gilded the old stone of the *mairie* and glinted from the bronze eagle atop the war memorial.

"I don't think I could leave this," Bruno said. "Besides, I've got the rugby club New Year's dance to arrange, and Stéphane expects me at the farm to help kill the pig next month. I've still got to sort out the contracts for the town fireworks on *le quatorze juillet,* and then there are the children who are expecting me to carry on teaching them to play tennis. On top of that, I came across this recipe I want to try, called *truffes cendrillon,* little pies with foie gras topped with truffle and baked in cinders. I was thinking of inviting you all to a Christmas dinner at my place with Florence and her children to welcome them to St. Denis."

"Dear Bruno," said Pamela, lifting her hand from Bruno's dog to cup his cheek and kiss him softly on the lips. "Don't ever change."

"Change?" said Bruno, returning the kiss. "I don't think St. Denis would let me."

Acknowledgments

This is a work of fiction and the characters and situations have all been invented by the author. While there is regrettably a growing amount of fraud in the truffle trade, particularly relating to China, the reputation of the famous truffle market in Ste. Alvère has not been tarnished. But my friends and neighbors in the enchanting Périgord have served as inspirations, guides and the most patient of teachers in educating a foreigner into some of the folkways of the land. They have taught me to pick and tread the grapes, to hunt and cook the elusive *bécasse,* to search for truffles and try to tell one variety from another. Above all, they have taught me the difference between food enriched with the real black diamond of Périgord and the wan apologies for the truffle you so often encounter in places that take their gastronomy less seriously. So my gratitude to the people of the valley of the river Vézère for the welcome they have given to me and my family and our basset hound is deepened yet further, along with my fondness for their way of life. I hope that the Bruno novels convey some of my profound affection and respect for the people of this valley, whose ancestors had the excellent taste to settle amid its gentle hills and fertile slopes some forty thousand years ago. Their descendants have never left, and I can understand why.

Acknowledgments

This novel is dedicated to a particular friend, Raymond Bounichou, a veteran of the gendarmes and of various other, perhaps less public, arms of the French state. Not only has he made me reassess the role of the *barbouze* in France's complicated recent history, but his endless stories have also triggered thoughts of many future plots. So Bruno should have some mysteries to solve in the future, even as he stands guard on all the traditions and peculiarities that make France and the Périgord so beguiling. But Bruno would hardly be Bruno without the devoted ministrations of Jane and Caroline Wood and Jonathan Segal, who whipped this book into shape with their customary and attractive blend of firmness, frankness and charm. I am most grateful to them, and to my wife, Julia Watson, and our daughters, Kate and Fanny, without whom I suspect we would not have made nearly so many friends.

A NOTE ABOUT THE AUTHOR

Martin Walker is senior director of the Global Business Policy Council, a think tank on international economics founded by the A. T. Kearney management consultancy. He is also a senior scholar of the Woodrow Wilson International Center for Scholars in Washington, D.C., and editor in chief emeritus of United Press International, for whom he writes the weekly syndicated column on international affairs, "Walker's World." In 2010, he was given the Swissglobe Award for building bridges between Switzerland and the rest of the world. Mr. Walker spent twenty-five years as a prizewinning journalist with *The Guardian*. He has also written for *The New York Times, The Washington Post, Foreign Policy, The New Yorker, The New Republic, The Times Literary Supplement* and other national and foreign publications. He divides his time between Washington, D.C., and the Périgord region of France. Readers can learn more about Bruno and his friends, his cooking and his region on brunochiefofpolice.com.

A NOTE ON THE TYPE

This book was set in Adobe Garamond. Designed for the Adobe Corporation by Robert Slimbach, the fonts are based on types first cut by Claude Garamond (ca. 1480–1561). Garamond was a pupil of Geoffroy Tory and is believed to have followed the Venetian models, although he introduced a number of important differences, and it is to him that we owe the letter we now know as "old style." He gave to his letters a certain elegance and feeling of movement that won their creator an immediate reputation and the patronage of Francis I of France.

Composed by North Market Street Graphics,
Lancaster, Pennsylvania
Printed and bound by R.R. Donnelley,
Harrisonburg, Virginia
Designed by Virginia Tan